PRAI

MW00720542

"I've read few novels with characters as particularized and whole, perceptions as amusing and alive. It takes the basic Canadian-fiction starter kit and assembles it with a lightning wit and energy that make the results wholly agreeable ... *Crossings* is a superbly realized novel."
—Douglas Hill

"That *rara avis*, the novel that makes you say, now here's a *real* novelist ... *Crossings* is a powerful novel of a woman discovering herself. And we discover a powerfully talented writer."
—*The Globe and Mail*

ARSENAL PULP PRESS | Vancouver

Betty Lambert

CROSSINGS

ARSENAL PULP PRESS
Suite 101, 211 East Georgia St.
Vancouver, BC
Canada V6A 1Z6
arsenalpulp.com

This publication is made possible with support from the City of Vancouver's 125th
Anniversary Grants Program, the Office of Vancouver's Poet Laureate Brad Cran, and
the participation of the Government of Canada.

The publisher gratefully acknowledges the support of the Canada Council for the Arts
and the British Columbia Arts Council for its publishing program, and the Government of Canada (through the Canada Book Fund) and the Government of British Columbia (through the Book Publishing Tax Credit Program) for its publishing activities.

Cover photograph by Herb Gilbert

Printed and bound in Canada

Library and Archives Canada Cataloguing in Publication:

Lambert, Betty, 1933-1983
 Crossings / Betty Lambert.

Originally publ.: Vancouver : Pulp Press, 1979.
Issued also in electronic format.
ISBN 978-1-55152-427-6

 I. Title.

PS8573.A385C76 2011   C813'.54   C2011-904107-3

Introduction
Claudia Casper

Betty Lambert's only novel is utterly contemporary, utterly shocking, razor sharp (I swear you can cut yourself while reading this book), and as original and controversial as the day she ripped the last sheet of paper from her typewriter and laid it on top of the manuscript.

Crossings re-entered my life when the wry firebrand Anakana Schofield, a Vancouver writer and critic with an avid interest in the city's working-class literature and labour history, invited me to join other writers to read at an event at the Vancouver Public Library in December 2010. Anakana, with the sharp eye of a literary immigrant from Ireland, was wandering the VPL's Canadiana reference section when she found a mention of *Crossings* and became intrigued. She found a copy and was bowled over by the passion, complexity, and commitment of Lambert's writing and the fact that "she did not turn away from depicting the difficult stuff."

When she spoke of the novel, Anakana was astonished by how few people had even heard of it. She decided to organize the VPL event, called "*Crossings*: A Return." During the evening, writers Annabel Lyon, Renee Rodin, Juliane Okot Bitek, myself, Anakana and performance artist Lori Weidenhammer read from their favourite passages, and Lambert's sister, nephew, and daughter spoke movingly and stirringly about the woman they remembered and had lost much too early at the age of fifty.

Now *Crossings* has been chosen as one of ten books reissued in 2011 in honour of Vancouver's 125th birthday, and at last this masterpiece will get the chance to take its proper place among the important literature of the twentieth century.

The city of Vancouver that plays a starring role in *Crossings* was a rough-edged port town with a resource-based economy and home to beatniks, heroin addicts, and slacker businessmen who skied or sailed in the afternoons. It was a pre-Expo Vancouver, when real estate prices were not the city's primary meme and False Creek was not yet a cluster of condo glass. You could still scare yourself looking down at the ocean through knotholes in the wooden sidewalk of the Cambie Street Bridge, and when you glanced to the east, you saw the sign for Sweeney's Barrels and great piles of peeled logs stacked dockside. Gastown's steam clock had not been installed, and bars still had separate Ladies' entrances and covered windows to hide the shameful activity of imbibing alcohol.

When Lambert wrote her novel the first generation of women for whom the pill was available from the onset of puberty was sexually active. Anti-war protests were taking place under the banner "Make Love Not War," a slogan whose meaning expanded to include the conflicts of race, gender, and class. Feminism and sexual liberation were hitting their stride, yet sexual assault, rape, spousal abuse, sexual harassment, and inequality flourished.

Fierce, brutal, often silent struggles were going on between the genders, and class conflict sometimes played out between men and women so that the wounds of class and the wounds of gender became morally entangled—pain and confusion abounded among the daisies and the guns and the long hair. In September 1975, Pat Lowther, the gifted Canadian poet and University of British Columbia instructor who had just submitted her latest collection of poems, *A Stone Diary*, to Oxford University Press, was murdered in North Vancouver by her husband. Lowther's publisher was a friend of Lambert's, and it seems likely Lambert would have known her and certainly known about her murder.

I arrived at Pulp Press in 1980, a young woman who had moved to Vancouver from Toronto with the pure but inchoate intention to write. By then Betty was the writer who had made the big time; the US edition of *Crossings* had been published by Viking in New York, and her plays were being produced by numerous theatre companies. Meanwhile, the contradictions of that era played out in the offices of Pulp. I do not describe the situation with blame. It was a time of sudden change; we were all reaching for new social ideals and hopes while anchored by the society we were born into and weighed down by our own ignorance and human limitations. The culture at Pulp Press was a culture of men. They were the writers and artists, the movers and shakers, and the deliverers of the most, and frequently the best, one-liners; they were also the ones who started, financed, and ran the press and who mostly made the final editorial decisions. And then there were the women: typesetters, editors, shippers, frequently also writers, often girlfriends and common-law wives, yet somehow we were more the audience than the actors. Also, amid all the drinking and chaos, there was physical violence against some of the women in relationships—it was known but not spoken of, left invisible and hush-hush in shadows, glanced at only when unavoidable. There was even less vocabulary and social context for such actions then than now (there is still no precise vocabulary—"wife abuse" doesn't cover girlfriends or women in more casual sexual relationships, yet the phenomenon is the same), and things are harder to see and talk about when we have inadequate language.

When I finally read Crossings in the mid-'80s I was astonished at the clear-eyed, brave precision of Lambert's understanding of the desire for self-annihilation, the potency of sexuality linked to it, and her scalpel-like ability to deconstruct the subtextual aggressions of class and culture. In Crossings, class and gender are fully weaponized. Lambert's story of a mutually destructive, erotic affair between a writer, Vicky, and Mik, an ex-con and logger ("You can't destroy me. I've been destroyed by experts") is unflinchingly non-judgmental as it tracks their protracted chess game of physical violence, intellectual superiority, and emotional dominance.

Betty Lambert was born in Calgary to a working-class family in 1933, during the Great Depression. "My father died when I was twelve," Lambert wrote, "and I was no longer working-class, I was welfare-class, and I was determined to get out ... Writing was a way out, but soon it became more than that, it became a necessity." She wrote more than sixty plays for radio and stage, produced to enthusiastic acclaim in Vancouver, Toronto, and New York, as well as dozens of stories. She was also a knowledgeable, energetic, and generous professor of English at Simon Fraser University. She was a socialist with a cutting wit and deep moral skepticism.

Lambert finished writing Crossings in 1976 or 1977 and was discouraged when the manuscript failed to find a publisher. She handed it to a friend, Brian Brett, who was about to retire from his partnership in the literary publishing company Blackfish Press, with the words, "maybe you can find someone for it." Brett writes, "I was in love with Betty, though she was almost twenty years my elder. She was so good, so hot, so smart, and had been a power in the sixties, but was left behind. It was near criminal. She'd gone from being a honcho to not being able to find anyone to publish Crossings."

Brett interested Stephen Osborne, founder of Geist magazine and one of the early and most committed instigators of Pulp Press (later reincarnated as Arsenal Pulp Press, publisher of this book, under the new leadership of Brian Lam). Osborne drove out to Brett's house in Tsawwassen one afternoon and, after much drinking of whiskey, a box containing the manuscript was produced from the depths of a closet. That night Osborne sat down at his kitchen table in Burnaby and opened the box with the intention of reading just a few pages, but he continued through the night, finishing the last page at eight o'clock the next morning. He realized he had just read a truly remarkable work.

Crossings was published in 1979 by Pulp and received a rave review by Canada's top book critic at the Globe and Mail, William French, who wrote, "Rarely has the complex subject of male-female relationships been dissected with such skill and subtlety ... Crossings is that rara avis, the kind of novel that makes you say, after the first few pages, now here's a real writer." The novel was picked up by Viking in the US and released under the title Bring Down the Sun. Lambert's career was on the rise again. In 1980 her radio play Grasshopper Hill won the ACTRA Nellie Award and a new stage play, Jennie's Story, opened to a standing ovation at Toronto's St. Lawrence Centre, won the 1983 Chalmers Canadian Play Award, and was nominated for a Governor General's Award. In February of 1983, Lambert was diagnosed with lung cancer. After chemotherapy she went into remission for several months and managed to complete a new play, Under the Skin, before the discovery of a brain tumour. She died on November 4, 1983, blinded by three tumours and unable to speak because of pneumonia. Days earlier she'd written on a notepad, "I want to write."

Biographical descriptions of Lambert's life include the sound of a typewriter being worked furiously. She was driven to write—she was a woman with a fire inside and a lot to say at a time when women still were not expected to say much; were expected, if they did insist on using their voices, to entertain, to emote, to speak about "women's issues"—love and child-rearing—but not about the desire to destroy, to annihilate the self, not about ethics and truth and the muddied waters of evil and good in which we all swim.

Lambert had not only the determination to write as a woman who thought and loved thinking (*Crossings'* narrator is frequently criticized within the text for being too rational, cerebral, and philosophical), she also had the courage to write about the volatile, primal, "reprehensible" (to quote Jane Rule's review) world of passion. Lambert's writing about sex is superior to most writers' and equal to any. The following passage describes Vicky midway between orgasms with Mik: "I was under the sea at last, slippery and silk, silver and single, whole, not moving, as salmon do, resting in their element, gills moving imperceptibly, breathing. His sweat on my tongue." She writes devastatingly well about bad sex too: "So. Benjamin Ferris poked it in one last time. Without a safe. Without consulting the little calendar, without a norform. He did it. Yes he did. Back and forth he went like a little man. Brave as brave. And ooops, here he comes, and he's out and running all over the sheet."

The raw, wild, primal life-and-death world of sex and babies infiltrates the politically correct, cultured world of early yuppiedom and academia, while separate from both realms and rising above them is the perceptive, probing mind of Lambert's narrator Vicky. Her cool voice, silently screaming like Plath's, like Kathryn Harrison's in *The Kiss*—the only way in which she truly exists is through her voice—anatomizes her libidinal participation in her own destruction.

The narrative structure of *Crossings*, daring and virtuoso in the author's effortless handling of time, darts back and forth across the narrator's life. Lambert uses fragments, repetition, recapitulation, and interruption, even ending paragraphs mid-sentence to contradict what has gone before. The narrative circles back around its story several times, like an anxious dog preparing to lie down.

Her main themes, honesty and truth, are even more relevant now than when she wrote the novel, given the wild explosion of plugged-in voices telling us "facts" and interpreting them for us. Lambert writes, "I thought truth was something you could work out, like the logarithms upon which a slide rule is premised. I thought if you could once discover the base, you could work it out from there. I thought if I could ascertain facts, it would all come clear. Multi-dependent, multi-causal perhaps, but there in some solid and satisfying way." Lambert's approach to her themes, along with her narrative structure and bold content, makes Crossings a contemporary novel. If I haven't made it clear yet, let me say now—this is in no way an old-fashioned or musty book. It slaps you in the face and wakes you out of your trance while pulling you deeper into the author's.

What kind of truth is possible given the unreliability of memory and the constraints of point of view? Vicky is haunted by the inaccuracy of memory, often correcting and changing what she has already written, sometimes with a straight-up correction, sometimes ironically, with a sly, double-edged wit. For example, when a psychiatrist asks Vicky about her hysterical pregnancy, "You do realize, Mrs Ferris? You do know you're not having a baby?'" she replies, "'Yes, I realize.' I wished he wouldn't smoke. It was bad for the baby."

Lambert wrestles with language, psychology, and philosophy and gives us lovely meta-textual moments by having other characters correct or contradict the narrator and accuse her of dramatizing, fictionalizing, inventing, dreaming, of having hyp-nagogic spells.

> The seventh version.
> 'The unity of plot does not consist, as some suppose, in its having one man as its subject. An infinity of things befall that one man, some of which it is impossible to reduce to unity.'
> 'Vicky always dramatizes,' says my mother. 'Must you always dramatize?'
> Francie said, 'But you lied!'
> Jeff says, 'You have fictionalized your whole life.'
> ...
> Sister Mary Joseph says, 'You have always been obsessed with truth.'
> The Nut Lady [Vicky's psychotherapist] said, 'Why did they tie your hands to the crib?'
> 'Because I bit my nails.'
> 'Why?'

Lambert was an intelligent, passionate, profound, potent and complicated writer, yet she was also delightfully irreverent, funny, and down-to-earth. "When they ask me later if I have been influenced by Bach, in the fugue-like contrapuntal technique, I want to say, 'Actually, it was I Love Lucy.'"

The main difficulty in writing an introduction to this novel is that I want to quote every line to you. Better just to let you indulge in this killing, brilliant, and raw novel, the crime of its near oblivion put right by Arsenal Pulp Press and the city of Vancouver's 125th anniversary.

CROSSINGS

I TOOK THE CATS and flew up to the island. All the time I was getting ready to go, packing, neatly, like a lady, I felt frozen. As if the trembling had frozen into a single shrieking note, high-pitched on a violin, so high that no one could hear, only the mad dogs of the universe.

And I moved calmly, neatly, precisely, like a lady, a small poised smile on my face, cold with that shriek of terror. I was putting myself in his hands. I was going to his territory. I was going beautiful, a sacrifice.

'You can't destroy me,' he had said. 'I've been destroyed by experts.'

I rounded up the cats and put them, yowling, into the big Mexican basket. I put my typewriter in the case. I took enough paper for the last story.

The big plane flew low over the water and we came in. This was the end of the world but there was still another plane to catch. When the man opened the luggage compartment, Peter spat at him. He had gotten out of the Mexican basket. Sally and Lolly were still inside, huddled, afraid, frozen. But Peter was enormous, puffed out to twice his size with indignation. 'I've got a tiger in my tail,' said the man and everyone laughed. I laughed too, and gathered Peter up, stroking him, saying, 'It's going to be all right.

It's all right, it's going to be all right.'

I found a taxi. He seemed to know all about it. We drove to the sea. I went down the ramp as if it were the most normal thing in the world. There was a man in a hut, at the bottom of the ramp. A little hut with calendars and a telephone. I hired the man to fly me to the island, as if it were something I had done every day of my life. I had just locked the door and walked away, leaving all my things, the fake Sarukhan rugs, the Renoir reproduction, all my stories, the bills that were going to come through the mail slot. I had walked away, as other people did, as Mik had done all his life. A shriek of freedom in my head. So this was what it was, freedom. To walk away and leave everything behind, to go to a man and say, Kill me.

A week before I had phoned him. It was a radio telephone and he had to take the call in the cookhouse. Everyone in the cookhouse could listen in. Everyone on all those lonely islands could listen in.

'It was all sound and fury, signifying nothing,' I said. But he didn't understand.

'What? What?' he said, his voice strange and crackling through the lost northern air.

'I'm not pregnant,' I said. And everyone heard. He was humiliated.

The men went into the forest and the women stayed in the compound. It was forbidden to go into the forest if you were a woman. Once I climbed the road into the forest, the cats leaping in and out of the trees beside me, running ahead and then dashing back, suddenly elemental, or following me, as dogs do, then rushing away again, their tails fluffed absurdly, scuttering back to the forest and leaping at me, the prey, arched-back, stiff-legged, doing the sideways daring dance of Siamese. I walked up into the forest until I saw them, the men, in their great yellow machines, grunting and roaring, tearing at the earth, ripping and gouging. I hid behind a tree and watched them, men alone in their secret world, and I was afraid. Men engaged in their mysterious rites, tearing great holes in the earth.

The ground shook beneath them. I felt the shudder in the tree I was hiding behind. Like creatures from some fantastic world, the men moved, grunting, laborious, in metal helmets and thick boots. No one human could have such large feet, it was impossible.

But that was later. Now I was going to the island, I was putting myself into his hands, great thick hands, hands that grasped you and brought you down, hands like weapons. Not fists. Nothing that looked like that could be called 'a fist.' A fist is small, with knuckles, the bones shine whitely through the skin. Thin and delicate. Mik's hands were weapons.

'You can't destroy me,' he had said. 'I've been destroyed by experts.'

Sometimes at night I cry God, God, and before my mind can stop it, He comes and holds me. Over each nipple is a tattoo: one says *Cream* and the other says *Coffee*.

Later, that day in the forest, I crept away, unseen. I went back to the compound and had tea with the boss's wife. She made doilies.

'How do you get them to stand like that?' I said. It was all mysterious to me, the world of women. Women who wait in compounds for men. I belonged nowhere.

'You starch them,' she said.

They were curved and bowed into elaborate arches and scallops, and they were everywhere, on the backs of the chairs, on the back of the sofa, on the arms, on the radio, on the side tables, everywhere. In their centres were ceramic fish or ashtrays, bowls and figurines. They said 'Campbell River, B.C.' or 'Victoria, B.C.'

But now the little plane is taking off. Inside it is wired. The chair I am sitting on is actually wired to the floor. Peter is yowling in the back. Lolly is mewing plaintively. Sally is stoic, resigned. I think, Held together with baling wire, just as the books have promised. This is 'baling wire,' and I am delighted to meet it at last. You never meet a brickbat, for instance.

'But what is a brickbat?' I said, nineteen and clever, all those years ago.

The old Marxists looked at me with scorn. But they never told me.

The world below us stretches deep and green and blue, miles of forest and sea and mountains. We thud through the great empty sky, and the white and the blue and the dark green ignore us. The man beside me is chewing a match. He drives the plane as if it were a car, as if it were nothing, as if every day he took someone like me to the island to be killed.

The wings go up on one side and down on the other. My stomach lurches, as if my body still cares for itself, as if it can still remember, and I am amused, as one is at a child who cries out in the dark. 'There, there, it's all right,' but the child too will die, one way or another.

Like a swallow, we come down toward the inlet. The forest rises to meet us, alerted now. The sun glints sharply through the glass and the man curses, ducks his head. I am wearing my grandmother's wedding ring. And here we are, an insect of wood and metal, moving calmly through gentle ripples to the dock.

Mik comes down the path to meet us. But he was not waiting. He must have heard the plane circling, but he is not waiting for us. He comes down the path now that I am on the dock. The man with the match hands out the typewriter, the Mexican basket, the suitcase.

Mik is filthy. Unshaven. Dressed in unfamiliar khaki and great tan boots. Even his face is grimy, streaked with grease. I know. He is so like me. I know everything. He wouldn't clean up, he wouldn't shave, he would not come down to the dock when he heard the plane circling in the sky. How could he? If he shaved, if he cleaned up, if he came running down, it would not be me. It would be someone else. I would not have come.

I don't think he says anything to me. He goes 'Hunh!' and picks up the basket, typewriter, suitcase, managing them all easily. I don't hear the plane leave. The world is deephued with gold from the dying sun, gathering now into navy blue shadows. We go up the dock, up the path. The stones are sharp under my elegant brown shoes. Alligator shoes, very expensive, someone gave them to me. Who? Oh yes. Barney. She said, 'They hurt my feet.' They hurt mine too, but I am so pleased to be wearing size five.

My hair is long now. And I am thin. I am small and thin and elegant in expensive clothes and alligator shoes.

Mik moves silently a little ahead of me, thick and silent, not looking back. It is time for the sun to go down. Now we are passing a large open shed. A man is working there. A Japanese. Caught in the last golden flash like a man on the stage. He straightens up, sees us, does a double-take.

Mik laughs. His great thundering laugh.

The first time I ever saw Mik, he did a double-take too, but then it was on purpose.

It is comical, this double-take, as if the Japanese has meant to do it, as if he saw at a glance the joke about us. But he hasn't meant it, he has just done it.

We have to cross a log bridge to get to the house. And the house itself is on logs, almost in the bed of the stream, only feet away from the lagoon. It is in deep shadow now, the house. I am to learn it is in deep shadow all the time. Morning, noon, and night. From the mountains and the forest. In the lagoon, jellyfish float lazily. Like blobs of semen slowly disintegrating.

Mik says, 'You can't swim there. They get on you.'

There is tarpaulin on the floor. Bleached white. Mik must have poured gallons of Javex on it, but he says, 'No, Dutch Cleanser.' It is powdery beneath my shoes.

'I chunked the joint out,' he says.

There is a door. I can see the small dark room. But I don't go in.

This room has a large wooden table and a wood stove. Ornate. Glistening blue-black from some special polish he has used. It has taken him every night for a week to get the house ready, and still he didn't believe I would really come.

One wall is lined with open shelves. On the shelves are cans of food. Pork and beans. Meat balls. Spaghetti. Salmon. Cabbage rolls in tomato sauce. Ravioli. Whole hams. Whole chickens. Hundreds of cans. I don't see French beans or even peas. No asparagus. No soup.

A kerosene lamp stands on the table.

Mik opens the Mexican basket.

The cats leap out. Lolly still kitten soft and white, tips of brown on her ears and her paws, the end of her tail. Peter crouches beneath the stove, massive, black, snarling. Sally looks for something to eat.

Mik takes me outside to show me how to get wood for the stove. He is establishing how it will be. He will make the fire up this time, but from now on I will make it up, as women in this world do. It is not my world anymore and he is letting me know. It is not my world where men politely make up unnecessary fires in unnecessary fireplaces. He shows me the round block of wood. He shows me the axe. He lets me try.

'Not like that!' He is disgusted. 'You'll cut your hand off.'

He makes up the fire, showing me how to bunch the newspapers first, how to lay the kindling, little fresh white slivers of wood, so clean and new.

And all the time he is silent, brusque and silent, as if this were nothing. As if his woman came everyday to his house, to his world, as if I were just like the others.

He shows me how to light the wick in the lamp. You have to be careful or it will become sooty and then you must start all over again. And you can't just wash the lamp right away. It will be too hot and it will break.

Now we are out on the little porch at the back. Here is the toilet. 'Watch out for the octopus,' says Mik, grinning. Grinning now because it is dark and no one can see him grin at me.

'Are there octopuses?' I say. Not risking 'octopi' right now. Afraid of him.

'Come up and zonk right in there.' He laughs.

The world is very still. The sky has fallen, now there is only a great black hole.

There is a hole in the toilet too. You sit there and everything goes down into the stream. Toilet paper and excrement. Sanitary pads. Mik holds up the kerosene lamp and I can see it all below. Cans. A broken chair. An old mattress. Papers.

'Oh!'

'Well, I had to chunk the joint out,' says Mik. I have made him angry. 'There ain't no garbage collectors here.' Yes, he is angry with me. I can tell because he is pretending to be stupid. Double negatives. I know he is going to punish me.

We come back into the house. Mik shuts the door. He laughs.

It is hard to remember sex. It is hard to remember in words. You only remember the words and the lighted places, and yet everything real goes on in the dark. You do not use words in the dark and so it goes. You do not say, as with baling wire, or brick-bats, so this is feallatio. So this is cunnilingus. They are probably not spelled right, those words. I have just looked them up and the *Webster's* doesn't have them. Nor the *O.E.D.* Historical principles indeed.

With Ben, of course, I knew all about sex. Ben would know how to spell fellatio and cunnilingus. We had a good sex life, Ben and I. When we were to be married, Ben bought two books: *The Rhythm Method*, approved by the Pope, and *Married Love*, by an Anglican minister in Toronto. Beside our bed for years, on all the rented tables or shelves. The circular chart that was in a pocket in *Rhythm Method*, a darling envelope in the back of the cover. I mean, inside the cover. You turned the chart around until you got the proper slot. It was very complicated at first. Safe days were green for Go; unsafe days were red for Stop. Ben also practiced three other methods of birth control: French safes, norforms, and co-itus interruptus. Simultaneously. Years later, when Edna said, 'But why didn't you trick him? Why didn't you just go ahead and get pregnant if you wanted to?' I didn't know what she meant. How could you trick a man into letting you get pregnant? How was it possible? Even if it were not morally indefensible, which of course it was, how?

We were all so free, so intellectual, so satisfied, we university girls. We never thought of asking real questions of each other. Do you have orgasms? Yes. So do I. Aren't we lucky.

I knew all about sex with Ben. Only with Mik, now, in the little dark room, do I know nothing.

There is a bed here. Low. On blocks of some kind. It is very damp. Musty. The flannelette sheets are damp, musty. The blankets are coarse. How did he get sheets? Mothballs. Smell of. He has my clothes off. The first time is just the punishment. It doesn't matter

22

that I came to the island after all. For a week he thought I might not, and therefore he must punish me. Mik doesn't rely on facts; he knows what is real.

He comes in me, bellowing like a bull, gripping my waist in his hands. Lifting me up to him, throwing back his head and hollering. We are deep in the forest. There is no one for miles, to the circle of the Arctic and beyond that, to the moon, to the great dark empty hole of the sky, like a wound in a dead man. A wound that doesn't bleed, dark and empty. That won't heal.

Over his right nipple, Cream; over his left nipple, Coffee.

Years later, I realize what the joke was. The joke was, must have been, if you asked for sugar. 'I've got another tattoo, baby,' or, 'I've another spigot'? Would he have said spigot? No. Mik never told me the rest of the joke. I never led into it. It seemed strange to me, a tattoo over each nipple. I didn't understand. I was embarrassed for Mik when we went swimming. It seemed terrible, to have signs, indelible, forever on your body, where everyone could see. Worse than varicose veins or even false teeth.

But of course we are not in the forest now. I only think that. We are in a house on logs, almost in the bed of a stream. A cluttered stream. A few feet away is the lagoon. Jellyfish float in the lagoon, dreamily, like fairy umbrellas, pale, translucent, deadly.

The mattress is on concrete blocks. It is damp in the little room but not so damp as our skins. I have always kept one part of my mind aware. With Ben, I mean. One part of me watched when I made love to Ben. I was in love with the way I looked. I was always on camera. With Mik it

With Mik it is

I am caught in the eye of a hurricane. All around the winds rage, in here it is still, calm, not a leaf stirs. It is terrible.

Was I subjugated? Yes, I suppose that is one word for it.

I am subjugated. Mik subjugates me. Dominates me. Makes me
Makes me

Yes. For him, the second time, there is victory in my coming.
I don't come the first time. That is just the punishment. When I
come he licks his finger and chalks up an imaginary mark on an
imaginary wall. That's one. That's two. That's three. He is pleased,
yes, but disappointed too, as if somehow this only proves me to be
a slut after all. Not a lady.

I come without dignity, noisily, moaning on a damp mattress.

Ben licking his fingers. Lick lick, all the fingers of his right
hand. Not the thumb? Yes, also the thumb. It was terrible to see
him do it, before he started to draw. Before he picked up a scalpel. Because he would do it, too, before he began to 'make love.'
Before he followed steps one, two, and three of *Married Love* by the
Anglican minister from Toronto. Moisten the lips of the vulva with
your fingers. Use Vaseline or prepare your fingers by moistening
them with your saliva. By the time he entered me, I was finished.
Boom. Shudder. Sigh.

'Did you come?'

'I'm sorry.' I used to say that at first. Later I didn't bother.

And he would withdraw and finish, his hand moving busily
up and down beneath the covers, finish alone, his back to me,
by himself. He didn't want to bother me, he said. 'I don't like to
bother you, Vicky.'

Sometimes he teased me about being trigger-happy. That's
what he called it. 'You're trigger-happy,' he would say. Men gain
power over you in many ways. I would come as soon as he entered
me, and then he could do it to himself, not bothering me. He was
so considerate. I shall never forgive him.

Now, in the dark little room, Mik thumping me down, his
great body tearing at me, gouging at the roots of my forest, the

great yellow machines, ripping and tearing in the sacred world of men. But of course this happens later. I don't think of the yellow machines now.

And now, now that he has determined my guilt, my defection, the innate capacity for betrayal in women, he gathers me to him, to his great thick strong chest. He says, 'I'm gonna pull you on like an overcoat. I'm gonna fuck you to death. You're gonna beg for mercy.' And laughter, subterranean, rumbles in his belly. I feel it rather than hear it.

I don't want to tell this.

I got asthma.

I hate it. Asthma is what they all get, silly, squalid, ridiculous people in novels. 'The middle-aged woman wheezed asthmatically up the tenement steps.' 'The asthmatic old man looked helplessly in the alley for returnable bottles.' Even elevators wheeze asthmatically. And lap dogs. 'Without makeup, she looked seventy. With makeup, and her asthmatic Pekinese under her arm, ninety.' 'Are you wheezy, Vicky?' the aunts would say. 'Do you feel wheezy?'

I have made it out to the tarpaulin in the big room. Away from the must and the damp and the mothballs. My mouth gaping like a mongoloid's, I rock back and forth, back and forth. Mik hears me, comes out, takes a look at me, and goes out the door. Thump crash bang. Over the log bridge. I can hear him. I feel shame. Oh god. But he has only gone to 'phone the doctor at Campbell River.' He tells him, 'Move your ass.'

He doesn't say, 'Are you all right?' He doesn't say, 'Do you want me to call the doctor?' He just does it. And the doctor comes, his sea plane thrumming through the cold misty air. Forty-five dollars. The precious vial of adrenalin. But it doesn't work. I am too far gone for adrenalin. Epinephrine. He is well equipped, this doctor. Ties my upper arm with rubber and shoots it in the vein. Whee. Leaves me a syringe and a pack of needles. A bottle of adrenalin. In case.

'You should carry an emergency kit,' he says sternly. But I have thrown mine away. The little black plastic box. The note from Dr Munston saying: 'Mrs Ferris is under doctor's care and requires a hypodermic syringe for her asthma.' To prove I'm not a dope addict in public washrooms. I threw it all away, my needles, my syringe, my rubber-tipped vials, the day of the divorce.

Because that's when my marriage really ended. When I said to Ben, 'I'd rather do it myself.' Like the woman on the television ad: 'Mother, I'd rather do it myself!'

Ben boiling the syringe, the needles, bubble bubble in the poached egg pan. Drawing up my nightgown. Slowly, oh slowly, pushing it in. So many needles, so many holes, suppurating, festering, turning gold and green with pus. So that once, by accident, arranging me in the oxygen tent, the nurse sees my hips and says: 'My goodness. What's that?' Thinking I have some loathsome disease. And Dr Soronski coming, cross with me, saying, 'The nurse says you've something wrong with the hips.'

Pulling up my nightie, saying, 'Mrs Ferris!' Disgusted. As if I had done it on purpose. As if I did the asthma on purpose.

But now the sores are almost gone. Deep craters of the moon when they healed. The red sores, the black holes, the ones that won't heal, the green and gold, all gone.

I don't hear the doctor go. The world stands still. I am paralytic with ecstasy. White all over, frozen, still, in a deep wide river of pure oxygen. Still and deep and frozen. Blissful. Forgiven.

Ben, in Mexico, sits by my bed and watches me die with typhus. After, when the landlady has got the doctor, he says to me: 'But I didn't know what to do. You were lying there, you were just lying there. And you know I can't speak Spanish. I didn't know what to do.' The landlady tells me what you were doing.

'He is sitting there, like this,' and she imitates you, hands flopped helplessly down, palms up. 'And ...' She raises an imaginary glass to her mouth. She shakes her head. 'It is fortunate I arrive,' she says.

You sat there watching me spew puke and shit and you couldn't think what to do. 'I was frightened,' you say.

But Mik just radios Campbell River and tells the doctor to get his ass moving.

He goes off to the forest about ten o'clock, leaving me alone in my wide white world, cold and pure. He gathers on his great bulky windbreaker and he says, 'Well, I got to hump it. See ya.'

That night we make love again.

And every night, all those nights, the first weeks, with the stars so multitudinous in the deep black hole of the sky. I leave the door of the toilet open so I can look up. Of course, there are no octopi. But there are heron, grey-blue, like statues, in the mornings. And a loon, maniac with misery, calling across the lagoon. And the jellyfish.

I used them later, in a story. Festooned like garlands on the pale white body of a woman, drowned. Drowned on purpose. Pushed in. Because she is paralyzed. The jellyfish cover her like gardenias.

One morning, after Mik had gone, I took the typewriter out of its case.

Mik had grumbled about my cooking.

'It's worse than the cook's!'

'But the cook makes marvellous meals,' I said. He had taken me there one night, perhaps the first day, when I was sick. 'Really, I'd much rather eat there. Is it some sort of tradition, to bitch about the cook? Because, really, the food is fantastic.' So it was. She showed me one day how she did it. How she prepared the vegetables in the mornings, and the pies. How she set the dough to rise. Her refrigerator was a large walk-in room, hung with great carcasses of pig and cow. She used real butter in everything. When I went up to the shower house I could smell that day's meals, glorious in the cool air. Great roasts and Yorkshire pudding. Bread stuffing for turkeys. She made breakfast, a huge dinner at noon, another huge dinner at night, and was expected to have pies, buns, cakes on hand for evening snacks. Her pastry could have won prizes. And yet she was spoken of in the most disparaging way. Not only was her cooking not fit for dogs, but she herself was reputed to be sexually insatiable. It was well-established that she spent every night draining the loggers dry in her room behind the kitchen. Yet, when I said, but who? Mik couldn't say. I was not allowed to speak to the men, except for Noddy, the Japanese; but he too seemed to regard the cook with loathing. She was dirty (her kitchen was the cleanest I have ever seen); she was a whore (through the open door to her room, I glimpsed books, a child's sweater on needles, a narrow bed); she was a disgusting old bag (she was about forty-five and her hair was dyed a rather impossible colour).

I'm not sure why Noddy was allowed to speak to me, or I to him. There had been a terrible scene the first week. I had been taking a shower when the men came back into camp. Mik had stormed and raged. I said, 'But no one could *see* me.'

'They know you're there,' Mik said. I was forbidden to take my showers between the hours of eleven-thirty and one-thirty. And not after four in the afternoon. In general, I never saw any of the men, except at a distance. Noddy was the exception. He was allowed to come to the house and drink my instant coffee and eat my pathetic biscuits, which he pronounced 'Great!' He treated me with such deference, such courtesy, that I was tempted now and then to do something outrageous. In that context, something outrageous would have been the utterance of 'damn,' or, of course, the statement that Mik and I were not married. When I did finally tell Noddy, he was so shocked he couldn't speak for a minute. I suppose I was a lady in the same way the cook was a slut.

I was allowed to see the women. They came over in the mornings, across the bridge, and we had tea. They told me their stories.

'Bent right back he was, bent right back. When they did the autopsy, they said it was spinal meningitis.' Her five-year-old son.

'But didn't you take him into hospital? Didn't you take him to Vancouver?'

The woman looked at me, not understanding. It was beyond her, that act of faith. Her child had grown hot, had screamed, had bent slowly backwards like a bow, the crown of his head touching his toes, and she had suffered this to happen. 'They had to break his bones to put him in the coffin,' she said. She said it without tears, with a kind of awe, a sort of wonder. It was what life did to you, that was all.

One woman said, 'I had a baby, you know, before.' She waved her hand in the direction of the forest. 'But he was real good about it. He never said a word. He made me give it up though. Like, I met him when I was in the family way. So you can't blame him. It was a girl. I never saw it. They take them away, like, if you're going to give them up. They don't let you see them. But they told me it was a girl.' She was quiet for a while, drinking her tea from the terrible old mug. 'It's better that way, not to see them. He never throws it up to me.'

Another woman, big, with a large red face and house dresses starched so thickly she sounded like a nurse, said, 'Like, on Love of Life, is that all written down?' She was looking at the pages on the table. Not reading them, just looking at them, as though they were artifacts of some strange world.

I didn't understand at first.

'I mean, is it all written down for them, like this, all these words, so they know what to say?'

'Oh, yes, they have a script.'

'You mean, they have to learn all those words by heart?' I could see she didn't believe me. No one could learn all those words by heart.

'I mean, I guess I just thought that was the way they were, in real life. You know. Like that Vivian Carlson. I mean, I bet you anything that's the way she is, I've seen her type before.'

And, 'Like they pay you for writing it up, eh?'

'Well, if I'm lucky. I mean, I don't know if ...'

'Like, what's this show?'

'It's called Festival. They do different plays. Different stories. It doesn't carry on.'

'Oh yeah.' She nodded. 'CBC. My husband, he won't watch the CBC.'

I didn't know what to say. 'Sometimes they have good things on,' lamely.

'He says they don't ever finish. He gets so mad. So you just make it up out of your head, like. I guess you get a lot of ideas from books.'

'Well, you're not supposed to.'

'I don't know how you do it.'

'Well, it's not really just out of your head. I mean, that one I did, I really know people like that. I mean, that did actually happen. They did break up, and she did go away with the best friend.'

'You mean, like, people tell you stories and you just write it up in good grammar?'

'Well, not ...'

'I could tell you some stories. Boy. If I ever wrote my life story, I'd make a mint. It'd be a best seller.' She laughed, slapping her thigh. 'My old man'd kill me though,' sobering. 'I don't know, though, nobody'd believe it. I mean, the things that happened to me! I should tell you and you can write it up, like in good grammar and good spelling. We could split it, we'd make millions. I'm not kidding. The things that happened to me.'

I think they pitied me, the women. I think they pitied the drabness of my house, the lack of doilies and leaping fish with 'Campbell River, B.C.' on them. And my mugs, they pitied my mugs. They all had thin tea cups, in different patterns and shapes. And they pitied Mik, too, for the dinners I probably fed him. When they came, I wasn't baking bread. I would hear the horn go and I would rush around opening cans, getting the stove going.

'Hey. I'm sorry. I forgot the time.'

'Jesus Christ!' But at first it was a joke.

When I was working, it was Ben who cooked. Ben who cleaned. A plate would appear on my desk. Tea. Coffee. I would eat, drink. The plate would disappear. The telephone would ring. 'She's working right now.'

That first morning, up in the forest, Mik endured much levity on the subject of my ill health. 'They gave me a hard time,' said Mik, but he was pleased, he was grinning. 'Bastards,' he said, but he was proud of himself. He'd screwed me so hard he'd had to call the doctor.

'Oh bunk,' I said. 'It was the damp and the mothballs.'

So we moved the bed into the big room, and we made love before dinner that night. Was that the night we ate in the cookhouse? Just Mik and I and the cook. Probably. When we came back down the path he says, 'Did ya see them give you the eye?'

'Who?'

'The guys.'

'But there wasn't anyone there. I didn't see anybody.'

'They saw you,' he says and laughs.

TRYING TO SAY what Mik was like, I cannot use the ways of the world I live in. I cannot tell you what Mik believed in, or what he thought. I know he liked John Wayne movies.

If you asked me, What was Ben's approach to Viet Nam, I would know. Ben did not approve. I always knew what Ben thought. He explained everything to me. We got married in church because it isn't right to hurt other people. My mother. But there is no sanction in the legal tie. Two honourable people (Ben and I) do not require the force of law to do the correct thing. 'We'll have the part where you say 'and obey' taken out,' Ben says. But he doesn't. If either of us wishes to leave, for any reason, the other must not attempt to stop him/her. We are not going to be possessive. 'Jealousy is a manifestation of the private property ethic.' We were going to have the perfect marriage. It was a surprise to us, the way it turned out.

AND LAST NIGHT, at the reception, Carla is shouting: 'That bastard! That ingrate! I shall put the curse of the Slav upon him! I am furious. He could let Elton do one small bit from Hamlet.'

'But what happened?'

Carla is hanging onto Elton protectively. 'He won't let Elton do one small scene from Hamlet for the Congress!'

'But has he that much power?'

'Oh Vicky won't believe anything bad of Griffith,' she says to Linda, who is sitting languidly beside them.

Elton leans toward me and says, 'I've told you. Griffith is not an honourable man.'

'He has always seemed an ethical man.'

Carla begins to shout. 'You can tell him for me, I am going to destroy him! I am going to put the curse of the Slav upon him, my grandmother's curse.'

'But you haven't said anything yet that ...'

'Elton was his friend! He defended him for years. He stood up for him!'

'You're a terrible nepotist, Carla,' I say, trying to make a joke.

'I don't care! I'm loyal to my friends! I love my friends. I'm going to destroy the bastard!'

'But what has he ...'

'Oh Vicky,' says Linda, smiling at me. 'Don't try to be logical.'

'You're so cerebral,' says Judy.

'But you've read William James.'

'What's William James got to do with Kate Millett?'

'No, I mean The Varieties.' I feel horribly embarrassed for Judy, an honours graduate in philosophy, up for promotion to assistant professor. 'You know, you can't invalidate St. Theresa's vision just because she imagines St. Michael or whoever doing it to her with a great ruddy sword.'

'But Kate Millett is a bisexual!' says Judy again. 'It said so in Time. She said so. You can't take a woman like that seriously. I mean, here she is, explaining my nature to me and she's a bisexual.'

I feel such anger that I do say it after all: 'That's an ad hominem,' grinding it out, smiling fiercely, expecting her to drop dead with shame.

'So I'm illogical. I don't care. That's just part of my feminine nature.'

Linda's husband, the turd poet, says: 'You know your trouble? As a writer? You know where you go wrong? You're a rationalist.'

'WE SHOULD SIMPLY PLEDGE ourselves to each other at the top of a mountain,' says Ben. The wedding has cost forty dollars and he is put out about this. We should have gone, simply, to the top of a mountain and pledged ourselves to live honourably together: I pledge to allow him/her to pursue self-actualization (but this can't be; this is from Maslow); I pledge never to become dependent, emotionally or financially, upon him/her; I pledge never to have children.

We did go later, that summer, to the top of Mount Rundle. On the shale near the top, Ben froze, clinging to the rock. 'I can't,' he says, between clenched teeth. 'I can't move.'

I go on, leaving him there. I am afraid too, but I am more afraid of being afraid. I go on and I come to the rim. I cling there, peering over the edge, a mile below to the forest and the river. Through the bright clear air I fall, lazily, turning over and over slowly, down to the diamond river and the velvet forest. The wind tears at me, and I cling to the rock. This is only the lower cairn. Up above me is the real cairn. Really to have made it, I must go up there. But I am afraid, and, behind me, below me, Ben has his eyes closed. We do not get to the topmost cairn. We do not pledge ourselves to anything. I go back, pry his fingers loose, help him down.

No. I do say something. Yes. I don't want to remember. Yes. I call back to him from the edge: 'It's only twenty feet!' Willing him to come. Shooting back down the shale the force of my will. 'Come on, Ben. It's only twenty feet. You can't give up now.'

I wanted him so much the day of my wedding.

I was eighteen and a virgin. Ben was twenty-eight. Ten years older than I to the day. And a virgin.

Seven years later, Ben said, his voice shaking with indignation, 'But you agreed. You agreed not to have children.'

And he took his sketches and tore them across. Throwing the thick creamy paper into the fireplace. The worst thing he could do.

All his work. All those months. And on top of the paper he poured out his glass of tequila.

'But if you wanted a baby,' said Edna later, 'why didn't you just trick him?'

I wanted to ask how, but I said, lofty, ethical, disdainful of women who cheated and lied, who manipulated men, women without dignity, lives without honour, 'I couldn't trick Ben. I've never lied to him. We agreed always to be honest with each other.'

My mother said, 'But are you in love?'

He was to be an artist. I was to be a writer. At first, Ben said he would do nothing if it was not art. I got a job in a newspaper circulation office, selling subscriptions by telephone. After a week, they hired me to file. A week later, they fired me. The editor, passing through, remembered my applying for a job as a reporter. 'We'd rather have a girl who'll stay on.' I got a temporary job selling shirts in the Hudson's Bay. The head girl was a big red-headed Brunnhilde. She told me off for letting my hem hang. She's still there. Still red-headed, curls piled elaborately on top of her head, as they were then. Still tall and bursting out of her clothes. When art jobs didn't materialize, Ben sold newspaper subscriptions door to door, the big plush bonus bunny under his arm. And cars, from a script: 'The manager will break my neck for offering you so much on your trade-in, but ...' He refused to take a permanent job. I was desperate for one. I knew it would be temporary.

My sister Francie says to us, 'But we never felt poor.' It's true, all those years of Welfare, we did not feel poor. Now I felt poor. There was no soap to wash my white gloves. How did you look for work without white gloves? That was poor.

We had landed in Vancouver with eighty-eight dollars. We found a room in a West Georgia rooming house for eleven dollars a week. Hot plate. You washed your dishes in the bathtub. Or I did.

I suppose other people carried basins back to their rooms. I counted the people who used the bathroom once. Twenty-eight. In the basement there were drug pushers. The Mounties broke down the door one night. It was all very exciting. I was sure I'd heard a shot, but perhaps it was wishful thinking. On the second floor, the two prostitutes lived. And Erica and Karl, six weeks out from Germany. Across from us on the third floor lived the Cinderella Man. That's what he called himself. Grey suits, old school ties—all the old schools, with an entree into any world you could imagine. Was I interested in becoming a journalist? He personally would speak to the editor of the Sun. Actually, don't tell anyone, but he was living here incognito, doing research on the drug scene for a series of articles. Did Karl want to be a bartender? Fifty dollars to sweeten the union steward. The Cinderella Man could fix anything. To our left, the son of a man who'd been murdered. A famous case. He showed us the book about it. His father had designed the Empress Hotel. I felt I was really living at last. This was life.

Six months later I took half a bottle of 222s. Ben watched me, refusing to interfere. After all, it was my life. It was my decision. Made of my own free will. After I passed out, he took what was

No. He took a few of what was left. There were still some in the bottle the next morning.

No. We were not drunk. I had fallen in love. Tra la. But of course I was not unfaithful. I? I could not love thee, dear, so much, loved I not Honour more.

And I got asthma.

While I was in the hospital, Ben got a job, and that job turned into another job, and it was permanent. I got better and went to university. We stay married. There are always a lot of people around and they all say we are so lucky. No, what they actually say is, I am so lucky to have a husband like Ben.

LAST NIGHT, at the reception. No one hears me at first. I turn the brass handle and I hear ding dong inside. But nobody answers. There is a lot of noise and music. A woman comes. 'I'm not the hostess,' she says.

The host comes belatedly; he says accusingly to the woman, 'I like to know who comes into my house!' And 'I'm sorry, I don't usually do that.'

When he introduces me to Ferlinghetti, I do it, the Victorian thing. I make Ferlinghetti stand up. He doesn't want to. He is sitting back in a low chesterfield and it is awkward for him, an old bald man, to get up. But he does.

The Russian poet is introduced to me. He is standing with his arm around a pretty girl. And, without removing the arm, he takes my hand. And he does that slow down and up thing with the eyes. It gives me a start. I find myself a corner in the kitchen, near the vodka. The Russian poet comes to me. 'You are a poet?'

'No.'

'They tell me you are a poet!' And he frowns toward the other room as if they have lied.

He takes the matches from my hand. I don't know what to do. I say, 'Oh. Do you want a cigarette?'

'No.' He lights my cigarette.

He says, 'It is too bad you do not know Russian, we could talk.'

I ask if being on tour doesn't affect the work. He turns to the interpreter. I say it again. The interpreter tells him.

'Yes. I try this morning. I can't.'

He is very good looking. This Russian poet. I say something about the reading. He urges me to come today. Ferlinghetti will read also, and Robert Bly.

He is making me nervous. He is looking too steadily into my

eyes. Someone interrupts. And I escape. Elton says, 'I hear he is a fast worker,' meaning the girl in the miniskirt. I say, 'I don't really approve. It must be bad for the work.'

I have been asked because Carla is a believer in nepotism. Given the task of rounding up Canadian writers, she has asked her friends. Even academics. Even Americans. One because his wife has left him.

But today at the reading, it is different. I go cold and the hairs start up all along my spine, along my arms. The Russian tells his poetry in a terrible voice. I know it is the declamatory style. But I feel the shudder anyway. And Robert Bly is not a silly red-faced man anymore. He has been sitting there like Walter Mitty in a red serape with black eagles. But now he is telling a poem about Viet Nam. And he is enormous. His hands become bloody. He waves them, he turns them into claws, and they are bloody. 'Do not cry!' he shouts at me, I think it is at me, and I feel ashamed, for I have been about to cry.

And Ferlinghetti is not a bald old man any longer. I am glad that I said that to him after all. What I said later. In the kitchen. I said, 'It is terrible. To be introduced. To make you stand up. I know all you want me to do is fuck off.' But in the kitchen he was merely embarrassed by this. The Russian poet, now, is a pure flame. I take Anna away hurriedly, after, I don't want to be invited to have drinks. I don't want it to be ruined. I want them to stay pure, for both of us. The real thing.

BUT NOW WE ARE in Mexico. It's Ben's turn to be free. I am twenty-five years old and seven years married. I ask for a baby.

The seventh version.

'The unity of plot does not consist, as some suppose, in its having one man as its subject. An infinity of things befall that one man, some of which it is impossible to reduce to unity.'

'Vicky always dramatizes,' says my mother. 'Must you always dramatize?'

Francie said, 'But you lied!'

Jeff says, 'You have fictionalized your whole life.'

'The story, as an imitation of action, must represent one action, a complete whole, with its several incidents so closely connected that the transposal or withdrawal of any one of them will disjoin and dislocate the whole.'

Sister Mary Joseph says, 'You have always been obsessed with truth.'

The Nut Lady said, 'Why did they tie your hands to the crib?'

'Because I bit my nails.'

'Why?'

'Because I bit my nails!'

'Why?'

'The poet's function is to describe, not the thing that happened, but a kind of thing that might happen, i.e., what is possible as being probable or necessary.'

We had been in Mexico for some months. A Venezuelan actor with flashing eyes had fallen in love with Ben in Mexico City, and we had left precipitately. Now we are living in seclusion in the village of Zapopan.

The walls around the compound are covered with broken glass. Jagged, menacing, they catch the pitiless sun in blinding bursts of fire, green and gold.

The flagging on the floor of the villa is maroon. You mop it with a rag tied around a stick. You dip the rag in oil. It gleams back at you brightly as if it were clean.

In the back yard, at the stone tubs, Maria Jesus washes our

sheets. Her thick arms, mottled with white patches, plunge up and down like pistons.

'But if your baby is sick, you must bring it to the clinic. Come tomorrow. Come tomorrow with the baby, Maria. Come at eight-thirty.'

I am doing volunteer work at the clinic in the village. It is free, but the villagers insist on paying. One peso. Eight cents.

When Maria Jesus comes, her baby in the rebozo on her back, the doctor is busy with a heart attack. I say she must wait but Maria Jesus does not wait.

Next week, she tells me, 'Better she should die. Better she should die than live my life again.'

The doctor at the clinic is small and brown, with a moustache. He does not speak English. That is, he does not speak English to the American volunteer ladies who come to the clinic.

My first day at the clinic, I make a mistake, but the doctor does not find it amusing.

'*Como se llama? Por favor?*' I manage in my textbook Spanish.

'Juan Maria Fernando Manuel Hernandez Servidora.'

'*Como se llama?*'

'Guadalupe Jesus Maria Garcia O'Brien Servidora.'

'O'Brien?'

'My father, he is Irish.'

I still don't twig. By the end of the afternoon. I have filed everything under S. Prolific family, the Servidoras. I look it up in my book. 'At your service.'

I show the doctor my mistake. He does not laugh.

I stay late and fix the file.

My second day, an American woman comes to the clinic. She is hysterical. '*Elle muerte, elle muerte,*' she says.

'I speak English.'

'It's my maid's daughter. Can you come right away? They're all screaming. She's been in labour twenty-four hours. I think she's dying.' And to the doctor, who has watched us impassively, 'Elle muerte.'

He tells me to get the instruments. They are in a dusty shoe box in the drug room. I hesitate, thinking I should wash them, but he says, 'Andele.'

I could look up the Spanish, I could make it correct. But that would imply I knew it well enough to write it. I didn't.

I was dressed in pink. Grace gave me that dress. Pink cotton, with a wide skirt, not gathered but flaring down over the hips and out in a lovely circle. A scoop neck and little tucks under the bosom. How the hell I got starch I don't know, but I did. Grace doesn't even remember it. She thinks maybe her mother made it for her, but she isn't sure. Anyway, she gave it to me, and I loved it. Even now Grace weighs only one hundred and five, so I must have been thin then too. But that was after the typhus.

Ben and I eschewed possessions. We did not want to be tied down.

When we came, the three of us, the doctor, the American woman, and I in my starched pink cotton dress, into the courtyard, we could hear the women screaming. They too were saying, 'Elle muerte, elle muerte,' rather like a Greek chorus. And all in black. Lovely.

The girl herself was lying in a hot, airless, sunless room. It used to be a chapel. High up in one wall was a cicatrice. This for air.

The floor is impacted earth, very hard, very dry, very clean. The furniture is Hollywood blonde. A bed, a dresser, a bureau with a huge mirror. Highly varnished with brass handles.

The girl lies on the bed fully dressed, with ribbed stockings. I used to wear them myself when I went to school. Her stomach bulges like some abnormality on a tree, a growth, a cancer.

Five women, counting the original American, crowd in after us. I am interested. They are screaming of death and blood and wringing their hands. They are wringing their hands, I say to myself. I have never seen anyone wring his hands before. I am scared shitless.

I say, 'Agua caliente,' in my teacher's voice and it works like magic. They are off like a flash to boil water. The silence is enormous. We are alone now. The doctor, the girl, me.

The doctor takes the girl's panties off. Thick white cotton, very clean.

He puts his finger up, feels inside. Then he sits down. On what? I don't remember. In the last version, I said, 'Then he sat down on a small wicker stool.' But I haven't a clue what he sits on. He sits there, cool as you please, and he lights a cigarette. He looks at me, his eyes gleaming with malice.

But the girl yells and I take her hands in mine and say, very calmly, very authoritatively, 'Usted no muerte. No. Les mujers estan nervioso.' I laugh at them. 'Muy nervioso. Estan loco.'

The girl laughs too, and, after a minute, I can disengage my fingers and take off my hat.

That hat. I just remembered that hat. I paid ten fifty for it in Army and Navy. Very finely woven straw with two black velvet ribbons. My god. That hat. But how, if I was not supposed to wear anything frivolous? How, if we never spent money on anything? It comes out of the blue at me. I took off my hat and I gave her a red nylon scarf to wipe her face with. Red? Must have been in my handbag.

I am absolutely calm. I think, 'It is an exam in Boolean algebra.' When I said 'Agua caliente,' I was terrified. But I am not terrified now. I am deadly with will. She is not going to die, I will not allow her to die. But I have never felt this way before, except in exams.

''Sted Ingles?' she says.

'Si.'

'I speak English,' she says, delighted. To prove it, she grips my hands again and says, 'Ouch!'

We are giggling like school girls. She is a schoolgirl. Nineteen. We pay no attention to the doctor.

'I like your furniture,' I say. I hate it.

'I buy it. Is from Hollywood, California.' I was right.

'It's very smart.'

'I study English at the Institute,' she says carefully.

'You speak it very well.'

'Verdad?'

'Si. Verdad.'

'Habla Español muy bien,' she says, returning the compliment.

'No es verdad.'

The doctor finishes his cigarette and throws it on the floor, grinding it out with his foot. The girl is shocked. So am I.

He takes something from the shoe box. Something which gleams through the dust. I think forever after it is a pair of scissors, but that can't be. Surely?

He cuts the vaginal walls and, with his hand now far inside, up to the wrist, his whole bloody hand for god's sake, he turns the baby.

There is a lot of screaming. She does not say ouch, she says, 'Aieeee,' very long and drawn out. My hands go to pieces. And all the time she looks into my eyes as if I can save her. I can save her.

''Sta bien, 'sta bien,' I say over and over. I think I am saying, 'It's okay,' but I think now it was likely, 'Be good.' Oh god. Ah, well. Maybe that's what she expected me to say, god knows.

And the baby comes out.

He snaps off the cord with his fingers. He doesn't tie it or do anything I've been led to expect. He just snaps it off and gives me the baby. And he looks amused.

It's solid. It is very solid. It is not soft. It is hard and solid and it squirms. Muscular. Furious. I saw children like that in the stone frieze in Chartres. The Massacre of the Innocents. Their faces contorted with fury. The way children would be if someone were to kill them. A genius made that. He knew all about children. They do not die, nor come into the world, content.

It is hard and muscular and it squirms against me, a hard real living baby. Complete.

'Es un niño,' I say.

The Hallelujah Chorus has just come on in my head.

'Un niño,' she says. Blissful. I give it up to her. Annunciato Ferris.

And we wait for the afterbirth, which is a great deal messier than the baby. The doctor sews the girl up with a needle and thread. Unsterilized. We will come back here in three days with the penicillin.

'Mañana,' I say to the girl but in fact I will be back tonight with the booties, the sweater, the flowers. And she will tell everyone that her husband gave them to her. Her husband with his other wife in Guadalajara, by the State.

She is his wife by the Church. He hasn't been near her for three months, and he won't be either, for another two. When she's ready to get pregnant again.

Out in the courtyard the women are standing around a great cauldron of boiling water.

'Agua caliente,' I say. 'Agua caliente!' I start to laugh. ''Sta bien,' I say through hysteria. 'Es un niño.' And, as they all start to converge with glad cries on the door of the chapel, 'No. No mujers. Elle—uh—sólida. Muy sólida. Que es la mere? La mama?' I can't think of the word for mother.

One of them, the blackest of them all, comes to me, laughing and crying, saying, 'Gracias, gracias, gracias,' and she falls down and kisses my hand. No one pays the slightest attention to the doctor, who is standing by the gate waiting for me. In years to come I will say, 'When I delivered a baby,' bringing it out casually. '*Usted, sólida*,' I say sternly. It doesn't surprise me that she has kissed my hand. Not at all. I *have* delivered a baby. It was all my doing. It was me.

They say, '*Vaya con Dios*,' and so on, and I go like the Holy Mother herself to the gate.

'*La primera niño?*' he says to me. Something like that.

We are walking down the dusty yellow road. Well, he is walking, I am floating.

'*Si. La primera.*'

'*La primera tiempo?*'

'*Si.*'

He laughs. '*Agua caliente!*' He shakes his head and laughs and stops to light another cigarette. '*Agua caliente!*'

He is laughing.

'*Como la cinema*,' I say, '*como les romans*,' mixing up French and Spanish as I always do when I'm excited.

He is laughing like hell. '*Servidora!*' he says.

'*Servidora!*' I say, and we are laughing in the hot dusty road, the dead heart of the siesta hours, laughing like lunatics.

I adore him. I want to throw myself at his feet and wash them with my hair.

In the meantime, Ben is drinking tequila. Slice the lemon. Sprinkle salt on the back of the hand. Lick. Suck. Gurgle. Lick. Suck. Gurgle. Later he will not bother with the refinements. Gurgle.

I insist we drive into Guadalajara, immediately, right now, to get booties and a little sweater, and the flowers.

We deliver them to the chapel and drive back to our villa, through the iron gates, parking under the high walls with the broken glass on top.

'I want a baby,' I say.

45

This all comes as a bolt from the blue to Ben. To me too. Although I can hardly believe I didn't know. I was just doing the fifth draft of the book. I mean, get this, for god's sake.

The book is ostensibly about Joe, who is upset about the Hungarian Revolution. A good Communist, he is all wrought up, he can't believe the news about Stalin either. Norah, his rather dumb wife, goes mooning about, when she is not attending classes in Boolean algebra, thinking of round fat squat pots. I'm not kidding. They have a friend, his name is Harold. Harold looks out for Norah while she's at university. He talks to her about his sex life. He says to Joe, 'How's the car, Joe?' Joe gets more and more depressed. He hasn't touched Norah for umpteen months. Norah has an affair with an English boy. Everyone thinks he's queer. She gets pregnant. While she's in hospital—can't remember why—Harold comes in all wrought up. Joe comes in all wrought up. Joe hits Harold right in the kisser, thinking it's all his fault. Norah smiles.

I mean, I wrote that, saying, 'Joe is a facet of my own character,' meaning it, and all the time Norah bumbles through the book like a bright morning star. I was a great believer in the artist as conscious craftsman. I mean, I really thought it was a book about a disillusioned Marxist.

I mean, the damn book starts out with Wilma and Mary and their frigging abortion party!

But I didn't know. I thought I had made a discovery, all in one afternoon in an abandoned chapel in Zapopan. Religious revelation.

I'm trying to get out of it. Telling this part. Deep breath.

'But you *agreed*,' said Ben. 'You *agreed* not to have children.' We were back now from our trip to the market in Guadalajara and the chapel. His face was no longer so flushed.

'I know, but I've changed.'

'But you said,' Ben said.

'I know, but now I want one.'

He went to the kitchen and brought back a glass of tequila which he downed at once, without salt or lemon.

'That's the end then,' he said. 'You have broken the contract.'

'All right,' I said.

I went into the bedroom and opened the upright wardrobe.

'What are you doing?' he said from the door.

'I'm packing,' I said. 'I'll catch the plane tomorrow.'

'Where are you going?'

'Home.'

'What am I going to do?'

'I don't know.'

'I can't get back alone,' he said. 'I can't. You know I can't.'

'You have the car.'

'I can't. It's 1,200 miles to the border. I can't.'

He was afraid. He was afraid of everything in Mexico. Venezuelan actors. The heads of pigs on market stalls, freshly bleeding, covered with flies. Gas station attendants whose meters never worked and whose prices Ben would never debate. I would. The 400-year-old mummies of nuns in the basement of the chapel in Mexico City. Hair and fingernails so long in death, their bones grinning through their skins behind the glass tops. I read that this is not scientific: the hair and nails do not grow after death; the skin merely recedes, giving one this impression. But then, those nuns must have been terribly vain. He was afraid of bullfights, though he went, where I would not. Of tarantulas, large as beavers, scuttering across the road near Mazatlan. The spiders in the Aztec village, yellow and orange and black, swaying in their webs across the village street, inches from your head; a village where the sun shone directly into the street only at noon, so high were the mountains, so perpendicular and mauve. The hare-lipped children, the cataracts, the beggars lying asleep on the pavements.

'You take the plane. I'll drive back.'

'I can't, you know I can't.'

I knew he couldn't.

But most of all he was afraid of the deep slit in the earth, I forget the name. It led five thousand feet to another world, far below our high plateau: a tropical world, where bananas grew. If you stood a quarter of a mile away, it was like prairie grass, uneventful. But walk near and there, at your feet, like something out of Jules Verne, an entrance to the centre of the earth. I'll remember in a while. If I don't think about it.

So I stayed.

I stayed and I went to the clinic. I finished the book.

One day we went for a walk to the, to the

If I don't think about it, I'll remember. 'Let's go down and see!' I said, excited all of a sudden.

Ben was perfectly willing. We started down. It was I who got asthma. It was I who made us turn back.

One night, waking, is that Ben above me, staring down into my face, propped on one elbow, his hand

No. I read that in a story. I imagined it. It was one of my hypnagogic things. But I did become afraid of spiders, as if Ben's fear were contagious. I had never been afraid of spiders. I would carry them out into the garden. I still do. I do again, I mean. But then, I was afraid. I would dream of them scampering, furry legs, over my face as I slept. And I wake and I see Ben above me, staring down into my

I see his hand and it has a thread dangling from it. But that must be a lie.

A year later I signed the papers to commit me to Essondale. In the meantime, we had come back to Vancouver, I had become pregnant. I had had an abortion.

Now I was enormous. Huge. I weighed one hundred and fifty-eight pounds. We agreed it was a symptom. We agreed I should commit myself.

The psychiatrist was a nice young sandy-haired man named Dr Hutchinson. Ben explained everything to him and he filled in the forms and I signed where he marked, in light pencil, X.

Ben was explaining that I understood this was a decision made of my own free will. This was voluntary committal, and I understood the significance of that.

I was very tired.

The doctor said would I leave for a few minutes, he had something to discuss with Mr Ferris.

I left. I sat in the waiting room. I didn't read. A long time seemed to go by, but then that might be me.

Ben came out, his face quite white. He looked shaken. I felt frightened.

'Would you mind stepping in here again, Mrs Ferris?'

I looked at Ben, but I couldn't tell what was wrong.

'Please. Sit down.' Everything had changed. 'Please.' I sat down. 'Would you like a cigarette?'

'I don't smoke.'

The psychiatrist gave what sounded like a laugh. But that might be me.

'There's just one or two things I'm not quite clear on,' he said. 'What would you do if you didn't go to Essondale?'

'What I was doing,' I said.

'And what was that?'

I held out my hands. They were covered with blue and white paint. Green enamel. 'The house.'

'You have taken a house I understand.'

'Yes. I've been painting it.' I kept my hands out as if he wouldn't believe me otherwise.

'You were going to move in, when?'

'End of the month.'

'One week, that is.'

'Yes. With my sister.'

'I see. You were going to leave Mr Ferris.'

'Yes.'

'You do realize, Mrs Ferris? You do know you're not having a baby?'

'Yes. I realize.' I wished he wouldn't smoke. It was bad for the baby.

He gave another short sound that might have been a laugh.

'You don't have to worry,' I said. 'I can write anywhere. Ben will be all right.'

'All right?'

'I mean, I can still support him.'

He didn't answer for a minute. 'Mrs Ferris,' he said finally, not looking at me, 'we don't like to put people in Crease if they're functioning.'

Crease. It was Crease. Not Essondale. Essondale is for the involuntary.

'You see, you are still functioning.' He seemed to be safe with the word. He used it again. 'So long as you can function, I wouldn't really like to see you go to Crease ...'

'All right,' I said. 'But I do want to leave him, you see.' I wanted to be absolutely honest. I was quite mad. I wanted him to understand the full extent of my madness.

'You know,' he said, 'I've read about these cases, but I have never actually seen one before.' This time I was sure. It was a laugh. 'I mean, where a relative comes in quite lucid, quite coherent, and the functioning ...' He thought better of going on. 'Mr Ferris and I have agreed,' he said, 'we have agreed, that perhaps he should have therapy.'

And that is how Ben went to Essondale. Crease. That is how Ben went to Crease instead of me.

Barranca. That's the word. I remembered.

So Jocelyn and I moved into the house. It looked lovely. I'd spent a whole month cleaning it, painting it, buying furniture from the Salvation Army and St Vincent de Paul's. The fake Sarukhan rugs. The Renoir reproduction of the girl with the cat. Blinds made to order. Curtains. It was a terrible mess when I found it. When I opened the door of the oven (the landlord sold me the stove for ten dollars), I was met with a solid block of green. I couldn't figure out what it was at first. It was mold. When I tackled it, like an idiot, with a bucket of Spic 'n Span, I got knocked clear across the kitchen, landing up against the glass-fronted cabinets. Actually, I didn't feel too bad. Wham. Right across the kitchen, as if some great fist had caught me in the stomach. I sat there for quite a while, and then I started to laugh. I was still laughing when I found the electrical shutoff in the cellar. 'Well, I got shock treatment anyway,' I said to the fuse box. In the crawl spaces under the eaves, the former tenants had thrown all their garbage. That took me three days. Razor blades. Apple cores. Incredible, and they were Germans. The panelling in the dining room was real mahogany. When it was oiled it came up beautifully. There were stained-glass windows at the entrance and in the dining room window. Even in the glass door on the built-in buffet. A dream of a house with a blue-tiled fireplace. And a garden. Rose bushes. A lawn. All for seventy-five dollars a month. I'd never spent so much, but Jocelyn and I were going to rent one of the bedrooms. I bought a lawn mower, a hose, a pitch fork. A shovel for the furnace. An axe. When I left, the landlord's wife complained. It was in beautiful condition, that house, beautiful. When she moved in. 'She's going to have to pay damages.' This to Ben.

We moved in, Jocelyn and I. And one week later, Ben signed

himself out of Essondale. 'I was wrong. I couldn't have worked there. Crease, I mean. They keep you busy all the time. It's ridiculous. They took away my razor.'

There was nowhere else for him to go. I let him move into the sun porch. Had to order a complete new set of blinds. Thirty-two dollars and fifty cents. Made the drapes out of a nice blue and brown striped flannel, eight dollars. The bed was the big blow: forty-eight ninety-five. I just gave it away two weeks ago.

Jocelyn and I slept in the big bedroom. We could still rent the other, with Ben in the sun porch. But then Francie, my youngest sister, arrived. Ben would spend hours telling her how he was going to commit suicide.

I can come back to this. I don't have to talk about this now.

It's a year later, almost a year. Yes, a year. I am divorced now. I'm in West Vancouver doing housework for a week and Jocelyn phones.

'We rented the room!'

'Oh good.'

'To a man.'

'Yeah, well, we knew that might happen.'

'Well, I figure we can use the money.'

'What's he like?'

'He's a clerk at city hall.'

I see a pale blond man, glasses, concave chest.

'That sounds all right.'

'So when you coming home?'

Mik tells me his side of the story later.

He'd been out of the Pen about eight months. Living downtown on Granville Street, in hotels that have names like the Helen's and the Queen's. He was sitting in the Helen's one day and he decided to go across the bridge. To sit in the Helen's is distinct from to crash at the Helen's. If you sit, you are in the beer parlor. *To go across the bridge* means to go straight, become respectable, get a job. He was just sitting there, boozing it up with the buddies, and it came over him, how he had to go across the bridge. When he got out of the Pen he was still gimpy, but Welfare fixed his back and then he did the odd bit of benny snatching and so on to augment his Welfare cheques. A bit of B & E now and then. Most times he crashed with one of the buddies in the Helen's. His buddies laughed at him, but he just up and did it. First he and Taffy got a suitcase from one of the rooms and stuffed it with old newspapers from the lounge of the Helen's.

'You can tell if someone's carrying an MT,' Mik said to me later. 'A guy forgets and hoists it,' he illustrated, 'so you got to stuff it.' All he owned in the world was the clothes he arrived in: a khaki shirt, khaki trousers, sandals, not the fashionable kind. Sandals with holes in them and buckled-down straps. Like children wear. That was all he had. Ben would have loved to have been so free.

In one of the newspapers was our ad, Jocelyn's and mine. We'd switched from the Female Only classified section to Men/Women. It was already two weeks old.

He borrowed a buck from Taffy. Then he humped the suitcase across the bridge. On the other side, he got a taxi to our house, with the buck.

'Your dumb sister!' he says to me. 'She never even saw me drive up.'

Jocelyn is a tall thin pre-Raphealite girl who moves through life in a Mr Magoo way, miraculously avoiding all pitfalls and mud puddles. It is a family joke. One day she inadvertently became engaged to an Arab exchange student. 'But we were talking about agrarian reform,' she said wonderingly, after he had made a scene in Acadia camp. 'He was telling me about his father's farms, and all I said was I would like to see them.'

'I come up in a cab and does she see me?' Mik said. 'Boy! Your dumb sister.'

He knocked at the door and Jocelyn answered it. Yes, she said vaguely, we still had the room, nobody wanted it. You had to share the bathroom, she supposed that was why. It was just a sleeping room.

'What a salesman,' Mik said. To me.

She took him upstairs. It was nice and bright, I'd cleaned it before going to West Vancouver, and it had new curtains. But it wasn't much, I guess. The bed cost ten dollars and the vanity, one of those elaborate three-way mirror things, was eight, from Love's auction. Jocelyn contributed the rug, a shag. There was a built-in cupboard arrangement for shirts and so on.

Jocelyn said to me later, 'Do you think that was all right? Sixty-five?'

Mik has asked for board as well as room.

'I didn't think he'd go for the share system,' said Jocelyn. We'd had actresses for a while and we shared everything four ways: food, rent, utilities. Our food never came to more than four dollars a week each.

'He asked for board too, so I said sixty-five,' she said to me on the telephone. She was worried about making a profit. Neither one of us believed in landlord profits. 'But I figure our time is worth something, cooking and putting up bag lunches and all that.'

Mik said, with professional tenantese, 'How about linen?'

'What? Oh, sheets, you mean? Okay. Sure.'

'My personal laundry?' he said, pressing his luck.

'Oh sure, just throw it down the chute there. Don't leave the door open though, Sally got excited the other day and fell down.'

'Unh?'

'Our cat. They were tearing around the place and she got excited and jumped into the laundry chute. She went all the way down. But it was okay, there was a whole week's wash down there. It was all right. It just scared her. Only we have to keep the chute door closed.' She was worrying the problem of bag lunches. Mik had asked for board and she'd assumed this meant bag lunches, so she was trying to figure out the schedule. If she did his bag lunch when she did hers, which would be reasonable and efficient, what chore would I then swap? Jocelyn was scrupulously fair about housework. She hated it, and still does, going Slam Bam Thank You Ma'am through everything. She was wondering if it would be fair to ask me to do two breakfasts to her one for bag lunches every night. I drove her mad with my nit-picking. She did everything she was supposed to, but I would wait eagerly for my turn at the kitchen, the wash, the bathroom, the floors, because now I could do it properly. She doesn't remember any of this. She says, 'I don't remember you being so domestic.' And, 'I left under the kitchen sink for you,' when I come to visit. 'God, Vicky, you've changed a lot. You never used to be so fanatic.' Our bedroom was schizophrenic. Jocelyn viewed it as not in the public domain and therefore never made her bed or put anything away. It was as though an imaginary line were drawn down the floor: on one side Dionysus rampant; on the other Athena couchant.

'I'm a clerk down at city hall,' Mik said.

'Oh, that's nice,' said Jocelyn. 'I'm a student, but I'm working as a waitress till summer school. I have to go pretty soon.'

But Mik was going to get the other part of the 'we' out of her. He'd gone this far and he wasn't going to stop now. He knew she couldn't be the real landlady.

'Your husband a student?' But he had looked at her hand.

'Oh I'm not married. I live with my sister.'

'Oh. She's the landlady, your sister.'

'We're both the landladies,' said Jocelyn.

He waited in the dining room while she found the extra key.

He couldn't believe it. He had to say it, even if she didn't ask.

'Uh, I'm short right now but I'll pay you Monday.'

'Oh sure.' She hadn't even thought about asking for money.

'I mean,' said Mik later, 'I don't think she should be running around loose.' Shaking his head. 'Neither one of you should be running around loose.'

We weren't very business-like, Jocelyn and I. One of the actresses had invited an actor to stay for the weekend and he'd remained for four months. At the end, Jocelyn said to me, in a cross voice—being materialistic always makes her cross; she has to get mad to do it—'I think we should ask John for something.'

We decided that it wasn't fair to ask John to pay toward the rent as he was sleeping in the sun porch, which wasn't heated. But he should pay four dollars a week toward the food, or whatever it worked out to once he was chipping in. And, 'Maybe he could do the furnace,' I said.

The furnace. My god. All that bit about the wood stove up at the island, I could make a fire. Every day I got the furnace going. Well, then, what was I doing, letting Mik show me how to ... Oh. Yes. Mik didn't know that I could make a fire. And I let him show me, helpless lady that I was.

Anyway. Jocelyn and I drew straws and I lost. John was quite pleased to pay four dollars a week, we should have asked before. He'd wondered once or twice. But he never did make up the furnace. They didn't have call until noon, and I start work early.

'Well,' said Mik, 'I'll just leave my suitcase upstairs then.'

He walked back across the bridge in a euphoria of success, burst into the beer parlor at the Helen's and said, 'I made it.' They didn't believe him at first. Then he did a B & E and went on a five-day bash.

The West Van trip had ended rather disastrously for me. I'd rushed back that morning to see the Nut Lady. 'You've got to put me away,' I said.

Now I was seeing a therapist.

When Ben signed himself out of Essondale, I had a long talk with the doctor in charge. Crease, I mean. Crease.

'You might need some supportive therapy yourself,' he said.

'But what's wrong with him?'

'The prognosis is not good,' he said. 'He's a latent homosexual.'

I didn't believe it. I still don't.

'We don't usually do this, especially if you yourself were to consider therapy, but we think you had better think about getting a divorce.'

'Can't he get therapy?'

'We don't recommend it,' the doctor said. 'But you might consider the clinic. It's free.'

Free. Yes, well, thank you very much but I pay my way. If it's free, how can it be good? I thanked him very much and went back to the house.

In the mornings, Ben slept. Around noon he would get up and go down to the dining room where Francie was working on her correspondence lessons. Like me, she was exempt from public school because of ill health. Actually, she could have gone, but she hated the confusion. It was easier to whip all the lessons off in one fell swoop and then concentrate on life.

I was upstairs at the desk but I could hear snatches of the conversation:

'What you do is get hold of some potassium cyanide,' Ben is saying. 'And then you put some in a tablet, one of those cylinder tablets you can put together. Then you get a lot of other tablets the same shape, colour, and you put them in a bottle and you take one a day, only they don't have anything in them, or maybe baking soda, and then that way it becomes habitual.'

'But how do you get hold of the potassium cyanide?' Francie says seriously.

'Yes. That's the problem. Vicky could have got it if she were still at the lab.'

And then there was the sure-fire bathtub method: 'But Ben, if you turn off the lights, you won't be able to see to get your wrists in position for the razor blades.'

'Oh yes, that's right,' Ben says. This is the one where he gets into a hot bath so he can't feel a thing, and the machine comes down, automatically, and *slice*. The lights had to be out so he couldn't see the water turning red.

Francie comes up from the States and I say to her, now, 'What else happened that fall? I can't remember clearly. What were Ben's great suicide plots?'

'Oh god, I don't know,' and she laughs. 'Ben was great.'

'Great?'

'He was so funny, even about suicide. The Rube Goldberg variations. He was so great.'

'I can't remember. About his jokes. I know he was funny. But I can't remember. It's not fair, not to put in how funny he was. But I can't remember. What happened? I can't remember. How did you go? I don't even remember your going.'

'I had appendicitis. Don't you remember?'

'Did you? Did you have them out?'

'It. I had it out. Don't you remember? I had to go home. They went swish! and it popped out.'

'I don't remember. I can't remember about your appendix.' And later, when she is having a bath, I go in to make sure. Yes. There's a scar.

'My god,' I say.

'Well, you were pretty far away, that fall. What a weird time! And I'm coming out of the ether and the nurse says, "How far gone are you, dear?" Because I hadn't had my period for four months.'

'Oh that's right, what was his name?'

'Carlos Johnston,' Francie says gloomily.

'Didn't I call the police because you were out late?'

'Yeah. Boy, was I furious. Don't you remember, Mom came out and took one look at him. Big black booger, and she whisked me home?'

'And he raped you,' I say, feeling the old fear; the old guilt. I hadn't looked out for her.

But Francie doesn't answer this. 'What was I?' She is sitting soaping her breasts in the tub. 'Was I fourteen or fifteen?' We work it out. Fifteen.

When Jocelyn came home from class, Ben would tell her all over again.

At least, that's how I remember those months. I wore an eighteen-and-a-half size dress. I was enormous.

But Jocelyn's version is quite different. One day her creative writing instructor phoned me and told me she'd written 'a very interesting play. About you.'

'Can I read your play?' I say to Jocelyn. She is cuddled up on the front room sofa with David. I am trying not to show how much this bothers me. Public displays of affection, ugh.

'No, Vicky. I couldn't.'

So I sneak it. One day when she is out, I take it from her desk and I read it. It's lying right on top, she trusts me that much. On the cover it has 'A' and 'Most interesting.'

Is that true, about Joss cuddling with David? No. They still don't. When he got home at Christmas, the most they did was touch each other lightly on the shoulder. David is even worse than me about public affection. It is all in my mind. They are just sitting there, but the charge is high.

It is called Merry-Go-Round and is all about a successful woman writer who lives in a big old house with her sloppy sister and her emasculated husband. She is beautiful and competent, and nags everyone about cleaning up the mess. Her husband sleeps all day and the beautiful writer comes into his room, picks up his canister of pencils and dumps them, crash! onto the floor. To wake him up. To make him feel guilty. When she isn't dumping canisters of pencils and nagging her sloppy sister, she is sitting at her typewriter going clackety-clack like a machine, making money. She keeps making logical statements with no regard for emotional truth. The husband brings her cups of tea. It is very funny and farcical and I would have given it an A too. Or an A minus anyway.

One day I hear Ben going on downstairs to both of them about the latest surefire way to do himself in. It fulfills all the requirements: it is painless, allows no reversal of decision, and does not leave a mess for anyone to clean up. I come downstairs like Armageddon.

'Look. Ben? Look. You just walk down to Granville Bridge and you just climb over the rail and you just push yourself off. I mean, I'm sick and tired of all this crap. If you want to do it, do it and get it over with.'

They are all horribly embarrassed for me. We don't know what to do with violence. We just feel so ashamed for the person. They don't know where to look. Ben gives me a pitying smile.

I register at the free clinic.

'I'm destructive,' I say in my first session. 'I told my husband to go jump off a bridge.'

About a month later, I am saying, 'You've got to get out, Ben. I'm destroying you.' Full of disinterested concern, that's me. 'I've talked to Ivan, he'll take you. Really, you'll be better off there.' It is all arranged. He is to leave Friday.

'You keep the car, Vicky,' says Ben.

'No, that's your car. You did the motor job.'

'Then you keep the hi fi. And the cats.'

'All right.'

'After,' he says, 'after, you can have the car back.' Meaning after he is dead.

On Friday morning I go out and stay away until noon. When I leave at eight the house is congealed. Francie and Jocelyn, where are they? I don't remember. When I get back, there is Ben, standing like a waif in the garden.

'I can't,' he says.

'You have to,' I say and go away for another four hours. When I get back, he is gone, and I am left with the hi fi and the thirteen cats. We did not believe in possessions. There was so little to divide.

Relief like a blessing pours through me. I go upstairs and work for a while. It is Jocelyn's turn to cook. At dinner, her eyes are puffy and red. Francie is in her bedroom. She won't come down.

'I had to,' I say. 'I had to.'

'I know,' Jocelyn says. 'But you just go upstairs and you ... you're like ... it's like you've got a steel trap for a mind. It's like ...' and she stands there, her lips shaking. 'I know you did. It's just ...' And she leaves the room.

I could never bear being unhappy. That was always my trouble. I'm still that way. If I'm unhappy I think something is terribly wrong.

I went upstairs and I wrote and I forgot all about Ben. I was trying to write a story about a man who commits suicide. About his family, really. How they are, after. How they try to understand it.

'You've got to stop giving him money now,' Jocelyn says later. That night. She has come down and said she was sorry. 'Why can't he go on unemployment insurance?'

'He's not eligible. He's in the executive bracket or something.'

'The executive bracket?' said Jocelyn. 'But that means he must have made a lot of money when he was working.'

'Oh I don't think so. It just means he was on the managerial side or something.'

'What was he making?'

'I don't know. He never told me.'

'Didn't you *ask*?'

'No. I never thought about it.'

'God.' We are drinking tea and there is a long pause.

'I sneaked your play,' I say.

'What did you think?' Jocelyn says before she remembers.

'It's good. I liked it. It's very funny.'

'Oh Jesus,' she says. 'Oh shit. Look. Vicky. It's not really true, you know. I mean, that's not the way I really see you. I mean, you make it up, you know. It starts one way and then you make it up to fit.'

'The form takes over,' I say. 'I know.'

But it is true. Everything you make up is true. Too.

'We'd better put an ad in,' says Jocelyn. 'Francie can sleep with me.'

So we put an ad in and we get the actresses.

Francie leaves, though I don't remember how. Jocelyn goes to classes. The actresses go to rehearsal. I work on the suicide play. November 14. The day I would have had the baby. I go on a diet. I start to lose weight.

But that isn't how I remember it. I remember it more dramatically. I remember a great rushing wind pouring out of me. I remember going down like a balloon. I've had to put in the diet, because that is also true. It is a fact. But

Somewhere in there Ben registers for teachers' training.

One night I wake. It is black in the bedroom. I can hear them making love in the other bed. Jocelyn and David. I lie there, afraid to move, afraid to breathe. They are making love, groaning and panting. The bed springs are jerking violently. How can she? In the same room. I lie there petrified with horror and shame.

The Nut Lady says, 'Are you sure?'

'I was right there.'

'Have you asked your sister about it?'

'No! My god. How could I?'

'Vicky,' she says, very gentle with me in these days, 'didn't this happen before?'

'No. She's never done that before.'

'Did you tell me about this before? When you were five? About your father and how he took your hands from your ears. How he said, "She's lying! She's awake. She's lying there listening."'

'Dear god. Then I am mad.'

'Talk to your sister,' says the Nut Lady.

'No! My god, Vicky, how could you think I could do it! Or David! David's so square he can't even dance with me in public. No! It isn't true.'

'I heard you. I heard the whole thing. It was real.'

'I swear!' Jocelyn says.

'I know. I know. I know you weren't there. I know. I just heard you, that's all.'

'What does she say it is?'

'Something called a hypnagogic vision. Where you externalize.'

'But why would you do something like that?'

'Daddy caught me listening once. Well, I was trying not to listen, but he got mad at me. She thinks that's it.'

Jocelyn says, after a while, 'Does it happen often? Do you get these things often?'

'I don't know,' I say. 'That's the trouble.'

But Jocelyn is still angry. 'Well, if you want to know, we only do it when we're prepared to take the risk.'

'What?'

'We only do it when we're willing to get caught,' she says, her mouth tight, like my mother's. 'That's what you believe, isn't it? That's what you think. You don't think it's right unless you get punished. Well, you can be satisfied about that.'

'What?'

'And we have never done it here, never!'

Oh Jocelyn. Oh my god.

I AM IN West Vancouver. The divorce is over. The play has gone on. The one about the suicide. The director didn't like the first draft. He has said, 'Oddly enough, it's very competent. It's just crap.' And, 'Tell me about your father.'

I tell him about my father and he says, 'Now go back and write it again.'

I go back and write it again in two days and two nights, nonstop. I break once to watch I Love Lucy. When they ask me later if I have been influenced by Bach, in the fugue-like contrapuntal technique, I want to say, 'Actually, it was I Love Lucy.' Last year I read a graduate paper on it. 'The motif of sterility and death can be seen in the carefully worked-out images of ...' I say, to the earnest woman student, 'I can't tell. It seems right, I mean, I suppose that's all there, what you say about the images and so on, but I didn't work them out like that. I wasn't trying for that.' She has got a B and wants me to tell her why she didn't get an A. It seems both amazing and ludicrous for that play to be written about, with footnotes and a bibliography.

I am in West Vancouver doing housework.

I am cooking and cleaning and babysitting for Gladys, the woman from the radio station. She is giving a recital.

For years she has been saying, 'I've wasted my life on that man.' I say, 'Well, why don't you give a recital?'

'I couldn't. It'd cost a fortune. We're living beyond our income now.'

'Well, I've got money. I'll back you. I'll be your entrepreneur.'

Gladys laughs. 'You don't have that much.'

'Sure I do. I'm rich. I got a fortune for that play.'

'It's too late,' Gladys says. 'I've given my life to that man.'

'You're singing better than ever. You told me so yourself.'

'But I can't afford to get help in. His Nibs would have a fit if I weren't here to serve him hand and foot.'

'I'll do it. I'll come and be your housekeeper.'

'Do you think we could?'

We get all giggly and make elaborate plans. I shall do the catering and rent the gallery, we'll get Boris to make up the programs, and Paul to translate from the German. 'Oh but He'll never agree,' Gladys says. She always capitalizes her husband.

But he agrees. 'It was never me, you know,' he says on the QT to me, but I don't listen.

I come on Monday and I make a lot of mistakes. I throw out the *schmaltz* she was saving. 'But it just looked like chicken fat,' I say.

'Chicken fat!' Gladys says. 'It *was* chicken fat!'

'Would you put it back in the frying pan?' says the husband about the limp French toast. He is lying in bed, being a genius.

Gladys encourages me and on Tuesday I do better.

By Wednesday I have ironed all the genius's shirts.

By Thursday the house is running smoothly. 'It hasn't been this clean in months,' says the genius. 'Why don't you live here permanently? ' says Gladys.

By Friday Gladys has her dress and everything is arranged.

And every night, I lie in their downstairs room and hear them making love upstairs. Or, I hear someone. Making violent love.

Saturday morning, Gladys screams at me: 'You want me to fail. You've done this on purpose. You've planned the whole thing.'

I've arranged for a dozen red roses to be delivered after the recital. The card says, 'See? It wasn't so bad after all.' She gets them before she goes on. Oh god.

I have missed a CBC cocktail party because of the housekeeping and Sunday a man arrives at the house to see me. 'You were the guest of honour,' he says. 'Didn't you know?'

'I was babysitting,' I say.

'Well,' he says, 'if the mountain won't come to ... etcetera.' He sits on Gladys's chesterfield and says extravagant things about the play. And offers me a job. A play for Festival.

After he leaves, Gladys comes out of the bedroom and says, 'I can't stand the act.'

'What?'

'The innocent act. "Oh Mr Winters,"' she imitates, '"but I'm really only little me. I really couldn't write a big important play for Festival. I'm really no good at all." I wish you could hear yourself. I wish you could hear how sickening you sound.'

'Did I say that?'

'And you bounced up and down and said "Goody!"'

On Monday morning I slip out of the downstairs room early. I haven't slept much, what with all the hypnagogic loving going on

upstairs all night. Down on Marine Drive I get the first paper.

Gladys Turner has great sensitivity of phrasing. One could only wish
she had a talent or at least a voice commensurate with that sensitivity.

I go back up the hill to the still-sleeping house, pack my suit-case, and catch the bus to the clinic. All the buses to the clinic. I am sitting there, in my blue jeans and T-shirt, when the Nut Lady arrives.

'You've got to put me away,' I say. 'I'm dangerous.'

She gives me a pill and lets me lie down in the little green room for a while. A green underwater room. The nurse brings me a cup of tea. Then I go home.

I am sitting in the front room and Mik walks in the door.

It couldn't have been that day. That day I was wearing a blue skirt and a fussy blouse. The red suede slippers. The day Mik walked in and did the double-take. But it seems to be that other day. The day I came home from the clinic. It can't be, because of the blue jeans. But it was.

The key turns in the lock and he bangs into the entry hall. A great thick red-faced man in khaki. A man with a bald head. He sees me and he does a double-take. But it is a joke. I laugh.

'You the landlady?' he says.

This is after the five-day bash. He tells me later he expected the lock to be changed.

'Yes.'

'You don't look like a landlady,' he says.

I laugh. He laughs. That's the start.

Mik wasn't bald. I just looked through my I. Magnin box of old photographs and found the one of Mik and me.

It's a street picture. There's a sign behind us, over our heads.

You can see 'ancy's.' And another sign: 'ot donuts.' Mik is two steps ahead of me, and I am leaning over, listing to starboard, so that I disappear behind his shoulder. He is wearing the sports jacket and trousers we bought that day with Ben's credit card. Not the day of the picture. That other day. The shirt collar seems to be too tight. Perhaps the top button is gone. The tie is subdued, with two small flecks. The sports jacket is also too small. It is wrinkled across his middle. The trousers appear to be black or dark blue. Surely not. And Mik has a tuft of hair right at the top of his head, and a little on each side, over the ears. Oddly, the tuft at the top doesn't vitiate the Mr Clean look at all. He stares at the camera, his right hand cupped, the cigarette turned inwards to his palm, a genie in mufti.

Sometimes people, going through my I. Magnin box, say, 'Is that *you*?' for I weigh 112 in that shot. And then, 'Who's *that*?' I always mutter something and shove the picture under the others, ashamed, as if it were an atrocity photo.

I am a person who remembers what I've paid for everything. The black winter coat I have on cost forty-eight dollars. When I bought it, I thought, 'Grace and Terence will approve. It's in good taste, anyway.' The handbag is a closely woven wicker with leather straps. It cost forty pesos in Guadalajara, one of the expensive shops on the Avenida de la Revolutione. It was a lot of money in Mexico, but only five dollars really. I went hot all over when I paid so much. I want to say Ben disapproved, but in fact I think he said, 'Go ahead. If you want it so much.' I saw it later in the Village Square for twenty-five. I remember how much I paid for Ben's suede jacket. Four hundred pesos. And the black suit I got him with my first short story money. Fifty in Bellingham, on sale.

But I cannot, even for consistency, tell you how much I paid for the clothes Mik is wearing in the photograph. Later, I will approximate the sum, when I ask for the money back, but I will never remember.

The clerk in Eaton's Men's Department took one look at us and called the manager. There was a long confab about the credit card.

'It's my husband's,' I said.

And Mik said, grinning dangerously, 'I'm her little boy.'

They couldn't refuse us. Ben's credit was good. I paid promptly every month.

Mik picked out the sports jacket, the trousers. Grey. Dark grey. Now I remember. And a couple of shirts and socks. The tie. Not that tie. Not the one with the two flecks. Another. A thin grey tie. And a lovely soft yellow wool cardigan which he ruined by tossing for its first wash in a coin machine.

'Will you take them or wear them? Sir,' said the clerk.

'I'll wear them. Sonny,' said Mik.

'Will you need underwear? Sir?'

'Yah. You run over and scrounge me a couple of ...'

I can't remember. I never took notes on Mik. Something outrageous.

Mik has his head out the curtains of the dressing room. He winks at me. 'What size?' says the clerk. 'For the jockey shorts? Sir.'

Mik gives him a look. 'Big.'

After, we are waiting at the counter for the clerk to wrap Mik's old things. He makes a great business of it, folding the khaki as if it were Harris tweed, enclosing the raggedy shorts with a piece of tissue paper before he raises them, with a small shudder, and puts them too into the package. Mik takes the neatly wrapped, carefully knotted, brown paper container from the clerk. 'Thank you veddy much,' he says, clicking his heels and making a Prussian bow. His hand comes up, his great fingers holding the knot daintily, his pinky crooked skywards, and drops the package into the waste bin beneath the clerk's nose.

The clerk sucks in his breath.

'Not at all, my good man,' Mik says and we are off down the aisle, not looking at each other, afraid to look for fear of the laughter inside us, walking very casually toward the shoe department.

That first day, Mik says, 'You don't look like a landlady.'

'Will you be wanting dinner tonight?'

'No. Oh no. I just have to get something from my suitcase.'

While he's upstairs Gladys phones.

'Have you seen the reviews?' she carols.

'Just this morning's.'

'The Sun's is better,' she says. 'But at least MacPherson understood the phrasing. Herbert did his proverbial roll in the aisle about the big voice bit. As if lieder singers should have big voices! But he's a well-known idiot, MacPherson. We've been counting up the ticket money and I think I can pay you back and make a profit too! Thirteen dollars and fifty cents.'

'That's wonderful.'

'Vicky, thanks for everything. Really. Hey, where did you get to this morning?'

'I had an appointment with the Nut Lady.'

'Oh. Gosh, I got up and I thought you were mad at me or something.'

'No. I, I thought you were, I thought maybe you'd be upset by the review.'

'Oh Vicky, don't be silly. They're good reviews really. Were you upset?'

'Yes. A little.'

Somewhere in all this, Mik leaves again, having checked his suitcase and found it completely untampered with, all the newspapers intact. There is some special way you can do this. With a hair laid a certain way across the inside of the lock. I forget.

The next day he moves in for good.

IT BOTHERS ME, that I lied about the wood stove up at the island. It seemed true when I wrote it. It seemed real that I did not know how to make a fire. I could see the smoke filling the cabin and Mik's disgusted face, puffed up and shiny with rage. I could see the balled-up pieces of newspaper, blackened and charred, the fire gone out. Perhaps I was transposing time and space, for when I began with the furnace in the house I did make mistakes. It took me a long time to become expert. I had a chopping block in the cellar. Paul got it for me. And I would put on my gardening gloves and set up the kindling and wham! precisely with the axe. It was very satisfying. I could keep the furnace going for almost twenty-four hours with only two or three visits to the cellar during the day and one last thing at night.

And yet I *know* I was totally useless with that wood stove on the island. At first I thought, Oh yes, it was the helpless lady bit, when I remembered at first, I mean. But it wasn't just that. In some way, more true than simple lying, I *was* helpless. I let it go out. Mik was angry with me. That also is true, and yet, how could it be?

Sister Mary Joseph says to me: 'You are obsessed with truth.'

The Nut Lady said to me: 'You tell me a fact and you think that is truth.'

When I was five, my mother caught me holding myself Down There. I was galloping through the house, giddyap, giddyap.

'What are you doing?' she said with that tight face my mother gets.

I took one look at her face and knew I must have been doing something heinous, something dirty.

'I was thinking of the devil,' I said.

I lie awake for a week of nights. In a cold sweat of guilt. It seems to me I have never been so wicked. I realize at last that I must confess. I will do it first thing in the morning. I cannot live with it anymore.

I go out into the kitchen. Linoleum on the floor. Maroon flowers. Worn in places, cracked. Under the sink, ghastly oozes of grey. Children see all the filth grownups can't: the undersides of things that aren't cleaned. I say, 'It was a horse.'

'What?'

'A horse. Not the devil. I was thinking of a horse.'

But she doesn't remember and gets cross all over again. Says, 'Don't be silly.'

My mother hated liars.

Jeff says, about the book, 'Oddly enough, I'm sure it will bear no resemblance to life at all. No one need worry in the slightest. You have always fictionalized everything that has ever happened to you. You make it up as you go along.'

MIK MOVES IN. I am working on a play about a man from the sea. He plays chess. So I must learn chess. I ask Paul to teach me.

I learn slowly. Paul explains the fool's mate carefully, over and over, but I keep opening to it. Finally, to teach me a lesson, Paul lets me play on, still in check. In the middle, when I think I am doing well for once, he says, 'Of course, you've been in check for seventeen moves.'

I sweep the pieces from the board. 'You bastard! You rotten bastard. You're banished for a week. I mean it. Get out of here!' And I go upstairs and slam the door. A tantrum. I have had a tantrum. Typically, Paul stays away a week.

Paul was Jocelyn's friend first. But he sort of glommed onto me. He is twenty-two then, and he too lives at Ivan's and Marie's. He and Ben get together and cluck over me, work out my problems, my neuroses. Paul is German and good looking, until he opens his mouth or walks. He has the classic fruit mince, up on the tippytoes. He can't help it, his father has the same walk. It's a deformity like any other but unhappily lacking in the ability to evoke sympathy. He is living off unemployment insurance while he gets ready to be a great writer. He is compiling a system of filing card references on Savonarola; this he does while listening to Wagner. Full blast. One day he is going to write the definitive three-act play on Savonarola. He finds me distressingly commercial. 'I can't see any point in being second rate,' he says.

Paul is the only person I know who consciously cultivates the art of the insult. He works on a crushing retort for days and then, having delivered it, rushes over to tell Jocelyn and me: 'You should have seen the look on his face.'

Ivan and Marie have other boarders. One is a poor boy taking his grade twelve from Surepass, the cram-for-exam school. Paul puts a poster on his door: 'Anus Mundi' and tells the boy it means 'Genius of the world.'

We are in the kitchen washing up. Paul is snorting into the dish pan.

'Actually, the language of the lower class is terribly rich in metaphor. It makes one consider the possibility that there is genius in the language. But my god! I hope you're taking notes, Vicky. What a find!'

At dinner I have mixed up *incubus* with *succubus*, and Paul has corrected me.

'Don't you mean he's an incubus?' My man from the sea.

'What's the difference?' Mik says.

'I beg your pardon?' says Paul, affecting to notice Mik for the first time.

'This whatsit? What you said, what's the difference?'

'The incubus is the male tempter,' Paul says. 'The succubus is the female of the species. She works at night.' He gives me a look to see if I see how clever he is.

Mik finishes his potato. He was a prodigious eater of potatoes. He put them whole into his mouth. 'Yah,' he says. 'I knew one once. You mean a lady gorgonzola.'

'A what?' says Paul, delighted.

'A lady gorgonzola,' says Mik, spearing another potato. 'Ain't that what you're talking about? Them guys run the boats in Venice. I knew one once, a lady gorgonzola, she run this gorgon up and down the carnals in Naples.'

I refuse to look up from my plate. I know Paul is bursting with glee. I sneak a glance at Jocelyn and she has a small curved speculative smile on her face.

'I believe the word is "gondolier,"' says Paul.

'Yes,' says Mik, 'that's the word.'

Now Paul is telling me about someone else he has demolished. 'I said, "Is that an ontological or a teleological argument?" You should have seen his face!'

I feel it happening to me. That coldness. 'What is the ontological proof?' I say softly. It comes over me like a demon, that coldness. I have no pleasure in it. I hate myself afterwards. It happened once in a philosophy seminar. I did it to a nice minister. The professor congratulated the minister on his interesting paper and asked for comments. I started out softly. That's how I know it's going to happen. I drew a few Venn diagrams. The professor said, 'Yes. Yes. I didn't see it.' And after, the minister says to me, 'I wouldn't have done that to you.' Robin said, 'For a nice girl, you have a surprising streak of sheer bitchery.'

Now Paul is trotting out St Thomas and so on, huffing and puffing, completely befuddled. I wait until he is quite done and then I say, 'I thought it went this way.' And spiel it off neatly, in a precise cold voice.

'Your trouble, Paul, is you mistake form for essence. You know the labels but you don't know the substance.'

'But I said that, about the attributes.' I just look at him. 'In effect,' he finishes lamely.

Then he goes into his big unrequited love bit. 'Kick me, beat me, any touch of your boot is sheer ecstasy.' He suffers beautifully from my cruelty. He is having an affair with Marie on the strength of his passion for me.

We finish the dishes and go back into the dining room to practice my chess game.

'Shall we play seriously?' says Paul, still smarting.

'All right.' I lose badly. I listen to Paul explain how, sixteen moves back, I took the pawn, unable to resist the sacrifice, but all along I should have seen that this left me open to attack. In taking the pawn, I had lost the chance to castle. And so on and so forth. 'I don't sacrifice without a reason,' says Paul.

We play another game. Paul keeps up a running commentary, quoting *Paradise Lost* at me to see if I can follow.

I have moved up my Queen. I am flagrantly careless with her because Paul cares for his so. I know I can shake him with sacrilege.

'"Whence and what art thou, execrable shape, that dar'st, though grim and terrible, advance thy miscreated front athwart my way?"'

'I'm waging war,' I say, '"by force or guile eternal."'

'That doesn't follow,' says Paul, catching me.

'"The next verse isn't apt,' I say, lying like a fish. I haven't a clue what the next verse is.

'True,' says Paul, eyeing me warily.

In the front room, the TV clicks off and Mik lounges toward the kitchen to make some coffee.

Paul says in a low voice, '"And what rough Beast, its hour come round at last, slouches toward Bethlehem to be born."'

It is horrid. It is too apt. Mik is a bit like the monstrous second coming, the rise of the mass man as it inundates the effete super-sensitive aristocrat. Brute, Neanderthal, lowering. I laugh.

Paul smirks at me. To him Mik is nothing more than an interesting specimen. Not real at all, certainly not real enough to be despised. Or loathed. Interesting, as an invertebrate is interesting, especially if it has assumed an upright position.

Mik comes back with his coffee mug and I, ashamed now, look up and smile at him. He nods at me and then leans against the frame of the sliding door.

Paul and I are still in the second game. Mik is behind Paul and Paul, after a few minutes, says, '"And at my back I always hear Time's winged chariot hurrying near."'

'Not terribly apt,' I say. I am in a good position by some fluke, but, being there, I can't see what to do with it.

'The pawn,' says Mik from the doorway.

And I see it. It's lovely. The pawn challenges *en passant* and Paul is screwed either way.

Paul sees it too. 'Do you mind?' he says over his shoulder. 'What is the charming expression? Would you please sixty-five?'

This refers to something that has happened earlier, before dinner. Mik and Paul have been talking in low voices, Paul uttering rather high giggles, and when Jocelyn and I carry in the food, Mik has said, 'Sixty-five.'

'Sixty-five?' Paul has said.

'Dummy up,' Mik has said.

Now Mik barks. A hard bark of a laugh. 'Okay,' he says. 'I'll "sixty-five."' He puts it in quotes and I look at him surprised. But Paul is trying to divert me with a knight attack, and I'm too busy to consider this new linguistic evidence. I fall for the diversion and I lose, but not without honour.

'Thanks, Paul,' I say. 'I guess I'll go to bed.'

'Let me show you where you went wrong,' says Paul.

'Oh, do we have to?'

Mik says, casually, 'Want a game?'

'If you'd resisted the knight attack,' says Paul, and over his shoulder, 'Sorry. It's not quite the same as checkers.'

Mik ignores this. To me, he says, 'You got no end games. You got no openings.' He never called me by my name. He always said 'you.'

'Oh,' says Paul elaborately, 'do you play?'

'I fool around,' says Mik.

'By all means,' says Paul. But first he explains my mistake to me. I say I'll make coffee. While I wait for the water to boil, I watch from the kitchen. Paul sets up the board. The white is facing Mik and he reaches for a pawn.

'Do you mind?' says Paul. 'Shall we play according to tournament rules?'

'Sure,' says Mik and takes back his hand.

Paul takes one white pawn and one black and hides them behind his back. Mik doesn't do anything for a moment and I can see Paul thinking he has done it again. Then Mik's finger comes up, slowly, and, just before it taps Paul's right shoulder, I see Paul wince. But it is a gentle tap. Mik gets white anyway.

Paul moves quickly at first. Then I have to make the coffee. By the time I get in with the tray, Paul is staring at the board. 'You're very good,' he says. He takes the regulation five minutes.

'Yeeees,' he says at last and moves his bishop. Mik doesn't hesitate. He moves and reaches for the coffee mug.

Paul gets up and gets himself a glass of water. He drinks eight glasses a day, religiously. Later, when I consider him seriously, Aunt Forbes says, 'Vicky, but I think there's something wrong with his bladder. He goes on the hour every hour.' But Uncle Forbes just says, 'Oh Christ, Vicky, not another.' It's a lie. I never considered Paul seriously. I just wondered if I should marry him, because of the baby.

The game goes on, very slowly when Paul plays. Mik moves without pausing. Paul starts to say 'J'adoube' when he touches a piece. Holding onto it and checking once more before he releases his hand. Finally, for no reason I can see, he says, 'I concede.'

He gets another glass of water. 'I can see where I went wrong,' he says from the kitchen. 'That first move with the bishop. Yes.' He comes back in. 'Want another? Best two out of three?'

'Sure,' says Mik.

They play for hours, and I watch. Paul concedes the second game. Then the third. He has drunk six glasses of water and gone upstairs four times.

'You play extremely well,' he says to Mik. 'Where did you learn?' Mik doesn't answer at first.

Then he looks directly at me. His eyes are very blue. Blue like the sea. I feel a shock in my body. 'In the Pen,' he says. At me.

Paul laughs from nervousness. 'I beg your pardon?'

'In the Pen,' says Mik, still looking at me. 'From a murderer. A professor. He was in for life.'

Paul says, 'And what were you doing in the Pen, might I inquire?'

'I never was no city clerk,' says Mik, still at me. And to Paul, 'I was doing ten for armed robbery.'

'How interesting,' Paul says.

But I say, 'Who did he murder?'

'His girlfriend.'

I drop my eyes first. Then I laugh. When I look up, Mik is laughing too, silently.

I WANT TO PUT this in next, though I know it didn't happen after Mik, but before. That is, I know I wore the dress to Gladys's recital, so I had it before Mik. But it seems to have happened after. And perhaps in some sense it did.

Edna came over one day and said, 'You've got to get some clothes.'

She was going through a bad patch just then, because of Sam. Until Edna was twenty-one she was a virgin, and dreadfully worried about it. And then, after Sam, he worried about her being a one-shot woman. 'I can't marry you,' Sam said, 'until you've got it all out of your system. Look at Vicky.'

Sam had a theory about me. All my troubles stemmed, he said, from my being a one-man woman. Had I experienced life fully before I married Ben, I wouldn't have turned out so flighty. And so, at Sam's urging, Edna trotted equably off to Ottawa where she was to have a summer working at the National Library and screwing as many men as she could muster. In September, she was to come home, It out of her system, and marry Sam.

In September, back she came. The wedding plans were firmly in motion and one night, a week before the ceremony, Sam said, 'Well, Love, and what did you learn in Ottawa?'

Like a fool she told him.

Sam cancelled the wedding. His final remark was, 'I'm not going to marry a slut!' And off he went to do his doctorate at

Berkeley. His dissertation is on the feminist movement, and I am glad to be able to say he has not yet completed it.

At this point Edna was recovering from a depression, going to a psychiatrist, and working in the university library.

'I'm going downtown with you,' she said, 'and I'm going to watch you like a hawk. If I let you do it alone, you'll end up wearing Mother Hubbards.'

Edna's taste in clothes had altered radically when she was in Ottawa. From saddle shoes and short socks she had emerged into patent leather pumps with high spiky heels. From tartan skirts and cardigans, she had plunged into astonishing blouses and short skirts. Rather, her blouses plunged into her.

'Just look at what you've got on!' she said.

It was a two-piece turquoise print, size eighteen and a half. The jacket had a little peplum. Jocelyn had given it to me for Christmas.

'What's the use of losing all the weight if you go around like *that!*' Edna said.

We caught the bus like two schoolgirls and went to the Hudson's Bay. I moved gingerly toward the half-size rack and took down a brown two-piece print, with a peplum jacket and little rhinestone buckles on false pockets. 'I can take off the buckles,' I said. 'I can take off the pockets for that matter.'

Edna looked at the tag. 'Eighteen and a half,' she said with grim satisfaction. 'It's good I'm into my aggressive stage.' She made me go into the dressing room. 'You just wait,' she said. 'I'll bring you everything.'

She brought a blue suit first. With a blue and white polka dot blouse. Size ten.

'I can't get into that,' I said.

'I'm starting you off easy. First we satisfy the prig, then we satisfy the beast.'

I put it on and a slender girl looked back at me from the mirrors. An elegant slender girl with long brown hair and no make-up. Large eyes. A girl in a blue suit. I turned and she turned. I smiled at her and she smiled back at me.

'Yes, that's all right,' said Edna appearing with a brown and white thin cotton.

'No. I think I'll take this one,' I said.

'Of course you'll take it,' said Edna. 'I knew you would. It's so damned prissy. Now get this on.'

'I can't. Look at the back. It isn't there.'

'So?'

I took them both, signing the cheque for forty-six sixty-five in fear and trembling.

'Now shoes,' said Edna.

'Oh I've got to have tea first. No, I've got to. I'm sweating like mad. I can't do anything else until I have some tea.'

But after the tea I bought high-heeled sandals, beige, with clear plastic inserts between the straps. Sixteen ninety-five. 'Plastic,' I said. 'My god, I've gone utterly vulgar.'

'Nothing that costs that much can be vulgar,' said Edna.

'I can't wear them in front of Grace,' I said.

I look back and I remember, in all those nine years of my marriage, exactly what I bought and how much I paid for it. The black winter coat, forty-eight dollars; the two yards of tweed for the jumper, two dollars and ninety-eight cents; the red perforated shoes with crepe soles, nine ninety-eight. Yes. I'd had to ask Ben for the money. I was broke and I had to have shoes to go to the scholarship committee. I had to ask him for ten dollars. He paid my room and board but not my clothes or books or fees. That was agreed. I hated asking him. I bought the most sensible shoes I could find. I figured they'd last me through my last year. They did, and I hated them.

The Mexican blouse and skirt: forty-eight pesos. The wicker handbag: forty. The navy blue suit when I started teaching: forty-eight dollars; the paisley dress: eighteen ninety-five in Bellingham. The black pumps: three dollars and ninety-five cents.

I had clothes when I married of course. And they lasted me all those years. A red shorty coat, a brown tartan skirt, the useless white linen two-piece I bought for the wedding, the two-piece blue suit Aunt Forbes got for me at the rummage sale. My mother went berserk over the tartan skirt. It cost eighteen ninety-five, and that was a lot of money then. A Nat Gordon.

'You're selfish!' she said. 'Through and through.'

But I was right about that skirt. It lasted. I gave it to the Salvation Army only three years ago.

The night before I was married, she said, 'If you aren't good to him ...' not finishing.

'What?' I said. 'If I'm not good to Ben, what?'

'I'll never forgive you,' she said, her mouth tight.

We were up in the attic room. The self-contained room with the stove and the sink. I paid forty dollars a month. For board too. But I could make my own meals if I wanted. She had come upstairs to ask if there was anything I wanted to know.

'I probably know more than you do,' I said.

'You probably do,' she said.

'From books,' I amended. She sniffed. My mother began to accuse me of losing my virginity quite early. She would see a bruise on my arm or a red spot on my breast and she would say, 'You're no virgin!' And so I was determined, out of spite, to be a virgin on my wedding day. Ben and I were getting married two months early because a week before, as we fooled around upstairs on my bed, It had slipped in for a second. Very limp, very scared It was. And just for a second. But now I considered myself no longer a virgin. Not even technically. My practice was to pet madly until I had an orgasm, and then to retire from the field, Virtue Triumphant. It was lucky I wasn't killed.

'Everybody thinks you're getting married because you have to,' Momma said.

'Well, Everybody can wait for nine months and see,' I said loftily. But I had a twinge of doubt. Was it possible? Surely not. But I went around those first weeks in agony, thinking maybe it was possible after all.

It was my mother's belief that I was born rotten and that losing my virginity would prove it once and for all. 'You wouldn't even suck!' she would say.

And, 'You're not in love with him, are you?'

'That's just in the movies, Mom,' I said.

She shook her head. 'He's in love with you. Don't you dare hurt him.'

Ben was in love with me and I did hurt him. My mother knew all about me.

About three days before I got married, she gave me a bill. An itemized list from the high school years: Kotex. Lustre Creme. One sanitary belt. One brassiere. All the things she'd had to buy besides food, which the Welfare paid for anyway. I never thought much about the bill, just paid it. Jocelyn got a bill too, when she finished university. And Francie got hers before her wedding. They paid too, without thinking.

'You know,' I say to Francie, 'that wasn't usual. The bill thing. No one has ever heard of it.'

'I know,' says Francie, laughing. 'I asked Jo Anne and she didn't have one. But that's just Mom. She felt like it was cheating the Welfare to spend money on stuff like O-Do-Rono. And, I mean, she thought we could use rags instead of Kotex.'

'She did,' I say and we go into peals of embarrassed giggles.

'Oh god,' says Francie, 'don't put that in the book. Please. I'll die.'

'And she kept them in the bottom of the clothes closet. Used.'

'Oh don't,' says Francie. 'Oh god. Don't. I know. Oh god. You know,' she says seriously, 'that's why I hate encounter groups. I think I'm going to say something like that, when I get excited. I'm going to say, "My mother used rags." I mean, they're all so middle class, those encounter group people, they don't have a clue.' And, 'But we never *felt* poor, did we?'

'No.'

'I know. It wasn't like Aunt Harriet's. I mean, there, you could *smell* the poverty. I mean, it was clean and everything, but it smelled poor. How much did she get for us anyway?'

'Sixty a month. But that was in the good days, when I got the scholarship. I got thirty-five a month for a straight Honours report.'

'Yeah. I got that too,' says Francie. 'Maybe it was because there weren't any books. At Aunt Harriet's. Did Mom ever look at your report cards?'

'No. She just signed them.'

'Yeah. Funny, wasn't it? She really hates the intellectual bit but I wonder what would have happened if we'd been dumb.'

I can't stop myself. 'It was I who brought the books into the house.'

But Francie says, 'Then it was something else. Like, table manners and speaking correctly and all that. It was a different feeling. We weren't poor.'

'Because we were going to get out,' I said.

'Yeah. Maybe that's it. Maybe it's the hope.' Francie is working with negroes in ghettos, trying to understand. 'I mean, we were white and we could get out,' she says.

But the money thing doesn't begin with my father's death. It's there even before, when I'm six and I say, 'I'm going to live with you forever.'

'Well, you'll have to pay room and board,' Momma says.

'What's room and board?'

'It's what you pay for eating and sleeping in a house,' my mother says. She looks very grim.

'But children don't pay their parents,' I say.

'Yes they do, when they're old enough to work. It wouldn't be fair.'

I'm horribly shocked. You don't pay your parents. It's terrible, to think of that. Momma becomes furious with me and we have a dreadful fight. She says I'm selfish and I say she's mean. She cries. She never forgets either. The day I said she was mean.

Mom is horribly honest about money. If the cashier at Safeway's gives her too much change, she gives it back. One day she caught Francie skipping school. In the distance she sees her, downtown, going into the Greyhound building with our cousin. Mom goes into Safeway's and comes over faint with it, just in front of the meat counter. She has a packet of lamb chops in her hand and she puts it back, feeling too ill to go through the cash aisle. Out on the street, a woman stops her and searches her shopping bag. My mother is furious. 'I was poor all those years!' she says to the woman, 'and I never stole one thing.' She hires a lawyer and sues Safeway's for defamation of character. She still has the letter in her cedar-wood chest on her bureau: the apology from the manager.

At least I would bet anything she had. And she has never forgiven Francie for lying that day. Either.

'It wasn't exactly a lie,' says Francie. 'I just didn't say I was going to look for a job.'

'But she got Aunt Foster to drive you to school that day. Because

85

it was so cold.' I can feel my lips going tight.

Francie and I are still hung up about money. When Aunt Car-rington died, she left terrible fearsome sums to all of us. But to me she left the most. Francie sent hers to Oxfam and Biafra, but I spent mine on the mortgage. Jocelyn paid off their bank loan. The last time Jocelyn and I went shopping together at Zeller's, she loaded up her shopping cart with knickknacks, toys for the kids, jokes for David, and, at the counter, she grins at me and says: 'Isn't it won-derful to have money!' But, later, driving home in the car with all our loot, she says, 'Still, it'd be hard. I don't know what I'd have done if she'd left me so much.' She chuckles, 'I guess you'll just have to suffer the guilt.'

'Of getting so much?'

'No,' says Jocelyn, 'of being loved so much.'

I BEGIN TO PLAY CHESS with Mik. He doesn't explain where I went wrong. He doesn't suggest I take that move back. He doesn't hold post-mortems on the game. He just beats the shit out of me. I stop writing. As soon as Jocelyn leaves for classes, I get out the chess board and we start to play. We play all day and then I start din-ner. After the dishes, we play all night. About two weeks later, Paul comes over and I beat the can off him.

It's summer now. One night Mik says, 'Let's go for a swim.' But I say I can't. I don't have a bathing suit. I do, but it's size twenty. The next day I go down and find one on sale for seven ninety-five. A vulgar leopard-skin one-piece. Two thin black straps on each shoulder. Size seven.

The next night we walk to Kitsilano and then beyond, down the beach to a lonely stretch of sand. Below the high cliffs.

'I haven't been swimming at night for ages.'

'Yah. It's nice at night.'

He takes off his sweater and shirt and I see the tattoos. *Cream* and *Coffee*.

I don't know what to say. I say nothing. I feel terribly embarrassed for him. I think I know why he has said, 'No, let's go on,' why he hasn't wanted to swim on the public beach. While we are swimming, the sun goes down. Now it is black, the water smooth and warm, silken. I go far out. Toward the deepest point of blackness, where the sky meets the sea. Where darkness oozes out of the water into the black hole of the night. When I come out, I am shivering with cold. My skin feels as though it will break off in icy hunks.

Mik is building an illegal fire. He puts his sweater around me and rubs me briskly. He does it roughly, efficiently. It is the first time he has touched me. I sit, his sweater on over my suit, and stare into the fire.

'Take it off, you'll just get cold again,' he says.

But I haven't brought underwear.

'Take it off,' he says, and throws me my jeans. So I do, wriggling out of the wet suit underneath the sweater, which comes to my knees. He is getting more wood for the fire and doesn't look my way.

'Aren't you cold?'

'Nah.'

On his back is a long white scar. 'Where did you get the scar?'

'Broke my back. Cat skinning.'

'Oh. Is that a spinal fusion?'

'Yah. Took the bone out of my leg.' He shows me the scar on his thigh.

'I'm the mechanical man,' he says. 'Got a silver plate in my head too. Right here. That's why I ain't got no hair.'

'What was that from?'

'The war.' He throws an immense log onto the fire. 'Got a pin in my hip too, from the broken back thing. So now you know everything.'

'How'd you break your back?' I say again.

'Cat skinning. I was a cat skinner.' He looks at me. 'It's a tractor. It turned over on me. And the company said it wasn't responsible, and Workmen's Compensation said it wasn't responsible, and I couldn't get no unemployment insurance, because they said it was Workmen's Compensation's problem.' He sits back against the log, beside me, not touching.

The fire is very warm and the sky very black. I am very aware of my body under the rough wool, without underwear. And of his body, not touching me. I keep looking at him, as if I am just speaking to him, but really I am looking at his body in the light of the fire. Thick and muscled. The tattoos. The small patches of hair around each nipple. Below his navel. His shoulders. His thighs. The bulge in his bathing shorts. His feet. He seems very ugly. Embarrassing.

'I was in this cast,' he says, 'from the top of my head to my knees. That was at first. Then I got just a body cast. That's how I got caught. For armed robbery.'

'You were wearing a body cast when you did an armed robbery?'

'Yah.' He laughs. 'I was sitting in the airport at Saskatoon, waiting for them with $8,000 in a suitcase.'

'Waiting for the police?'

'Yah. I'd stuck up a bank. I figured if Unemployment Insurance and Workmen's Compensation and the whole fucking lot of them wouldn't ...' He stopped. 'Sorry.'

'You mean you did it on purpose? To get caught? To be put in jail?'

'It seemed like a good idea at the time.'

'And you did it in a body cast?'

'Yah, you should have seen the description they sent out: One body cast, 250 pounds, on one body, 230 pounds.'

'Did you really use a gun?'

'Nah. It was from Woolworth's. It doesn't make any difference though.'

'That's terrible. That's the worst thing anyone's ever told me.'

'Yah, well, I asked for it. So how'd you know, about spinal fusions?'

'I was a polio. In the crippled children's hospital. The girl next to me had one. She got up one night and tried to get out the window. Tried to walk through the window with this huge body cast on, in her sleep.'

And I tell him that story and he laughs.

'So what was wrong with you?'

'Oh I had it all down one side.'

'You look all right now,' he says.

'Oh yes, I was all cured.'

'Your legs don't show.'

I hold them up. 'I rode one stirrup all one summer for that leg. It was awful at first.'

'Yah? You had a horse?'

So I tell him the story of the horse, and he laughs.

'I said to my mother, "It's out there, in the back yard," and she laughs. "Oh yeah." She almost died when she saw it. But I'd been saving for a year. I told her I was saving for a horse, and it was my money, I'd earned it.'

'What's the bit about the one stirrup?'

'Well, when I got out of hospital, this one,' and I lifted it, 'was like a table leg. I'm not kidding!' because he is laughing. 'So I took off the right stirrup and rode that way all summer. And it came back. My leg.'

'Yah,' Mik says. 'You can't tell the difference.' And, 'You must have been one tough kid.'

'So how were you in the war?'

'My buddy and me, we signed up when we were fifteen. Lied about our ages. I was in Italy when I was sixteen.' And he tells me stories about the war.

'I come up and this guy, he's yelling and hollering and he says, "For christ sake, kill me." His balls is blown off. So I take out the pistol and I shoot him through the eye.'

And, 'I see this German bastard crawling away, his ass in the air, and I shoot him like that, in the asshole.'

'You must have been one tough kid yourself.' Mik laughs.

We walk home through the soft air and he does not touch me. In the front room I say, 'Well, goodnight,' and he says, 'See ya.' And picks up the newspaper. Up in our bedroom I think of Desdemona and how she said, 'He told me stories.' But then I think, But who is Othello, which one? And I laugh too, softly, so Jocelyn will not hear.

One day I come back from the Nut Lady and I take down the bottle of meprobamates and I chew them, one by one, sitting on my bed. Looking at Jocelyn's.

I don't think about what I am doing. I don't give it a name. I just start to chew them up, one by one. They taste terrible. Jocelyn's bed is a mess.

When I came in a few minutes ago, Mik and his friend George were in the front room. They were drinking beer. I said hello and came upstairs. I can't remember what had happened with the Nut Lady. I know I had the dream again last night. Neon blue. Water. The baby in the neon blue water and the mirror cracks.

As usual, Jocelyn's bed is unmade. A week ago I gathered up all her things, from all over the house—boots, stockings, books, nose drops, her grey wool blouse, bloody panties from our closet floor, pearl nail polish—and dumped them in the middle of her bed. On the comforter I made her out of foam rubber and nine yards of orange cotton. The comforter leaks. The foam rubber is all over the floor. And the dust. From here I get a good view of under her bed. Arrgh. The afternoon light is pitiless. All the things there, for a whole week. She just crawls in under them at night. Kafka is on top. *Crime and Punishment* is on the floor, she has stepped on it, its spine is broken. *The Magic Mountain* is on the floor too, with a cup of old tea on top, making a stain, no doubt. The new black skirt I gave her for Christmas is crumpled hopelessly at the bottom of the bed, wedged in between the mattress and the bed posts.

I get under my blankets, lying down, still chewing.

I feel very light, very peaceful. The ceiling is neat.

The door bursts open and Mik comes into the room. His face looks as though it has been boiled. I hide the pill bottle under my pillow.

He has never been in here before. I am ashamed of the mess.

He is drunk.

He kneels down beside my bed, not touching me, and he says, 'I love you.'

And, 'I only ever loved one other person in my whole life. Gil. And I killed him.'

I am not able to say anything. I just lie there, looking into his face.

'He was clean and good, like you. His name was Gil. We were in Palestine and there was this fight and I heard him yell. He yelled "Mik!" and I come running. I had this knife in my hand and I come round this corner and there's this fucking Arab coming at me and

I let him have it. In the gut. And after, when they put on the lights, it's no Arab. I never loved anyone else like that. You're like my mother's kitchen cupboards. All clean and good.'

Later, Mik denies the whole thing. He never came into my room. He never killed Gil. Yes, he had a friend called Gil, but he never killed him. He never said he loved me.

I've been over it and over it. I've told myself it was just another hypnagogic vision. And I've answered, 'But I'd never use the kitchen cupboards metaphor.'

I don't remember his leaving. I remember waking up and coming downstairs.

I remember Jocelyn saying to me, 'What's the matter with your eyes?'

I remember saying, 'I'm sorry about the pile. On the bed.'

I remember she doesn't answer for a while. Then she says, 'Okay. I'm sorry I'm such a slob.'

'I shouldn't have done it.'

'I'd have left it there till kingdom come,' she says.

When I go up again, later, the pile is gone, both our beds are made, everything is mopped and clean. There's even a safety pin in the comforter.

When I'm sure Jocelyn is asleep, I masturbate. I pretend Mik has just burst into the room and he has said, 'Now I'm gonna give you a baby.'

ONE OF MY PROFESSORS phones and says, would I like to come over for a few days to the island.

I go, with my typewriter, and I work on my play and he works on his article.

It is very quiet, very peaceful. Sometimes we swim. One night he says, 'Let's swim nude,' and we do, our fingers and toes shooting sparks in the phosphorescent water. I'll never forget that, the dark red water and the flashes of lightning coming out of my fingers and toes.

He says, 'Homer was right. The sea is the colour of wine.'

We were very peaceful together, this good old man and I. He hates liars. He honours what he calls 'the Real.' In the evenings we read each other what we have written, and drink gin and tonic, listen to Stravinsky. The night comes down and I feel very safe. I sleep in the guest house. One wall is glass, and when I wake in the mornings I see arbutus trees, their barks curling softly away from the clean undersides.

He is a good man, a kind man, and he asks me about my marriage. What went wrong. I hate it, when people ask me, but I don't hate him. I want to tell me, I want to tell him the truth.

'But it's so hard,' I say. 'I don't really know myself. I was unfaithful to Ben, you know.'

'Were you?'

'Yes. Do you remember Robin French?'

'That English boy? The one with the bare feet?'

'Yes.'

'I thought he was queer.'

YOU AGREED,' SAID Ben, that night in Mexico. 'You *agreed*.' And he took his sketches and tore them across. Threw them into the fireplace and poured the glass of tequila over them. The worst thing he could have done.

We had gone to Mexico so that he could be free at last. To be an artist.

He had worked all those years and put me through university.

Now it was my turn to support him. He tore the sketches across and threw them in the fireplace. All the sketches. All the work of months. So very few. So very bad.

After that night, he never touched me again. Not until the end. I would brush against him at night and he would wince away as if I were a cattle prod. We had used to curl up together, his arms around me, my face against his chest. Ben was very hairy. I loved the way it curled up at the neck of his shirt, like furry spiders' legs. But I had liked spiders. I would pick them up and carry them out into the garden. If you love them, they don't bite.

I finished my book. Clackety-clack. Ben drank. I went to the clinic.

One day the doctor says to me, 'Shall I tell you a comedy? Shall I tell you what they call you? The villagers?'

My Spanish has improved. We have got to the point where we can tell each other comedies.

'What do they call me?'

'La gringita virgita.'

The little American virgin.

'But I'm not American,' I say.

And, after a minute. 'Nor am I a virgin.'

'Que?' Or whatever it was. I've forgotten it all. That looks French.

He is staring at me, his eyes very Indian again. 'But you wear no ring?'

'No. We don't believe in rings. The bull, he wears a ring in his nose, is it not true?' But my Spanish isn't good enough for this comedy. The doctor does not laugh. I don't know how to say 'principle' and 'freedom' and 'private property ethic,' though I am certain he would understand if I could. He is a Marxist, the doctor, though he wears a medal around his neck.

'My husband, he does not wear a ring,' I say.

94

'Your brother?'

'My husband. *Sposo*. No brother.'

'*Sposo? Verdad?*'

'Yes, for seven years. Since seven years.'

'You should wear a ring,' says the doctor. He looks very cross.

'But *you* wear too many rings,' I say, meaning the medal and the party card, but he does not laugh.

'All these times, since so long, I have called you "*señorita*."'

'But you call all the American volunteer ladies "*señorita*."'

'That is a comedy, because they are so old and fat.'

One day Ben says, 'I want to go home.' We leave the next day. I send a message with the only American lady I can trust. I give her a key to the morphine cupboard. 'That's why they came, you know,' I say to her. 'All the women from the colony.' I am very indignant. When I found out, I did a thorough inventory and put a lock on the door. The volunteer rate dropped alarmingly. But this one still came so I give her the key. And the message for the doctor. I am ashamed to tell him myself. I feel as though I am deserting him.

We drive back through the long high deserts, past the mauve hills. We stop for a while with his mother, with mine. My grandmother dies while I'm there. I sit by her bed for a long time but at the end, Uncle Forbes sends me out for cigarettes and I go, knowing. When I get back it is over. Aunt Foster gives me Grandma's wedding ring.

Back in Vancouver I go to work full-time in the lab, and take a philosophy course toward my Master's. I withdraw my thesis, my novel about the Marxist and the wife who wants a baby. I say I do not believe in creative writing degrees. The acting head is delighted; he has fought the program from the first. Everyone thinks me very noble and high-minded. But the truth is, I am ashamed of the book. I do not quite know why. I only know that when, at last, I gave it to Ben to read he said, 'It's very interesting.' I never sent it out. I put it away in the trunk.

Ben buys me two Siamese cats. And a television.

Peter is the male and the female is Molly. But one day we hear a car screech, and she is dead. She lies in the road, all the air gone out of her, looking so small. And Peter pines. He refuses to eat. So we get Sally. At first she pays no attention to Peter at all. Very practical, Sally was. She checks out the food dish, the water pan, the kitty litter, then she circles Peter. Pouncing at him. Sidling up stiff-legged. But all Peter does is howl and yowl and say, 'Leave me alone, my heart is broken, I want to die.'

And she circles him. 'Go away,' he spits. 'Go away and let me die in peace.' Sally circles. Round and round, closer and closer. When we go to bed she is sitting on Peter's head. From under her rump come the most appalling noises. Indignation mingles with self-pity. When we get up, there he is, weak and wobbly, eating.

A Siamese is the only other animal who likes to do it all the time. Besides humans, I mean. Maybe monkeys are like that too, I don't know.

But I mourn Molly. Her death seems an omen.

By January, Sally is pregnant.

I go to work in the mornings and Ben makes sake. He has a large green bottle with spigots and hoses and it is all very complicated. When he isn't making sake, he is drinking it. When I come home, my supper is ready. The apartment is spotless. Ben is drunk.

One evening, after the philosophy seminar, I am walking back across the quad with Robin and I say, 'What do you think about this magic business of Sartre's? If there were a bear, could you really make it disappear?' I remember because later he quotes me, laughing, saying, 'You were so intense.'

I didn't understand. It still seems to me a good thing, an incantation against bears.

One night I give him a lift, and we sit out in front of the Varsity Grill for three hours, talking about Life. Robin tells me how he was put in an English jail for three months, for being a conscientious objector. 'I forgot to fill in the forms,' he says. 'So it became an issue.'

I tell him about wanting a baby.

'Doesn't your husband want children?'

'No. He says the world is over-populated already.'

'I think people should be able to have babies if they want them,' says Robin, after a moment's judicious thought.

He tells me about the sorority girl he's in love with. I've seen her. She's got shoulder length blonde hair, which turns under smoothly; and she wears cashmere sweaters with matching skirts. It's hopeless and he knows it, and I, looking at him, think it's hopeless too.

Robin is thin and smells. He has terrible acne and often forgets to wear socks.

I cry a bit before he gets out. Then I drive home.

'The supper's ruined,' Ben says, furious. 'Completely ruined. You could have called to let me know.' He has that silly look on his face. I know he's drunk but I'm too far gone to care.

'I want a baby.'

I haven't said it for almost a year.

But Ben says, 'If you're going to start that again, I want a divorce.'

There is a great sighing whoosh in my head. I sit down, still in my coat. The television is on. I seem to be watching it.

'I mean it,' says Ben. 'I'm getting a divorce. I'm leaving you.'

It occurs to me that I really do not want Ben's baby. Ben has terribly thin skin. When we used to make love, the marks from my fingernails would rise up in white welts on his back. I wouldn't want a baby with thin skin.

'I'm leaving tonight,' says Ben. 'I'm warning you. If you bring that up once more.'

'I want a baby.'

'I want a divorce!' Ben says.

All right. All right all right all right.

'I'll go down to Berkeley and stay with Sam. I'll give you grounds.'

Yes all right yes yes oh god thank you yes.

Ben stomps off into the bedroom. It's a basement suite as usual. He has to go down two steps into the kitchen and up two steps into the bedroom. I hear him opening drawers. I see him come back down into the kitchen and up two steps to the basement door. I hear him getting down a flight bag.

I am still watching television. It seems a queer thing to be doing, sitting in my black winter coat, forty-eight dollars. I was wrong. Neither Grace nor Terence liked it, good taste or not.

Ben comes back into the front room. He is wearing his Mexican shirt and the suede jacket I gave him. But it's February. It's going to be cold, driving down to Berkeley.

'I'm all right,' he says. 'I really am leaving you,' he says.

'Have you got enough money?'

'I've got enough,' he says but I don't think so. I don't think he can have more than ten dollars.

'All right,' I say. 'I'll get a baby somehow.'

'I know about it already. You've been going to bed with that beatnik. That Robin French. I know.'

I shake my head. 'No. But maybe I will.'

'Well, I'm through with you. I'm really finished this time. I mean it.'

'All right.'

'I think you are mentally ill,' says Ben and goes, closing the door softly after him.

It was our first fight. We've never fought before. I turn off the television.

Not wasting a moment, I telephone Robin, who, miraculously, is home. Then it must have taken longer than I thought. He had to eat and walk down the hill.

'Look,' I say, 'did you mean that, about people having the right to have babies?'

'Sure. What's up?'

'My husband's left me. Will you give me a baby?'

There is a long pause. 'I'm not in love with you, Vicky.'

'I know.' I'm not in love with him either.

'We'll have to have a gentlemen's agreement about this,' Robin says.

'All right,' I say. I'm used to gentlemen's agreements. I've been a gentleman all my married life.

I call a taxi and get off at the address Robin has given me on the phone.

It's a house right across from the beach. Locarno Beach. A rather large, new, imposing house. Robin lives in the rec room. I don't go in at first. I cross over the road and look at the ocean. Moving lugubriously in the fog. A moral idiot. The fog horns sound from across the water. Lonely. The loneliest sound in the world, a fog horn on a foggy night. In February.

Robin lets me in the basement door, going 'Shh, shh' because of the landlady upstairs. I can hear her TV droning on like a retarded child. It is very chilly in this rec room. My heels are congealed with cold. My marrow has burst into ice crystals. Frostbite appears on my fingers.

There is a large stone fireplace and a chair. A table. A hot plate.

A mattress lying on the floor. I just get undressed and lie down on the mattress. I spread my legs. The mattress smells awful, like Robin. Rancid.

Later I use the shower to pee down. The bathroom is upstairs. I thank whatever gods that I don't have to have a bowel movement.

That's all. It's very jerky and very quick.

I think, I hope it doesn't get his acne.

Robin has to creep upstairs and muffle his voice to get me a taxi.

Then I go home.

Old bacon grease gone nasty, I think. That's what he smells like. So that's sin. So that's adultery. Some fun. Big deal.

As soon as I get home, I get down the ironing board. No, I get it out from the basement. I iron Ben's shirts. I spray starch them and iron them and fold them carefully, for easy packing. Ironing was my one domestic chore and I did it well. I enjoyed it. I was professional about it. Jocelyn still says, 'But you like ironing,' as if it were some perverse sexual thing.

'It's hell now, with all this drip dry stuff,' I say.

I put on Haydn and then I put on Bach and I ironed away. Then I wrote a cheque for $128, payable to Mr Benjamin Ferris, signed V.E. Ferris (Mrs).

It's an odd figure. I can't imagine why that figure. Maybe it was half what I had in my account. I don't know. That seems logical. Half what I had. Or maybe it was what he would have got on welfare, if he'd applied. God knows. I remember all the numbers so well, with such a mean fidelity of spirit. The book makes me remember. I'm not going to get away with anything.

Along about two o'clock, the key turns in the door and there he is. The prodigal husband. Crying.

They'd turned him back at the border. He hadn't enough money. I feel my selfishness harden inside me, like a jewel. Yes, a jewel. Strong and invincible. A great gleaming emerald, harder than diamonds. Burnt in the sun for a million years. Hard and ruthless and bright. I've never felt it before, this coldness my mother spoke of, but now I feel it. Yes, there it is, my power and my safety. Me, inside there, hard and cold and brilliant. Yes! Me. Victoria Ellen Carrington Ferris. There I am. Impermeable. Impregnable. Cruel. Vicious. Dangerous. It shines through me with a deadly radiance, as light through your fingernails. I wonder he doesn't throw up his hands to shield his eyes.

'I ironed your shirts,' I say.

'You always iron your troubles away,' he says. 'You always do that.' He is trying to smile, trying to forgive me.

'They're all done.'

'I'll just have a cup of coffee. I can go to Ivan's.'

'There's a cheque for you. On the desk. Cash it tomorrow morning and then go to Sam's.'

'All right.' He picks up the kettle but I take it from him.

'I'll make it.'

He sits down and waits for the coffee. Bach's Brandenburg comes to a stop and the record goes zzz zzz rrr rr. Ben goes to put up the arm.

'Will you take back the Haydn?' he says. He means to the music library. 'And the Scarlatti?'

I'll take them back.

'You always listen to the Brandenburgs when you iron.' He is trying again.

'I know nothing about music. I like them, that's all. They're so neat. Like calculus.'

'You like good things though,' says Ben.

But he lies. I like *Bye Bye Birdie* too.

The cats come out of the bedroom, yawning, what's going on? Sally's tum is full and round.

'I hate to leave the cats.'

I give him his coffee. I can't remember what he took. Isn't that strange. But I say I'll get it, whatever it is, sugar or cream, or both.

'Let's talk, Vicky.'

I am still standing. I start to fold up the ironing board. 'There's nothing to talk about.'

'Yes, there is. I was upset. You were late for supper and I had it all ready. I was upset. You should have called.'

I don't admit it. I don't admit anything.

'And I'd been drinking.' Big news.

'The point is, we're in no position to have a child right now.'

Right *now*? Oh you bastard.

I can feel Robin's semen on my legs. Cold and sticky.

'Until I get a job or start making money from my art.'

'You made money from cartoons.'

'You know I want to do serious work.'

'You could do cartoons. I do murder mysteries.'

Yes. Well, we all know Vicky, the big sell-out. Ben sighs.

'We must try to be reasonable.'

'You *said*!' I scream. 'You said you wanted a divorce. You said you were going.'

Grace says to me, 'You listen to the words, Vicky. You don't listen to what's going on underneath.'

Even Anna says, 'What did she say?' and when I give the words, she says, 'But how did she say it?'

All right. I knew. Like I knew Ben didn't mean it when he said go ahead, practice free love. I knew he wasn't going to leave. I knew he didn't want a divorce. But the bastard held me to my word. I would hold him to his until hell froze over.

'You *said*, you *said*, you *said*.' Over and over.

'Let's not have a scene.'

Not have a scene?

'It's too late,' I say. 'It's too late now.'

'No it isn't. Vicky.' He is crying again. Oh god, how I hate to see men cry. Like my mother. Saying, 'Forgive me, forgive me,' say you forgive me.'

It goes on for hours. Neither one of us says anything crude or vulgar, or accuses the other of bad behaviour. Except for that one moment, we don't raise our voices. I don't, I mean. Ben never does. The main point is simply: I *agreed*, he *said*. I promised. He said. On and on.

ALL RIGHT. Let's be fair. I can explain Ben. I suppose. Part of it, anyway.

We'd been married six weeks. We were in Banff. Ben was driving a bus and I was taking a scholarship course. His mother and dad arrive from back east.

The first great trip of their lives. They get themselves a little cabin and Ben and his dad go fishing. The father is an undertaker and he makes jokes about people who, just as he is about to slice them from their gullet to their zilch, sit up, not dead after all. Ho ho. He is wearing a belt snitched from a corpse. 'You never see the waist anyway,' he says.

I ask if he takes their rings and watches. The mother looks at me as if I've said something in terribly bad taste. Not so bad as stealing belts, lady.

She is helpless and envious and goes around saying, 'Ooooh, ooh, I wish I looked like you, Vicky.' 'I wish I was as smart as you, Vicky.' 'I wish I was as brave as you, Vicky.' One day, believe it or not, she says, 'I wish I were as young as you, Vicky.'

She's afraid of everything. Bears. Moose. High roads. Mountains. Rivers. One day the car breaks down and we have to hitchhike into Lake Louise. She's afraid to put out her thumb! 'oooh ooh. You're so brave, Vicky.' Shit.

Christ, I was wonderful and she hated my guts.

I take it and I take it and I ... and one day I say, 'I am younger than you are, Winnie. It's a fact of life. Don't worry. I'll get old.'

Her lips quiver and she ducks her head. Tries not to show how hurt she is.

'What did you do to Mom?'

Like a beaten animal. Quiver quiver. I was a saint. I should have pushed her into a river, off a mountain. Couldn't get her on the chair lift.

She limps. With a small embarrassed smile, she limps around the cabin. Cooking for us. Arthritis. But when Ben was a child she told him it was cancer. Caused by, guess what, his birth.

'But didn't you ever see a doctor?'

'No, I was too afraid of doctors.'

In Mexico, we get a letter saying, 'I've always wanted to travel. You are living my dream. I am a gypsy at heart, just like you, Ben. If only I could see all those wonderful places. Vicky describes them so well.'

Out of revenge, sheer revenge, I send her a cheque for the plane fare.

We get it back by return mail. Oh she couldn't. Oh dear. Oh saints alive. Who would make lunch for Edwin? Oh my goodness, it's so kind, but she always babysits for Vera on Tuesdays, oh my goodness, she was so surprised, but if anything ever happened to Edwin while she was away, they're both getting on you know. I write a letter, pointing out the sheer absurdity of each and every one of her arguments, and accuse her of cowardice.

Ben persuades me not to send it.

He grew up believing his mother to be dying of cancer of the bone, and himself to be the cause of it.

'She didn't know.' Ben turns on me his saintly smile. 'She never meant to worry me.'

'She meant to worry you.' But I don't think I say it.

I could even explain her, I suppose. 'With Vera,' she says, 'when my water broke, I was so ashamed. I kept trying to clean it up and more kept coming, all over the floor. I didn't want Edwin to see. I thought I'd dirtied myself.' She tells me she took quinine for all her children, but it never worked.

Ben told me that once, when he was about eight, he'd almost fallen into an old abandoned well. He was playing in an empty lot and suddenly, beneath his feet, the ground opened up, and he fell, grabbing the edge at the last minute. 'All I could think of was, If she ever found out! She'd have died of a heart attack.'

I would have run home and reenacted the whole thing for my mother's benefit. I did this so often that when I came in one day, from a fall with the horse, blood from head to toe, she said, exasperated, 'Oh Vicky, what have you done now?'

'I kept everything from her,' Ben says. 'She worries so.'

I DON'T REMEMBER HOW I got him to leave that night. I think I persuaded him that we needed 'time to think things out.' I think I said we needed breathing space. I could feel him suffering at me. Pain stood out on his forehead like sweat. Part of me swayed toward him. This was Ben, it was Ben! And I wished a dark empty hole would open into the universe, and he would fall into it, missing the sides, unable to stop, down, down, into oblivion, where I could never feel him hurting anymore.

'But what will you do?' he said.

'I'll be okay.'

'But what if you get an asthma attack?'

'I can give myself a needle,' I say.

'But you get air in,' he says.

That's true. I just realized. That story about the sores on my hip? That was my doing. Dr Soronski came on the scene two years after the divorce. The sores were my doing. I did get air in the needle. Ben never got air in the needle. So all that is just another lie. All that imputation of bad needlemanship. Just another lie. It was my fault.

And he left, in the thin gleam of February gold, driving away into the fog, the cheque in his pocket, the fourteen shirts in a suitcase.

I had a shower and douched. I said to myself, Well, I've done *that* anyway, as if douching made it less culpable, gave Ben an even chance somehow. And maybe, too, I was giving me a chance. I felt a bit like Mik must have, sitting in his body cast on the bench in the Saskatoon airport with the $8,000 in the suitcase: Well, it seemed a good idea at the time.

I got out to the lab on the dot of eight-thirty. I was never late. I must have hitch-hiked. Ben had taken the car. All day, my head floating above my body, I titrated.

I worked in a tar-paper shack with a girl called Marcie. It was one of those temporary structures built after the war. I was out last Wednesday. It's still there. This was the job I'd had through university: Tuesdays, Thursdays, Saturdays, Christmas and Easter holidays, summers. My first boss is now Sister Mary Joseph. I went through her conversion with her, a long agony of love, me playing devil's advocate. I was just her general dog's body at first, but when Sister Mary Joseph left to enter the silent order, I found myself with five assistants. Marcie had been one of them. When Ben and I left for Mexico and freedom, Marcie became the boss. Now I was her assistant. Dr Mercereau, who dropped in once a day to check the results, said, 'You prove my point, Mrs Ferris. It is all a great waste of time to give technicians a university degree. You fill their heads with theories and then forbid them to exceed instructions. Now, you, you are intelligent and know nothing about chemistry. I can trust you never to innovate.' I was dependable, I was never late, I never exceeded instructions. I measured and weighed and calculated, and argued God with Marcie.

It was somewhere about noon. I was titrating, sitting on a stool in front of the window. This was Sister Mary Joseph's idea: to put the apparatus in front of the window; once in a while, she said, we should look up from the meniscus to the sky. I may be wrong—it may be too good to be true—but it seems that that day Marcie was having a struggle with her virginity. She was a good Catholic, Marcie, from a huge family of good Catholics, and it was a serious matter.

Through the window, beyond the titrating apparatus, I could see the soft slanting parallel lines of the rain, making congruent angles with the evergreens. Beyond were the experimental gardens, lush and misty with spring. Gently burgeoning. We wore white laboratory coats and made coffee on a Bunsen burner. It was warm and safe in the hut, and the rain made a reassuring thrumming on the roof. Down at the end of the lab, the retort flasks bubbled merrily. We were safe, enclosed, there was order in the world.

The hut next door was the men's lav, and behind that was a little room where the hapless English teaching assistants met students and worked up notes for their freshman lectures. From the window I saw Robin going in the back door.

At lunchtime, he called for me. And we walked in the rain, talking about his paper for philosophy. He wanted to read mine, the one I'd done at Christmas. 'What did you get, Vicky?'

'I hate people asking that,' I said. 'Marks means nothing. I refuse to discuss marks.'

Grace and I went through years of this, each of us cracking down top grades in our respective faculties, and each of us not only refusing to discuss the grades, but refusing to look at them when they were posted in the halls. It was a point of honour not to look. We despised the 'Whajaget' types. The only mark we ever discussed was the foul French mark we got in our first year. It was acceptable to discuss failure. Besides, we knew it wasn't womanly to be bright.

Robin said, 'But Dr Gowan advised me to read it. Your paper.'

I felt a clutch of panic. I was sure Robin was brighter, more incisive than Dr Gowan; he would see through it right away.

'And if the mark means so little, why can't you tell me what it was? Making a mystery only gives it importance.'

'All right. I got 136.' We were graded out of 150.

'Was that the highest?' said Robin.

'I have no idea.'

'Oh I expect it was.' And he went into one of his dances, skipping into the long wet grass and picking early crocuses, putting them behind his ear. I stood, old and fat, awkward, watching him, laughing. He was like a faun, clumsy from birth still. I felt centuries older.

We talked about Wittgenstein. I said Russell was all wrong, of course, and Robin said 'Really?' in a way that made me feel an absolute fool.

I thought that was all there was to it. We'd done our necessary twenty minutes, that was that. It was gentlemen's rules; he'd said.

But Robin, as he left me at the lab door, said, 'Shall I come over tonight?'

I was surprised. 'Oh you don't have to,' I said.

'I'd like to,' Robin said and my guts lurched madly. I was in love. But that night, in my arms, he said, with a painful precision, 'I don't want you, I just want.'

We were all so honest. It was the great virtue.

He was a poor lover. Thin. Bony. Young. For the first time in my life, I had no orgasms. Not that he noticed. I felt so old and fat and helpless and I adored him so. If I saw him in that large baggy dirty forest green sweater, loping across the mall, my body would go thwunk! as if I'd walked into a cattle fence. My body recognized him before my mind did. It became an issue in the philosophy seminar.

'Can one feel pain before one knows the word "pain"?'

I said yes and Robin said no. He was in a strange mood and asked me in a snarky way if I could cite an example. I went into a long rambling anecdote about how I'd gone to the dentist that week, how he'd said he could tell by my eyes I was in pain, something about the pupils contracting, but how I hadn't been in pain at all. It came out all wrong. Robin said, in his most English voice, that while we all admired Mrs Ferris's courage in the dentist chair, he couldn't quite see the relevance of the tale, however cleverly told, and he himself was the first to bow to Mrs Ferris's dramatic ability which could make a ballade of a bicuspid; nevertheless ...

And when the minister had given his paper, I demolished it.

Robin said, 'For a nice girl, you have a real streak of bitchiness.'

I told no one about Robin although one day Jocelyn came over and found him in the basement suite. She was in third year then, living at Acadia Camp. Years later, she said, 'I just didn't believe it, I guess. He was so pimply, Vicky.'

But someone else guessed, a boy called Rod Slitvitz. His real name was Morris Slitvitz but he changed it to Rod Slitvitz when he joined the Kabalarian Society and worked out his numerals.

Somehow Ben and I always had young men like Rod Slitzvitz and Sam and Paul around. Sam, who was constantly analyzing his motives, for instance, would say, 'You're my surrogate family. I get all the comfort of married life, and none of the worries. I sleep with you vicariously, and at the same time you're my mummy, pure, inviolate, virtuous.' He would come over, say, 'How's the car?' to Ben, and tell me of his latest love affair. But I suppose the real question is why Ben and I put up with them.

Rod too was in the philosophy seminar and this particular night was to give a paper on the free act. He had come over beforehand, to rehearse it in the front room.

I remember sitting there in the old striped chesterfield, trying to follow Rod's reasoning. He believed that the act occurs without cause, no matter how carefully one can elucidate cause. And to illustrate his point, he drew from his jacket a pistol and shot me.

I see the puff of smoke and a long time later hear the loud crashing bang. And I feel, quite surely, the thud of the bullet hit my chest. Death spreads through me like a visitor. I am immensely weary.

Rod stands there, shaking, a clean-faced boy who never eats meat because he wants to rid himself of lust.

'Oh I'm sorry,' I say. For I know now that he loves me. There is so much love in the world and all wasted. I look down at my chest, expecting a great spreading patch of red. There is nothing.

'Blanks,' says Rod unevenly, 'I rented it this afternoon.'

We both laugh a bit nervously, and I say, 'But Rod, that doesn't prove anything about causality or lack of it.' My god, I'd argue syllogisms on my death bed.

'I don't care,' Rod says. 'I'm going to do it tonight. I'm going to shoot the bastard.'

'Oh god, Rod,' I say. 'I'm stagnant.'

Rod sat down to consider this bit of news. After a while he said, 'I'll marry you. But I can't for four years. I have to get my PhD first.'

'That could be a bit late,' I said and made him supper.

As he munched on his carrot sticks, Rod said, considering, 'When I'm married, of course, I can go back on meat.'

And we went to the seminar, and Rod shot at Robin, who turned white beneath the spots. And Dr Gowan was puzzled but gave Rod an A.

Rod was the only person I told. He carried the secret around as if it were he who was pregnant.

I went to work every day and I read the Tractatus and I mailed off cheques to Berkeley. Ben wrote that he was doing postcards for the tourists and had seen a large statue of the crucifixion.

Sally had her kittens. At first she was more outraged than anything else. Outraged and humiliated, like Winnie, when her water broke. I found her trying pathetically to clean up the mess, scraping at the puddle with her paw. Siamese are the only cats you don't need to housebreak. Terribly anal neurotic. Then she began to whirl around and around, trying to bite whatever it was that was cramping her. She looked up at me indignantly as if it were all my fault.

I'd read in the cat book that you must separate the male from the kittens, for fear he'll kill them. So I put Peter out in the basement and locked the door. By the time I got back to the chesterfield, Sally was mewing nervously. She crawled, broken-backed, into my lap and uttered a long despairing howl, her ears slicked flat against her head. 'There there, there there, it's going to be all right,' I said. She began to pant laboriously.

There was a great crash at the basement door. And all the winds of hell broke loose. Peter was flinging himself bodily against the wood; and I could hear his nails going ratchety-ratch as he tried to claw his way through.

'What's all that racket down there?' yelled Mrs Flynn from upstairs.

I dashed out to the kitchen and eased the door open a fraction. 'It's the cat having kittens. I've got to keep the father out or—' But he had levered his way through and was past me, a flash of brown and black, screaming like a banshee.

When I got back to the chesterfield, the first kitten was out and Peter was enfolding it in his mouth.

'You stop that!' But he was licking it into life, gently as a caress.

Sally sniffed at the sodden white lump and decided to have nothing further to do with either of them.

Peter's pink tongue went rasp rasp, and the lump gave a great sighing mew and pushed its nose into Peter's belly fur. 'Oh you sweet old thing,' I said and he gave me such a look, long-suffering and responsible, as the kitten began to suck.

Sally, meanwhile, was having a nap. By the time the second one started, she had given herself a shake as if to say, Oh yes, now I remember what it's all about. She heaved and grunted and moaned and panted and howled.

Peter, cautious of the kitten still hanging on somewhere in the region of his left testicle, would reach out to give her a pacifying lick on the ear, but she, ungrateful bitch, would spit and hiss and bat him as if it were all his fault. But he went on licking haplessly, in a hangdog way. When the new one came out, she ate the sac dutifully to get her milk going but again it was Peter who had to lick the bundle into life. Sally began to purr, deep machine throbbings of pride. Look what I've done! thinking she was through. And off she wobbled to the kitchen to get herself something to eat, leaving Peter with two white rats sucking his fur.

And back she came to sniff them, snarl, hiss, saying, Who are you? And up and cuddle down on top of them, not for their sakes, but to get Peter to wash her instead.

There were four born that night. I left them, curled into an exhausted cocoon of domesticity, and fell into my own bed. Sometime in the small hours the beggars dumped their brood under my covers and went scuttering off, fancy free as ever, through the kitchen window for their sunrise romp.

I woke up to sharp little claws kneading my flesh urgently, and questing mouths in search of suitable tits.

It was really spring now. The daffodils were up and I had missed my second period. Mist rose in clouds from the early ground and Mrs Flynn gave me baleful stares and complained of cat dirt in her flower beds. 'When's your husband coming home?'

Of course she knew about Robin. Sometimes I saw her peering out behind the ecru curtains upstairs when we went out in the mornings.

And one night I come home from work and there's Ben's car out front.

'The kittens are marvellous,' he says.

'Yes, aren't they lovely?'

I move out the next day. Where did I sleep that night then? I must have slept beside Ben, it must have happened. I can't remember. Perhaps it didn't seem terribly important by then. We must have talked. Yes. He told me about his silk-screening process, something new he'd devised, the postcards he was going to make. San Francisco was wonderful. Sam was going through a bad time. He wanted to marry Edna, but all he could think of was all those men in Ottawa. Sam thought that maybe if he and Edna did a pilgrimage to Ottawa, visited all the shrines as it were, the stations of the cross, then maybe he could exorcise the experience. Edna acceded to this piece of lunacy, incidentally.

I borrowed Ben's car and went looking for an apartment. And found one almost right away. On the ground floor. With a window that looked out on the leaves of trees instead of their roots. God, how I hate basements. Within walking distance to work. The dark green sofa made up into a bed and there was a walk-in closet for cooking. I don't remember moving. Ben must have helped me. It was hard to say goodbye to the cats.

'Don't tell Rod my address,' I said. I didn't want to think about being pregnant. I didn't want Rod around asking me what I meant to do. He'd become very solemn lately, very portentous.

I was working on calculations one day and Robin came in and we had a cup of coffee together in the little office in front of the lab. It was Marcie's office, but I used it when I was making up the reports.

Marcie came in, rather breathless and wind-blown. 'Oh,' she said. 'Oh. Excuse *me*.' And she rushed out again, into the lab.

'Come have coffee,' I called.

But she didn't answer.

When Robin had gone, she came in again, her face very red, her lips tight. 'I wish you wouldn't have him in here.'

'Why not?'

'That's my desk. This is my office. It's not yours anymore.'

'I know, but I always do the calculations here.'

'It's my desk and my office and I wish you wouldn't have that person in here.'

'Oh.'

'It's disgusting,' Marcie said. 'I can't bear the sight of him. Ben's such a fine person.'

'I didn't know you knew.'

'I don't see how you *can*, Vicky!' She began to cry. 'It fills me with such'—she took a deep breath; she'd been rehearsing it for some time, I think—'It fills me with such moral horror.'

Moral horror. Moral horror. My god. Moral horror. I think I laughed.

When I wrote this first I put in, "'You insufferable little prig," I said.'

But I didn't. I never know what to say. I don't believe it, for one thing. But I wish I had said that. 'Marcie, you insufferable little prig.'

I did take off my lab coat. I did leave the calculations half-done. I hope she made a botch of them. As usual.

I went back to my ground-floor apartment, and I closed the drapes, and I didn't come out again.

Oh I must have. Yes, I did. Of course I did. It just seems like I didn't.

The day I took back Robin's forest-green sweater, I saw Marcie. Yes. I went into the lab and picked up my things. Yes. And she said, 'Well, I'm not your precious Sister Mary Joseph. I suppose she'd have forgiven you.'

You're right, Marcie. She did.

I began to write a play about a witch and a girl caught in a tree and a warlock who rescues her when the nights are short. It was supposed to illustrate some fine philosophical point; I was going to read it at one of the evening seminars. But the witch kept talking about the long nights.

Robin came over once but I worried about the landlord, and he made the sheets dirty. I don't think he ever took a shower, that boy.

I stayed in the room and I didn't see anybody. Or so it seems. Where were they then, Grace and Edna and Jocelyn? I don't remember. I don't remember seeing anyone at all.

Except Ben. Ben came over a lot.

I borrowed the car one night and asked Robin to go for a drive with me.

When I stopped beside the Pauline Johnson Memorial, he said, 'Whew! I thought you were going to kill us both.'

'Was I driving fast?'

He laughed.

I wanted to show him Siwash Rock in the moonlight. We stood at the barricade and I told him a story: 'Once upon a time there was an Indian maiden and an Indian brave living on this peninsula. But they were of different tribes. Her father, a chief, said he would kill them both; his father, a chief, said he would kill them both. They ran away together, to this spot.'

'And what happened?'

'They killed them both. The brave became Siwash Rock. It means "Clean Fatherhood." The maiden was taken into the sea.'

'And what is the moral?' said Robin.

'I don't know.'

I never told him. It's some comfort to know that. That I kept the gentleman's agreement to that extent. The legend is probably a lie. I probably made it up.

I drove him back to his rec room. 'You don't love me, do you?' I said, having to know, having to hear it.

'No. I don't love you, Vicky.'

The next day I took him back his forest green sweater. I threw it across his desk at him. He said, 'Does it have to be this way?'

For an exit line, not so profound as I would wish.

I took the car back to Ben's place. I didn't go in. Just left the keys in the ignition and walked away. I resigned from the philosophy course.

Someone did drop by to see me. A graduate student. Very practical and down-to-earth. Would I clean up her thesis, spelling and grammar, all that. A hundred years later, she says to me, 'I could see you were dying to talk about it. But I wouldn't let you ... Talking would only have vitiated the whole thing. I said to myself, Let her stew in it. When it gets bad enough, she'll go back to Ben.'

I don't remember dying to talk to her about it, dying to talk to anyone about it.

I hugged the little round lump inside me to myself at night. I woke and retched and my breasts ached. And every day was a victory, another step closer to the point of no return. I'd heard that when you reached the fourth month, there was no turning back.

I sold the play about the witch.

I sat in the room and the third period passed.

Ben came over to see me.

I sat in the room and the fourth period passed.

Ben came over. 'I've arranged for us to see a marriage counsellor,' he said.

And I, secure at last, said, 'I'm pregnant.'

He didn't believe me. 'Have you seen a doctor?'

'No.'

'Then how do you know?'

'You know.'

I don't remember. Why did I go to the marriage counsellor? Because I felt so safe? Because it would shut Ben up? Because it would show my good faith? I don't know. I went to the marriage counsellor.

His name was Mr Brockington and he said he had never heard of a marriage like ours before.

I acted the smart ass. I answered sardonically. I made cynical clever talk.

He said, 'You're behaving quite selfishly, you know. You're having this baby for entirely selfish reasons.'

117

'If she's having a baby at all,' said Ben. 'I think it's all hysterical.'

They were together in this, Ben and Mr Brockington. Older and wiser. Men.

Ben and Mr Brockington had long conferences about me. Ben would come over to report that Brockington thought I was almost psychotic. Brockington thought I should have an abortion.

'He *said* that?'

'You *said* I should have an abortion?' This in a private interview.

'I think you should certainly consider the possibility.'

'You think I should murder my child?'

'Now Mrs Ferris.'

'I want to hear you say it.'

'All right. Very well. I think, yes, you should seriously consider an abortion.'

It hadn't occurred to me that this might happen.

'I'm in my fourth month,' I said. Smugly.

'Yes, if you are in fact pregnant.'

'I am pregnant.' And, 'You realize you are suggesting an illegal operation?'

'I realize that you are, at this moment, too sick to become a mother.'

I didn't go back to Mr Brockington. I went to a doctor, a Dr Webb, and I said, 'Help me have a baby.'

Dr Webb was young and kind and he didn't give me a pelvic. He said women know when they're pregnant. We talked about marriage and had a few laughs. He told me he was happy, you know, not wildly happy, but happy, most of the time, he and his wife got along. And she'd put him through medical school, he owed her a lot.

He gave me some pills to help me sleep.

When Ben knocked. God. I can hear that knock.

Duh duh-duh *duh*-duh *duh duh*.

I didn't answer the door.

I pulled the covers over my head and I bit my knuckles and I did not answer the door.

He knocked and knocked and I did not answer the door.

Then the envelopes began to come. Slipped under the door. Long white envelopes in Ben's fine artistic hand. Black ink.

Clearly, as to an idiot, the letters spelled out the alternatives: A) I could have an abortion; he had made inquiries; they were relatively easy to procure: Jocelyn's boyfriend knew someone. He had told Jocelyn! B) I could come back home and have the baby and he would accept it legally; or C) I could have an abortion and then he, Ben, would give me a baby.

It was all terribly fair. I always read them, waiting until I was sure I heard him move away from the door, I always read them. Like a fool.

It's all right, look, it's all right. Just type it, and copy what you've got down. Don't think about it. It'll be all over soon.

There's something. I forget. Something about the play. Yes, I had to do re-writes. Yes. I had to do a re-write and the knock came at the door and it wasn't the knock and so I answered it, because I had the play in the typewriter and I wasn't scared and it was the professor, come to see how I was getting on and would I give a lecture to his engineering class on creative writing, yes, I would, that'd be fine, and then the knock comes, and it's Ben, and the professor looks at me as if I'm mad, not answering the door like that. So I have to let Ben in. The professor leaves. Ben asks me to give him a urine sample. Just to be sure.

He gives me a bottle. A huge bottle. A jam jar. I'm to do it in the morning, first thing. I'm not to drink anything or eat anything after supper.

Yes, All right, I will. I'll put it outside the door. Okay. Yes.

Okay. No, I won't eat anything or drink anything after supper. Yes, first thing in the morning.

And I do. I put that bottle in a paper bag and I leave it outside my door. I hear Ben's steps coming up the hall. I hear them going away.

Three days later, the knock comes.

I open the door. Doom is written all over his face. He is carrying another brown paper bag. It has brandy in it. A bottle of Liquor Store brandy.

'You'd better have a drink,' Ben says. So I do. I'm scared all of a sudden.

'The test is positive,' he says. He has come straight from the gynecologist's office. 'You're pregnant.'

I am pregnant. It hits me like the news of my father's death. I am pregnant. Dear god, how has this happened?

I think I cried. Yes. I cried. I was terrified. I was really pregnant. How had it happened, incredible. I had another drink.

Then I am in the car and Ben is taking me home.

'You'll have to make all the arrangements,' he is saying. 'It's your decision. It's a decision you have made of your own free will. That has to be understood.'

I am not saying anything, so he says it all again.

'I want you to say it, Vicky. It's important that you realize this is your decision.'

'This is my own decision.'

'Made of your own free will.'

'Made of my own free will.'

We pull up in front of the house. I see Mrs Flynn behind the curtains, watching my downfall. 'It's of my own free will,' I say, 'and I shall never forgive you.'

All right. I phone Jocelyn's boyfriend and he tells me to go to the White Spot at eleven-thirty Thursday morning. I drive to the White Spot on Thursday morning, and I sit for an hour in the car. Finally a man gets in on the passenger's side.

'I can't do it for two weeks,' he says. 'I've got my mother-in-law staying.'

'That's too late,' I say. I want it over and done with. Now.

Ben takes me to a doctor's office. He has got the name from a drugstore. A doctor's office on East Hastings. Dr Weinstein. An old man with shaky hands. No, he doesn't do them himself. Dr Weinstein tells me to go to the corner of Commercial and Broadway at noon on Tuesday. He tells us some funny stories. 'I've seen everything,' he says. He tells us about the girl who works in the bank. How she wrapped it up when it came, wrapped it up in tissue paper and ribbon and sent it to him through the mail. 'I've seen everything,' he cackles.

I go to the corner of Commercial and Broadway on Tuesday at noon. I wait. A woman with red hair drives up in a Morris Minor and tells me to get in.

She drives around and around through back streets and alleys and finally we stop behind an old clapboard three-storey house. An old house, very Vancouver, remodelled into suites. We go up some wooden steps. The kitchen is very clean and scrubbed. The linoleum has maroon flowers. There are plastic roses in vases and little plaques on the wall, 'Kissin' don't last Lovin' do.' No. That's not right. No. 'Kissin' Don't Last Cookin' Do.' That's right. Doilies on the arms of the chesterfield. The chesterfield is in the kitchen.

I put $100 on the arm chair. No. There isn't an arm chair. I put it on the table. Oil cloth. Red and white with little baskets of flowers in the white squares. Yes. And a plastic container for paper napkins.

That's all it cost to murder my child. $100.

She had black hair and green eyes and very pale skin. Freckles. No acne. Very Irish.

We go into the bedroom and I take off my panties. There's a board on the bed, and under the board are newspapers. I get down on the board and spread my knees. The newspapers rustle.

'Relax' says Agnes. Her name is Agnes and she has red hair. She is English, and on D-Day she celebrated with a Canadian soldier.

'Relax, dearie.'

And there was no one to help her, so when she got TB—

'Relax, dearie, I can't get it in.' She is holding a long orange tube and she has a stainless steal thing up my   It goes in and then she releases something and it forces the walls.   Stainless *steel*, I mean. Of course.

'So when I got TB, I decided I would help other girls in trouble, you see. *Please* try to relax, honey.'

'What happened to the baby?'

'Oh she's quite grown-up now. Sixteen years old. She's at school. Right now. Please, honey.'

She is putting up the orange tube. 'It's to let the air in, you see.'

And she gives up and says, 'Look,' and turns her back to me, pulling her magenta sweater over her red hair and there, like a long cicatrix on her back, is where they took the lung out.

She's dead now. Agnes. I read about it in the newspapers. They got her in the end. She committed suicide. I wonder what happened to the daughter. I can't remember how to spell *daughter*. *Dauhgter*? *Daughter*. That's what it says in the dictionary. I don't believe it. It doesn't look right.

'So I couldn't nurse any more. I'm a nurse by profession. I would have been, that is, if I hadn't got TB. Sweetie, you'll have to relax.'

And the tube goes in.

'I've helped a lot of girls. But one time I quit. It was this girl. She said she was only two months gone. Her father was a professor, a real big shot. And her mother, she swore the girl was only two months gone. A big girl. You couldn't tell to look at her. Anyway— I wish you'd relax. We're almost finished—when it came out, it was seven months. I mean, it was *alive*. I was so *sick*. I mean, it was—Relax! Dammit. Honey, I can't do this if you keep clenching up on me like that.'

'What did you do with it?'

'I put it in this can? Like a big coffee can? With lye? And I gave it to the mother. I said, "Bury it." I thought it was up to her, the way she lied to me. I couldn't do a case for six months. It really put me off. You married?'

'Yes.'

'I just wondered. You're not wearing a ring.'

'No. I'm married. My husband's out of work.'

'Yeah. It's really bad this time of year.'

And it's over.

'Now you just go home and scrub the floors. Tonight you'll start to bleed a bit and then it'll all come out. Here, give me your number and I'll call you.'

Three weeks later and five tube insertions later, I am still dog-gedly pregnant.

'I don't think your wife wants to lose this baby,' Agnes says to Ben. Now she is here, in our bedroom, looking at me doubtfully. 'I think that's the trouble. She just don't want to lose it.'

I remember what I did in those three weeks. Between visits to Agnes. I wrote a new play. About a man and wife who go to Mexico. His name is Max and he goes to Mexico for his health, for the good of the sun. His wife, to keep herself busy, works as a volunteer in the village clinic. She meets a doctor. Max urges her to go to a bullfight with the doctor.

'No. I should hate it,' she says. I don't remember her name.

'My wife's a good woman,' Max says to the doctor. They sit in the long mauve nights playing canasta. 'It's so difficult for her. A sick man for a husband.'

Ben takes me bowling. I refuse to scrub the floors.

'She was above me, you see,' Max explains to the doctor. And the moths flutter against the lamp and die. 'I wasn't her class.'

'That's not true, Max,' says the wife. I could look it up, her name.

I sat and I went clackety-clack and Ben made the meals and washed the dishes. Everything was back to normal.

The wife goes to the bullfight. She likes it. She goes to bed with the doctor.

'How brown you've become,' Max says to the wife. 'It's the sun.'

Above my desk, pencilled in faintly (Mrs Flynn's wall, after all): 'Endow thy thoughts with words that make them known.' I was a great believer in the responsible artist. The teleological principle in art.

'How brown and strong you look. It has done you good, the sun.'

The doctor says, 'There was a woman today. All cut to pieces. Her mouth and her eyes and her ears. Her *como se dice*, her nostrils?'

'Ah the poor woman!' says the wife.

The doctor shrugs. 'She had taken a lover. Her husband did it.' He puts down a card. 'Yes, it is an important thing, to have a good woman for a wife.'

'We are more civilized in our country,' says Max.

The tube hung down from my vulva. Nothing happened.

'All right,' said Agnes. 'Let's see what this does.' She kneels on my stomach. Back and forth she rolls, her knees like two terrible engines. She is very thin.

And I dream. Electric water. Neon blue. A mirror. Myself in the mirror. And in an instant, it shatters. Breaks into pieces like the world.

I wake. I go into the toilet and the blood comes. And into my hand, the baby.

You cannot tell of course if it would have had black hair and green eyes or pale skin with freckles. But it is a baby. You cannot tell if it would have been a daughter.

I wrapped it in some toilet paper. The pains are quite bad. It takes a long time for the afterbirth. I sit there on the toilet, holding the baby in the tissue paper.

When I go out into the front room, I am still carrying it. 'It's over.'

'Are you sure?'

Yes.

And he takes the tissue paper parcel. And he takes the scalpel. The one he uses for the silk-screen. And he goes into the other room. Down two steps. Up two steps. He is in the bedroom now. He is there a long time. A long time. Then the toilet flushes.

That didn't happen. That. The scalpel. It did not happen.

Yes. It did. It happened. It happened.

Ben said it was only right for me to pay the $100.

Listen. I am going to tell you now the most fantastic thing I ever did in my whole life.

You ready for a joke? I am ready for a joke myself.

One night, about two weeks later, Ben is working on his silk-screen.

There he is, working away with the scalpel, the same scalpel, and I go into the shower and I have a good scrub. I douche myself out. I've stopped bleeding.

I put on the green nightgown he bought me that first summer, eight years before. I come into the kitchen and I say, 'Ben? You promised.'

I said you'd get a kick out of it. Lovely. My god. I mean, you've got to hand it to me. I don't know what you've got to hand to me, but whatever it is, you've got to.

So. Benjamin Ferris poked it in one last time. Without a safe. Without consulting the little calendar. Without a norform. He did it. Yes he did. Back and forth he went like a little man. Brave as brave. And ooops, here he comes, and he's out and running all over the sheet.

'I can't, I can't,' he says.

Along about four a.m. I get a doozer of an attack.

'Are you wheezy?'

I nod.

I hear him out in the kitchen, busily running water, opening the fridge, putting the needle and the syringe into the poached egg pan. My word, doesn't he sound happy, puttering away in there. I hear the squeak of the vial as he pushes it in.

And in he comes, prick at the ready, poised to plunge.

'I'd rather do it myself,' I say.

'But you get air in,' Ben says.

Yes.

And and and.

Actually, Ben does very well once he gets away from me. He phones me one day in May and he says, 'I'm going to Mexico again.' He is off to build giant sculptures on the northern plains. Peace messages to flying saucers.

'But Ben,' I say, 'isn't that a bit loony?'

'Everything is,' says Ben, 'if you look at it the right way.'

He is going with three women and one teenage boy. They are to be his assistants. 'So if you want to divorce me, you'd better do it now. Because I'm never coming back. Her name's Rosa Manson and she's a poet.'

I trot off to the lawyer's the next day, and in three weeks I'm divorced.

I AM HOME FROM Bowen Island and the professor. Brown and glistening from the sun and the salt. In my white and brown dress with no back.

And there he is. Mik. Sitting at the dining room table. I can see him from the window, as I stand on the porch. I grin. He grins. He's playing chess with Paul.

So we all play chess. Mik beats Paul. I beat Paul. I play Mik. Mik beats me. But I say, 'Give me another chance.'

They've been drinking beer. Paul goes out and gets a twenty-six of something. Mik pours me a glass and I drink it down.

'I'm going to beat you,' I say. Mik fills my glass again.

And we play. On and on. I don't see Paul going. I finally win. I've gone beyond drunkenness, into a mad sobriety of vision. I win. Checkmate.

I stand up. The room does a rather peculiar thing. It moves. I am flat on my face on the floor. Dead drunk.

I throw up all over the floor. 'You let me win.'

Mik is mopping up the mess. 'No. You won.'

'You let me.' If he says yes, I'll kill him.

'No. You won.'

I'm on the sofa. Somehow. Yeeach. Mik comes in with a   With a fried egg sandwich! Whoops.

'Eat it. It's the best thing.'

Arrgh.

So he eats it himself. Right in front of me. How can he? I stink to high heaven.

Edna says to me of a lover: 'He held my head when I was sick, and I thought I'd love him forever.'

I think of Mik eating that fried egg sandwich. A foot away from the ghastly mess of my stomach. That has to be love.

I remember too Mik making love to me when I had my period.

But I'm getting ahead of myself.

But, oh Mik, it's awfully good to see you again. I've been away from you so long. Pages and pages.

He gets me some black coffee and I do the big confession bit.

'I'm not clean and good. I just want you to know. Not like your mother's kitchen cupboards.'

Mik waits.

'Had an abortion. Not my husband's either. So now you know.'

'So?'

'What you said. Other day. 'Bout Gil. Just want to get it straight. Don't make me into some fantasy.'

'What did I say?'

'When you said you loved me. You know.'

Mik shakes his head. 'What day is this?'

'Day you came into my room. You know. Day you told me 'bout Gil. How you killed him.'

'I never came into your room.'

'You came into my room and you said. You told me. You didn't?'

He shakes his head.

'You had a friend called Gil?'

'Yah.'

'You killed him?'

He shakes his head.

'Oh.'

I think it all over.

128

'All right. Just so long as you got it perfectly clear. What I am.'

'What are you?'

'Destructive.'

And Mik says, 'You can't destroy me. I've been destroyed by experts.'

I DO STUPID THINGS. I mean, really stupid things that it embarrasses me to tell about. I fall in with the innocent game. At dinner I tell Paul that he's inept at social intercourse, and pretend I don't see Mik cough and choke on his milk.

I say, 'So what's this sixty-nine you're always saying?'

'Sixty-five,' he says, not cracking. 'It's rule number sixty-five, on the cell door. "Prisoners will cease and desist from making loud noises," etcetera.'

I'm not sure what I'm up to, but whatever it is I don't like it. So one night, coming back from the beach, I say, 'I know what sixty-nine means. I was only letting on I was dumb.'

'Oh yah? So what does it mean?'

'It means doing it upside down.'

For some reason this amuses Mik even more. He throws back his head and hollers.

'No. I know all the words. Look. You have, you've made me up, and it's ridiculous. I can say all those words. Oh go fuck yourself.'

That's the first time I say it to Mik. This time he laughs even harder.

'What's the matter?'

'It's the *way* you say it,' he says. 'Like a kid saying "poo."'

'But you've got to stop apologizing every time you let something slip. You do, you know. You're always apologizing as if I'd never heard such language before.'

'Have you?'

This stops me. Really, I haven't.

'You like to think you're wicked. You don't know nothing, baby.'

This makes me furious. 'Don't patronize me. Don't you dare condescend to me.'

'Look.' He sits down on the sea wall and rolls a cigarette. 'Last week I was across the bridge. My buddies and me, we had this hooker in the room. There was five of us rammed it to her.'

I refused to be shocked. 'So?'

'So she never felt a thing. She was out cold.'

This does shock me. 'How could you? I mean, wouldn't that be worse, her not knowing?'

'I didn't want her awake. She had a face like a horse's ass. I hung her head down over the edge of the bed so I wouldn't have to see.'

I don't know what to say. The sea moves normally, gently swells on the beach. Children play with red balls. Gulls dive and scream. A summer's night. He's right. I don't know nothing.

'Once Gil and me, we had this Italian hustler. We made her do it in the mouth. It's safer that way. Anyway, Gil did it first, and then me. When I was finished, Gil slapped her on the back and made her swallow it. God. She was mad!' He chuckles, remembering.

'But why would he do a thing like that? Lord, what a filthy thing to do! I mean, it's not filthy to swallow it, of course. In some societies they think it's good for the complexion. But he must have thought it was the worst thing he could do to her. It was an act of degradation.'

'"An act of degradation,"' Mik says, rolling it around in his mouth, tasting it. Then he laughs.

'I mean, he obviously did it to make her feel disgusting.'

'She *was* disgusting.' Then he looks at me. 'You didn't have to do that,' he says. 'I know what "degradation" means.'

'Then why do you talk like that?'

'Like what?'

'Like "You don't know nothing" and "I ain't goin' nowhere" to Paul? Even to me.'

'Paul expects it,' Mik says. 'So do you.'

I shoot a look at him. I couldn't risk him full face in those days. He is staring out at the water, his face hard and lined, his eyes dangerous. Now he turns to me, and he does not smile. I look away.

'You just don't know,' he says. 'I seen things ... saw things at Ortona you wouldn't believe. I don't believe now. But they happened. I did them.'

'Ortona? Where's that?'

'Italy.' He gets up now. 'Let's go.' He's walking ahead of me, fast, and I have to run to keep up.

'Hey. Wait. What's the matter?'

He slows down.

'Did I do something, to make you mad?'

His mouth twitches. 'Naw. It's just, when you said "Ortona", like you never heard it before.'

'I haven't.'

'Yah.' He nods. 'Yah. It's just, Ortona was ... to a guy in the war, Ortona was ... like you said Thermopylae to some old Greek.'

'Oh.'

We walk for a while. Then he says, 'You haven't got me right either, have you?'

'Apparently not.'

The sun has gone down. Now the air is soft and dark.

'Yes,' I say. 'I thought you were illiterate.'

Mik stops in his tracks, and for one moment I think he's going to hit me.

It's a deep thrill in the groin, and I hold my breath. His face is in the shadows. Then he laughs. A huge wondrous laugh. Mik's laugh. A long deep roar from the gut.

We go on walking.

'You know,' he says innocently, 'you remind me of this lady gorgonzola, they got a very high smell to them. You heard about the smell of gorgonzola?'

Now it's my turn to suppress a snort. 'No, I'm sure you mean a gerontium. I mean the boats. Not gorgons. Gerontiums. A gorgon's a kind of cheese. Very smelly.'

But I know I've lost that round.

'No, I know what you're thinking of, but it's not gerontium. Gerontium, that's a kind of purple ointment they give you for the clap.'

I laugh and Mik says, quickly, not to lose it, 'Maybe I'm thinking of an orgon. Nah, that's a place in the States, got all the roses.'

'No!' I'm recovering slightly. 'You're thinking of organza, it's some kind of orgy they do in the South Pacific.'

'I thought that was onanism,' says Mik.

'No, that's a religion. You take an onastic order.'

'Yah, you're right,' says Mik. 'Order of Saint Succubus.'

I collapse. I stand there, holding my stomach, laughing like a lunatic. Mik says, 'Come on, you're stopping traffic.' But I laugh helplessly all the way home.

In bed that night, I say, 'Joss?'

'Unh?'

'You remember that night, when Paul was here, and Mik said a gorgonzola was a gondolier?'

Jocelyn laughs.

'Did you know he was putting it on?'

'Sure. Didn't you? "Up and down the carnals"!'

I don't say anything.

'Didn't *you*?'

'No. I'm as bad as Paul.'

'Got to watch those stereotypes,' says Jocelyn sleepily. And, 'I kind of like him.'

'Mik,' I say to say his name.

'Mr Clean,' she says and laughs again. 'That supercilious little prick.'

'*You* passed Paul onto me!'

'You didn't have to take him.'

'You really like Mik?'

'He's funny.'

AND GUESS WHO COMES back from Mexico.

'How did the sculptures go? Got any response?'

'We didn't get a chance. We were going to live like natives, but you need a work permit.'

'So how's Rosa?'

'Well, she had to have an abortion in San Francisco. We stopped off at Sam's and did it.'

'Yours?'

'No, I don't think so.'

Neither do I.

The teenage boy had disappeared. The other two women took off separately, hitch-hiking. Ben sold his car in San Diego.

'I thought you were never going to come back.'

Ben ignores this. 'As far as I'm concerned, Vicky, we're still married.'

'I could show you the papers.'

'That's all it is, papers. We're still married. Spiritually.'

'So. You never contacted the flying saucers.'

'Paul tells me you've got this man living here. This ex-convict.'

'That's right.'

'I hope you know what you're doing.'

'Yeah. Well.'

He looks at me with those mournful suffering eyes. 'I love you, Vicky.'

'How are you doing for money?'

He has just one request to make of me. Only one. He wants to do a head of me. In terra cotta. Will I sit for it?

I sit for it. He has the stuff all out there, on the porch. He knew I couldn't refuse.

He is working silently, intently, and Mik comes in the door. A large, noisy man, Mik. Crash. He stops dead at the sight of us.

Ben gets up and puts out his hand, then pulls it back, smiling apologetically. 'Clay. Sorry. I'm Ben Ferris.'

Mik stares at him.

Ben, explaining, says, 'I'd shake hands only my hand's all over clay,' and he offers it to Mik. Proof.

Mik stands there and finally Ben gives a nervous laugh.

'Vicky's been telling me about you,' he says. Mik shoots me a look, and I want to say it's a lie.

'I hope we can be friends,' says Ben.

'Yah?' says Mik and lumbers over to the stairs and up to his room.

Ben looks at me sorrowfully. 'Has he paid you anything?'

'He's looking for work,' I say.

'He hasn't paid you anything, has he?'

'So how's Rosa?' I say.

'Fine. She's a fine person.'

'You two still together?'

'No. Didn't I tell you? She went to Mexico City.'

'Oh. I thought you said that was Ida and Stephanie.'

'No. Rosa went too.'

'But I thought you said she had an abortion at Sam's.'

'That was on the way down.'

'You mean you *all* stayed at Sam's, you and Ida and Stephanie and Rosa, and the boy, what's-his-name? All of you?'

'Lionel. His name's Lionel. Sam's changed a lot.'

I bet.

'Sam's become rather conservative.'

Ben is wearing sandals, the fashionable kind, a new Mexican shirt. Beads.

'How much did you get for the car?'

'A hundred dollars.' Ben is bending now to the head. Looking up at me carefully, bending again to the clay. A spatula in his hand. I was going to say scalpel, but it wasn't.

'So how're you off for cash?'

'Oh Vicky,' Ben says, 'you always were so materialistic.' And later, 'Can I leave it here? I don't think I'd better do any more today. Can I leave it here and come back to work on it?'

'All right.'

And before he leaves for Ivan's, Ben touches my arm. A feathery touch, like Archimedes ... if you have the proper fulcrum, you can move the world.

'I just don't want to see you get hurt,' he says. And, 'I like your hair. You're very beautiful, Vicky. I love you. Just remember that, I love you. I always will. We're not divorced.'

Ah god, god, god, ah god.

Mik comes down and finds me sitting there, staring at the head.

'What's those?' he says.

'What?'

'The hair, the way it's spread out. Like snakes.'

I laugh. 'Medusa,' I say. Mik is right. The hair spreads out like snakes. The face is dead. The eyes are staring, sightless, and the neck is cut off. Medusa, after Perseus cut off her head.

'The little creep,' Mik says.

'What?'

'He's a little creep.'

'It's how he sees me.'

'Yah. He's a creep.'

One night we play chess and Mik bets me breakfast in bed if I win: I lose.

So I take him his breakfast on a tray. It is the first time I have been in his room. Everything is very neat. The clear thin sun of nine o'clock is coming in under the blinds. The house is still. I waited until Jocelyn left.

Mik is lying there, under the chenille bedspread. His chest is bare. He is smoking.

On the tray is a slice of papaya, a lime cut in half, a cup of coffee. Black. Mik took his coffee black.

I put it down on the chair beside the bed.

I am wearing a black velvet pantsuit. London Shop. Forty dollars, half-price. They weren't called pantsuits then. That's an anachronism. Lounging pajamas? I seem to have been spending a lot of money on clothes lately.

Mik is smoking. He doesn't move, just lies there, looking at me.

I go to the bottom of the bed, and say, 'Do you want to make love to me?'

Looking straight at him. Making an official pronouncement. I haven't thought this out. I haven't planned it. I just say it.

'Yah.'

I undo the frogs on the jacket. I take the jacket off. Drop it to the floor. I take off the pants. Let them lie. I take off my brassiere, my panties. Mik lies there, smoking.

Goosebumps. My hips. The scars. Moon crater white. I am shivering, my teeth are chattering. I know I am ugly, standing there in that pitiless morning light, scarred, purple, covered with goosebumps.

I lift the covers and get in beside him. He is very solid, and very warm. Enormous, like a whale. I am frozen to the marrow. My heels are congealed with the cold. If he touches me, I know I shall break off in slowly oozing lumps of meat.

Mik says

I haven't put this in before. It didn't fit. I know it happened, but it didn't fit with the story. So I ignored it. I said it wasn't relevant.

I still don't understand it. Why he said it. It wasn't true. Why would he say such a thing? But I will put it in, because it was said, because Mik said it.

Mik says, 'I'm not hung like a bull.'

And he puts out his cigarette.

He is all over me, large and heavy, a great crushing weight. I make all the polite little noises to show I am enjoying it. And Mik comes in me, roaring and bucking like a stallion, his head thrown back, hollering. It is all very embarrassing.

'Did you come?'

'Yes,' I lie. I think he'll be upset if I say no.

Mik lights a cigarette. 'No, you didn't,' he says.

And then I find out that men can do it more than once.

My legs are cramping from the cold.

Mik puts out his cigarette and kneels, begins to suck me.

'No!' I say, pushing at his back. I try to push his head away. But he holds my thighs tighter.

And Mik's face comes up, looms into mine. 'No?' he says.

And I pull his head down to my loins.

And then he is in me, lifting me up with his wild surging, and I am moving too, moving to him, with him. I have never known this before. This mindless rhythm of my body, up and up, meeting him perfectly, wanting him in me forever. 'No?' he laughed and took me beyond words.

'I'm gonna fuck you to death, baby.'

And I came and came again. And he said 'Uncle?'

'Uncle,' half-laughing, half-crying.

'Okay!' Mik says. Throwing himself down beside me. We lie like that for a long time, just breathing. 'Christ,' he says once.

And now he swivels around and kisses me there, licking me, growling, burying himself. I take his penis in my mouth and hold it. We lie there like two barbarians who have killed each other on the field.

'Ortona,' I say and laugh weakly.

He says, 'You're bleeding like a stuck pig.' He is pleased. 'Jesus, you're bleeding like a stuck pig.'

I can't lift my head. I bit him.

'Christ,' he says and pulls it out to examine. 'I'm raw!' Pleased again. Somehow proud. 'I'll be humping around like some cripple.'

And, 'I beat you. Eight to six.'

'You counted!'

'Damned right.' He snorts. He slaps me on the bum.

'I'll beat you,' I say. 'Yet.'

'You think so.'

'I'll kill you.'

'You're a bleeding corpse.'

'I bet you can't even stand.'

'You're asking for it.'

'I'm gonna destroy you,' I say.

And he leaps on me. And he is all over me, in me, crushing me, and he says, 'How's that?' kneeling upright in the middle of the bed, holding my thighs around his middle, working my hips back and forth in mid-air, so that I am jerked about like a rag doll.

And a long time later, he says, 'I think that was dust.' And, 'Give up?' But I can't speak. 'I want to pull you on like an overcoat,' he says.

And, 'Hey. You alive down there?'

'Bastard,' I say, finally.

He laughs. 'Tough guy.'

The papaya was ground into Jocelyn's shag rug. I don't remember how it happened.

We went for a swim that night, after dinner. A sedate dinner except for one moment when Mik said, innocently, 'What's the matter? You got a boil on your bum?' Jocelyn looked at him, surprised. 'Your sister,' he said, 'she's twitching.'

The salt stung. Blood was coming down my thighs. I watched it swirl away in the water, thin dark threads. Mik swam far out, huffing and blowing like a walrus. I floated.

'What's the matter?' he said, coming up and ducking me. 'Can't take it, eh?' So I swam far out, and he went round me in circles, calling, 'You'll never make it!'

I went to bed, my own bed, and fell asleep without a pill.

When I came downstairs in the morning, Mik was waiting in the kitchen. He took me into his arms and held me, looking down into my face, calling me a name I can't remember. He kissed me, a long gentle kiss, his mouth hard and dry. It was the first time our lips had touched.

He made my breakfast. I sat, waiting in the dining room, in the warm morning sun. Bacon and eggs and fried potatoes. Toast and lashing of butter.

'Eat up. You're gonna need it.'

I ate up. Then he took me upstairs. I could hardly walk.

Later: 'You won't admit it, will you?'

'What?'

'You liked that?'

'Yes.'

'It didn't hurt?' He is propped up on one elbow, looking down at me.

'No.'

'No. Want some more?'

'All you've got.'

And he called me the name I can't remember.

And later: 'Enough?'

'Why? You tired?'

And later: 'Say it.' His hands around my throat. 'Say it, or I'll just keep humping you.'

'It hurts.'

'What? Louder. I can't hear you.'

'It *hurts!*'

And he laughed.

That day or the next or the next, I don't remember, he took me to see some people. A linoleum carpet. Big maroon flowers. A man. A woman. In an apron. Little blue flowers on the apron. Beer. Mik talking. The woman talking. Upstairs. An upstairs. An upstairs apartment. A television set and a lamp that went round and round. A fire. A lamp that pretended to be a forest fire, the light going round and round inside so that the fire sprang up, consumed the trees, died down sprang up, died down, round and round. A lamp on the television and the maroon flowers, large fleshy petals, on the floor.

It was cool, the linoleum against my cheek.

And then I was in a dark room, in a bed, and the woman was bending over me. She was asking me to drink some of this hot tea, it would make me feel better. 'Men are brutes,' she said.

And a taxi. And Mik in the taxi, grim.

Jocelyn saying, 'What's the matter?'

'She's got a stomach ache.'

I slept for thirty hours.

And he woke me and took me to his room. Afternoon light. Green. Dim green light.

I held onto his shoulders as if I were drowning. The great crashing of the waves was Mik, the storm and the thunder, and all the winds of chaos. 'I love you,' I said, over and over. 'I love you.'

He took me across the bridge to meet the buddies.

'Wear that blue suit,' he said. I wore the blue suit and put on my white gloves and the sandals with the plastic inserts. I did up my hair in a great coil in the back.

We were sitting in a room in the St Helen's. There seems to be a lot of men there. Mik is ignoring me. Sitting over to one side of a stove. Talking to the men. From time to time I look to him, but he doesn't look to me.

Someone is cooking chicken on the stove. And someone else is giving me a piece of toilet paper, folded neatly for a napkin. And I am holding a piece of chicken, very greasy, in the toilet paper. I am trying to eat it. I wipe my fingers on the toilet paper, but it is too greasy. I am given another piece of toilet paper.

No one says anything rude to me. Once someone says 'shit' and then 'Excuse me.'

Someone says to Mik, 'Right off the banana boat.'

'So you're Mik's landlady?'

'Yes.'

It is all very uncomfortable. No one seems to know what to say to me. They are talking to one another as if I were not here, and yet I feel that I am here, very much. Someone says, has anyone seen the benny snatcher? I gather this is a proper name of some kind. But the Benny Snatcher isn't here today. Someone called Taffy is here. It all sounds as if a foreign language is being spoken. The banana boat is mentioned again and I ask if they are longshoremen.

'Longshoremen?'

'Well, if you've been unloading bananas.'

But it is the wrong thing to say. Everyone is laughing at me.

I have the feeling that I must keep my knees pressed firmly together, that I must on no account cross my legs. And I do keep my knees together, pressing them so hard that they turn white. It is a very uncomfortable position.

Mik leaps up suddenly and heads for the door, not even looking at me. He actually goes out of the door, leaving me to say thank you very much for the chicken. I gather up my gloves and head after him, like a puppy dog.

I trot after him down the street. He is walking ahead of me. I feel I have done something terribly wrong but I can't imagine what it is.

We are walking across the bridge. Mik has no money for a bus.

'Please. Mik. Wait just a minute.' I'm out of breath. I stop to lean over the parapet and look down to False Creek.

He comes back, his face very red and cross.

'Did I say something wrong?'

Mik barks, a short angry laugh.

'But you seem so angry.'

'No, you didn't do anything wrong.'

'But what is it?'

He looks down at the lumber yards and the tug boats and then up to the horizon where red and blue sails swing nerveless into the white glare of the sun.

'Nah. You did all right. You're just, like George said, you're just off the banana boat.'

'What was that about the banana boat, I don't understand.'

He shoots me a look. 'Green. Like bananas.'

'Oh.'

He swings away but I hold my ground. 'But what did I do! You tell me! You tell me then. What did I do wrong?'

And I grab his jacket and hold on. 'You tell me!'

'You want a punch out? I'll give you a punch out.'

'You tell me what I did.'

'You went down there. You went down to that place.'

'But you asked me. You were with me.'

'Jesus.'

'What is it? You tell me.'

'You went in there and you sat like ... like butter wouldn't melt in your cunt. Like some ... you sat there and your legs were so tight together ...' Then his mouth quirks. 'The bastards gave you a piece of toilet paper for a napkin!' He is struggling with his mouth. 'And Taffy apologized for saying "Shit." He apologized. Jesus.' Now his mouth breaks. I am hanging on his mouth. 'They were *scared* of you. Like you was glass. Like you'd ...'

He throws back his head and roars.

'Is that why you took me?'

'What?' He is still chortling, shaking his head.

'Like a slave in chains. To show me off. That's what it was all about, wasn't it? What did you want? Did you want me to spread my legs and say, "Okay, boys, one at a time"?'

His face is stone. He turns and walks away, too fast for me to follow. When I get home, he is not there.

But I don't care. I hate him. I don't understand what I have done. I don't understand why he is angry. Go then, go, to hell with you!

I go to bed and take three pills.

He is gone before I get up in the morning. Perhaps he never came home at all. Very well. I work on the play.

The man from the sea. 'When they found me, everyone was dead,' he says. And the girl says, 'But why were you alive? Why were you saved?' 'Because I am a carrier.'

At five-thirty, Mik lurches in, filthy, grinning. He has a job. He has been digging ditches all day. He has a job.

He goes off in the morning with a bag lunch. He comes home at night and eats dinner like a somnambulist. 'Potatoes,' he says, shoving his empty plate toward me. 'Potatoes.'

There must have been one night when I moved into his bed. I don't remember. There must have been one night when I stopped the pretense and moved into Mik's room. One particular night. But I can't remember. I don't remember what Jocelyn said, if she said anything.

I worked on the play, and Ben came over to work on the head.

I sat there, and Ben worked, and I smelled Mik on me, his sweat, his body, his love, and I felt safe.

One night Mik came in and gave me all the money he owed for board and room, and more besides. And a shoe box. Inside the shoe box was a pair of high-heeled slippers. Cinderella shoes. With rhinestones in the clear plastic heels.

I said, 'What's the extra for?'

'That's for the house,' Mik said.

'But you don't have to give me anything for the house.'

'That's for your keep. I'm paying for you now.'

'No.' And I gave the money back to him.

'I pay for your keep now,' said Mik, handing the money back to me.

'No, I couldn't. I pay my own way.' And I put it on the mantel.

'They look great, eh?'

I laugh. 'Well.'

'Well what?'

'I can't wear them, Mik.'

'Why not?'

'They're vulgar.'

He tears the money into pieces. And goes crashing about the front room, smashing things. There is glass all over the floor.

'Two can play at that game!' I say, and take down the Renoir and put my foot through it. Wham bang crash, around we go, knocking everything down. I remember aiming at the television screen with my foot, but pulling back just in time. I am laughing crazily, but thinking to myself: Well, we can scotch tape the money.

Jocelyn comes in screaming and heads for the telephone. 'I'm calling the police!' she says, but Mik is there before her and pulls it out of its socket.

Jocelyn is holding her head and saying, 'I can't bear it! I can't stand it!'

Mik slams out of the front door. So hard that it comes right off its top hinge.

'I can't, Vicky, I just can't!'

'What?'

'The violence!' She is crying. 'I can't take it anymore.'

But I can't imagine what she is talking about. This hasn't happened before.

What violence?

The police arrive. Jocelyn had got out, somewhere in that time, after Mik pulled out the telephone wire; she has phoned them. I explain it was all a misunderstanding. I go to the telephone box at Safeway's and ask for a repairman for our phone: just an accident. I clean up the mess. The Renoir isn't damaged, it goes back into the frame. I gather up the pieces of money and put them back on the mantel. And I wait for Mik to come home.

But he doesn't. A day goes by, and then another.

I make an appointment with a gynecologist for a diaphragm fitting.

'How long have you been married?' he says. I am wearing my grandmother's ring.

'Nine years.'

'And this is your first diaphragm?'

'Yes.'

'What made you decide to, uh, change your method?'

'I've heard it's more pleasurable for the man.'

He gives me a look. 'What method were you using?'

'French safes.'

'I see. Nine years,' he says. I can tell he thinks I'm up to no good.

He explains how to put the thing in. There is a long-handled plastic affair, and you snap on the rubber cup, here, on these knobs at the end, and you put the jelly in, here, and then all around the edge. And then you shove it up and give a flick of the wrist, and bob's your uncle. There was something about waiting for twelve hours before you took it out.

Mik didn't come home.

Finally, I get into my white and brown dress with no back and take a cab across the bridge. I start to make the rounds of the beer parlours.

I have never been in a beer parlour alone. There are separate entrances for men and women: Ladies and Escorts, the sign says. I stand at the entrance and wait until a waiter notices me.

'Have you seen Mik O'Brien?'

'Who?'

'Mik O'Brien. He's a big guy.'

'Big Mik? Yeah. I seen him. He was here yesterday.'

'Could you look in the Men's and see if he's here now?'

'You want I should look?'

'Please.'

And off the waiter would go, into the men's section, and back he would come shaking his head. I would say thank you, not knowing enough to tip, and go on to the next one.

Finally, someone followed the waiter back. A cadaverous man with sores on his lips. 'You looking for Big Mik?'

'Yes. Have you seen him?'

'I seen him this morning. With George. You know George? I think maybe they're down to the Chink's.'

'Where's that?'

'The Chink's. Down the street.'

'Is it a restaurant?'

'Yah.'

I find Mik in the last booth. George is with him. Mik looks most peculiar. His face is all puffed up. He is just sitting there, in front of a plate of bacon and eggs, moving slightly as if there is a breeze.

'Well, you idiot!' I say.

George looks up. He too has a plate of bacon and eggs, but he is eating. 'He ain't feeling so good.'

'Come on,' I say. 'I'm taking you home.'

George says, 'I've been trying to get him to eat something.'

'You stupid clot,' I say.

His head twitches. He lifts it, as if he is smelling the wind. 'Is that you?' he says. His voice is like sandpaper.

'Yes, it's me.'

He pushes at the table but its legs are bolted to the floor. It creaks ominously.

'C'mon, Mik, none of that,' says George. And to me, 'He ain't feeling so good.'

But Mik is out in the aisle now and swinging. His great fists go whizzing over the top of my head. Swoosh swish. Missing me by a foot. I start to laugh.

'I'm gonna kill you,' Mik says. Swish swoosh. 'Rotten bitch.'

'Duck,' says George. 'He's not kidding.'

'Neither am I,' I say. 'Don't be ludicrous.'

'"Ludicrous,"' Mik says, tasting the word. Then he winds up and wham goes his fist, a mile off.

The Chinese is dancing up and down behind us, saying, 'Not in here. Please. You get him out of my place. Please.'

'Oh don't be ridiculous,' I say to Mik and put my shoulder under his arm pit. 'Come on, now, I'll get a cab.'

He's still bashing away at mid air. George says, 'Why'n't you go home, Vicky? I'll bring him along later.'

Swish swoosh.

'You grab his other arm,' I say. And George does. We march him out to the front door, where I pause, and try to manoeuvre my purse so that I can pay for the breakfast.

'No, no,' says the Chinese, 'on the house. Please. Just get him out of my place. I don't want no trouble.'

We prop Mik up against the restaurant door and I go out to the curb and hail a cab.

When I come back for Mik, he tries it again. This time his fist comes quite close, so I slap his face. 'You stop that, you big goof!'

George is saying something. I can't hear him. We get Mik into the cab and I give our address to the driver. I wave goodbye to George, who is standing there, still trying to say something. 'Okay,' I mouth. 'Thanks a lot.'

We are almost home and I start to laugh.

'What?'

'"Boiled,"' I say. 'Your face, it looks boiled. I wonder if that's the etymology.'

I got him upstairs and took off his clothes. He kept swaying his head back and forth like a bull in the slaughter house. I ran a hot bath and tipped him into it. I shaved him. I got him to drink a cup of black coffee while he was still in the tub. Then I got him into bed.

He went right off to sleep. I felt rather tired myself, so I took off my clothes and crawled in beside him.

When I wake up, there he is, sitting up in bed, smoking.

He's looking at me.

'What'd you do, scalp me?' he says, feeling his face.

'I shaved you.'

'What with? A dull knife?'

'I don't feel the least bit of sympathy for you. You're a drunken sot.'

He looks at me.

'An obstreperous drunken sot.'

'"An obstreperous drunken sot,"' he says. And, like glory, the laugh comes, pure gold, a god's laugh.

We lie there a while. He takes a nipple in his fingers speculatively. 'I couldn't get it up if I tried.'

'We'll see.'

I go into the bathroom and put in the diaphragm and the goo, but he's right, it's impossible.

He had lost the job, of course.

His buddies came to see him the next day. They sat downstairs in the front room, drinking whiskey. They were quite noisy.

At one point, a buddy, on his way back from the bathroom, paused at my half-open bedroom door. 'How're ya doing?'

'Fine.'

'What're ya doin'?'

'Marking papers.' I waved at the pile on my desk.

'Yah? Oh yah, that's right. Mik was saying you're a teacher.'

'No. I'm a marker. It's just spare time work, like.'

'Yah?' He came into the room to see, putting down his glass which, for some reason, he had carried up to the bathroom. On the top of the unmarked pile.

He peered down at the paper in front of me. "'Non seq.'" he read out loud.

'Well, it's just an abbreviation. Like, it's short for non sequit ... it means he's made a dumb argument. It doesn't follow. What he's said.'

'I guess he's gonna fail all right. All them red marks.'

'No. No, he gets an A. Maybe an A minus.'

'Yah?' The buddy looked at me suspiciously. 'I'd hate to see what you do to the guy that fails.' He laughed.

'Well, here's one,' I said, taking it out from the other pile.

'But that ain't got nothing on it. Just a little squiggle. Can they read your writing?'

'Not always.'

'Jesus, and that one's gonna fail?'

'Well, this one's not worth bothering with, you see.'

'Yah?'

When he left, taking his glass, there was a great ruddy ring on the front of the top paper. 'Well, that's the last straw!' I said out loud.

I went down the stairs like Aimee Semple Macpherson. 'All right. That's enough. The party's over.'

They didn't seem to hear me. So I picked up the whiskey bottle from the floor and took it out to the kitchen.

I waited. After a while, the buddy who'd left the ring on the paper came wandering in, his glass still in his hand.

'Sorry,' I said brightly. 'It's all gone.' Waving at the empty bottle on the counter.

He wandered back toward the front room and then I heard Mik come clumping toward the door. He didn't come in, just stood there in the doorway.

'Where's the booze?'

'Somewhere on its way to the Pacific Ocean I should imagine.'

'What?'

I waved my hand at the bottle. 'I dumped it down the sink.'

He didn't say anything. Just stood there. Then he turned and went back to the front room. After a few minutes, the buddies all left.

I heard Mik coming back again. And again he didn't come into the kitchen, just stood very still in the doorway, well away from me.

'That was a dangerous thing to do,' he said, very quietly.

'I said it was time to go! Nobody paid the least bit of attention.'

'I never knew anybody do that, my whole life,' Mik said.

'I told them politely and they just went right on!' I was indignant.

'Pour a twenty-six down the sink. A whole twenty-six.'

'It's my house and I don't care for a bunch of punks carousing about.'

'Men've lost their lives for less,' Mik said.

I laughed.

He seemed more wondering than angry. 'Poured it down the sink? You're not kidding?'

'Well, it seemed to work.'

'I got them out,' he corrected.

'Well?'

Mik considered this. Perhaps he too thought it wasn't worth bothering about.

'George told me. About the Chink's.'

'I hope he did. Did he tell you what a proper idiot you looked?'

'He told me what happened. What you did. How you just ...' He seemed at a loss for words. 'He said you were just standing there. In front of me.'

'Well, I knew you wouldn't hurt me.'

Mik sighed.

'I mean, you were missing by a mile.' I imitated him, swinging with my fist. 'Over my head!' And I laughed again. 'You were just trying to scare me.'

Mik shook his head. 'I couldn't *see*,' he said. 'I was blind drunk.'

'Blind drunk.' So that was what it meant. Literally blind. From drink. But I didn't really believe him. I shook my head. 'No, subconsciously, even so ...' But he had turned on his heel and gone. I heard the front door close gently, and his feet going down the porch steps. Very quietly for Mik.

He didn't come back for hours. I was in bed when I heard him coming up the stairs. He came into the dark bedroom and took off his clothes, all but his shorts, and climbed in beside me. I loved the way he was, so warm and big.

'Hi.'

'Hi,' and he called me the name I can't remember. He had a pack of ready-mades and he lit one.

'Where've you been?' because he didn't smell of beer.

'Went over to the old lady's.'

'Your mother's?'

'Yah.'

'I didn't know you had a mother.'

'What'd ya think, I sprung full-growed from the dung heap?'

But he wasn't angry.

'You never said you had a mother.'

'Well, I got one.'

'Where does she live?'

'Out past Commercial there.'

'Is your father alive?'

'Yah.'

'Have you got sisters and brothers?' I was sitting up now. It was true in a way. Mik was to me a solitary phenomenon, without antecedents, without periphery.

'One sister. A brother. The prick. My brother, the second lieutenant.'

'Lieutenant,' I said, with the 'f.'

'Unh?'

'Well, we don't have to give way to the Americans in everything.'

He snorts. 'You know something?'

'What?'

'I've decided to marry you.'

'Who says!'

'I says.'

And later, 'What's that?'

'A diaphragm.'

He raises himself up on one elbow. I can see his face a little. It's dawn now.

'I got one. The doctor gave me the smallest size.' I offered that, an excuse. I don't understand even now why that should have mollified Mik. But it did.

'Yah?' And he puts his fingers in again, to feel. 'I thought you smelled funny. Like a hospital.'

'I think I use too much goo.'

'I like the way you smell. Better.' But he made love to me again, only when I took it out, the next day, the cap was full of blood.

I KNOW I'VE AVOIDED talking about My Therapy.

Her name was Miss Haggerty but I called her the Nut Lady.

'Well? What does the Nut Lady have to say for herself?' Mik would say.

'She says I want you to do me in.'

'Yah? You tell her how you do *me* in?' And he would laugh.

'What does your Nut Lady say about your progress?' the producer would say.

'She says I write out my anger. She says my writing enables me to avoid expressing anger in real life.'

'You tell her to keep her Freudian mitts off your work!' And, 'You tell her to keep her analysis confined to your mental aberrations and to eschew literary criticism.' And, 'All writers are nuts. Just take care she doesn't cure you.'

'How's the Nut Lady?' Jocelyn would say.

'She says I've got this mother complex about you and Francie.'

'Well, she sounds pretty cuckoo, but she might be right there.'

Grace got her fourth degree and went to work at the clinic. Her office was right next door to the Nut Lady's. Or, I think it was.

'But, she's quite short, Vicky,' Grace said.

'She is not, she's huge, she's ten feet tall,' I said.

'Oh Vicky.'

'She's tall and she always wears elegant clothes and her apartment is never in a mess. I know the type.'

'She is *not* tall,' said Grace. 'She's about your height. And she's got one of those horrible sweaters, white with embroidered flowers?'

'She doesn't! She wears Italian knits, absolutely plain, and all from Marty's at 200 per.'

'Oh Vicky, you're so funny.'

Grace says to me, last week, 'Aren't I in your book?'

'No, it's all about me. A big ego trip. You're there, but shadowy. The perfect lady. You and Terence.'

'Terence! What a good name for him.'

'I can't write about you.'

'Why not? Why don't I get a part?'

'I don't know you well enough.'

'You've known me twenty-three years.'

'That's why,' I say.

Grace was always perfect to me. Like her name, gracious, perfect, good. I was certain that if Grace had orgasms (which she wouldn't), they were lyrical affairs, having nothing to do with sweat or stink or maroon wrinkled lips.

I'm telling her about last summer and how, in twenty feet of clear blue Aegean, the wine steward started to masturbate himself with my feet.

'Good heavens! Your feet! What were you doing?'

'Lying on my back, trying not to drown!'

'Good heavens! What did you *do?*'

'I said to myself, What would Grace do if this happened to her?'

'Ooooh?' on a half-rising resentful note. 'And what *would* I do, did you decide?'

'I decided you wouldn't have got in the situation in the first place.'

'I don't know about that. But feet—no, feet aren't my fetish really.'

'I guess they were the wine steward's.'

'Apparently. So what happened?'

'I said "*Parakalo.*" And then I said "Stop!"'

'What does that mean?'

'It means "please."'

Grace laughs. 'It looks like you learned the wrong phrases from that book. Isn't there one for unhand me? Or unfoot me?'

'Yeah, I just learned all the polite ones.'

'So what happened?'

'Well, he wouldn't stop, he just went on treading water like mad, so I kicked him.'

'Good heavens!'

'Yeah, he almost drowned. It was an awkward position to kick from. I got him right in the balls.'

She said to me once, 'You always make yourself the clown. You always did. Even in the hospital, you made jokes about the bed pans and the enemas.'

'Jesus, don't read my case history, Grace,' I said that summer.

'No, I won't. Why not?'

'You're in it. I'm jealous of you.'

'Whatever for?'

'Ah, you and Terence, you're so perfect. Every time I go to your house, I think I'm going to break something.'

'Break what?'

'The thermostat or the fridge or something.'

'Don't you know, I'm jealous of you?'

'Of me?' I feel frightened.

'I always have been.'

I think of her that year, when she came to school, new and scared. She lived with her mother and father, just down the street from Grandma's. In the mornings, her mother kissed her father goodbye. Grace had a yellow cardigan and a yellow-y plaid skirt, to match. And a pearl, one pearl, on a thin gold chain. Someone had given me a red and white sweater, with antelopes running madly all over it. And a green skirt. I looked like Christmas all year round, very hardy hand-me-downs, last forever. I was back with my mother then, by hook or by crook, mostly crook.

'I'm jealous of you because you act out,' said Grace.

Once, in second year, I pretended to be a homo and stroked her leg. She leapt away with a shriek and I flushed all over.

Years later, she said, 'Do you remember that time?'

'God yes.'

'We were both so scared.'

'It was you who yelled.'

'If I *were*,' said Grace, 'I don't know anyone I'd like better.'

'I thought I was, that day,' I said gloomily. 'I came over all queer.' We laughed.

'You see, I love you.'

'I love you too,' says Grace.

And, 'So? Why aren't I in your book?'

Ah hell.

'Joyce says she could write me up in a minute.'

'Joyce writes everyone up in a minute.'

And that summer, 'I couldn't read your case history,' Grace said. 'Who would I tell my troubles to? I couldn't start treating you like a patient. Good heavens. But you really should stop calling her your Nut Lady.'

'Why?'

'For one thing, she doesn't like it.'

'But she's the lady, I'm the nut.'

'I don't think she quite sees it that way.'

'I know, it's part of my defensive mechanism,' I said.

'Well, it is, isn't it?' Grace believes in what she calls 'the intro-duction of reality.'

Of Mik she said, 'He's terribly *male*, isn't he? He exudes a sort of virility.' But when they came over, Grace and Terence, we all sat around making polite noises at one another.

'You never said anything, about you and Ben,' she said.

'I couldn't. If I'd said one thing it would have all smashed. I mean, it wasn't a virtue. It wasn't the good old upper-lip bit. Other people natter and complain but that's because the fabric's strong. They can pull all they please. But with us, it was a crystal vase, our marriage. One flaw and the whole thing shatters into pieces. I didn't say anything to anybody because I didn't say it to myself. I never admitted anything. Sometimes, when I was writing, I'd get close and then it scared hell out of me. It's like, in the writing, if you don't watch, you tell the truth and then, you're right there on the edge, and it's all blackness. And I'd draw back, even in the writing.'

'Yes,' said Grace, 'we were going to have the perfect marriage too.' But this was years later, when she divorced Terence.

Last week, Grace says, 'You know, when you told me, finally, that all those years you were faithful ... seven years? Was it seven years?'

'My god.'

'I couldn't believe it. The way you went on. You and Ben. The way you talked about free love all those years. I thought you two were having a gay old time. I thought you were both really whooping it up. And then when you told me you'd been faithful!—It was very provocative, intellectually. It was provocative,' she laughs, 'in all sorts of ways.'

I don't pursue this. 'Yes, well, we never talked about anything real, did we?'

'We thought it was real.'

'Oh yes,' I say, 'we were all so bloody honest.'

'Weren't we?'

She lives with a tall blond psychiatrist now. I say to him, 'Jake?

Tell me. Did you ever fight with your wife?'

'Hell no,' says Jake. 'Christ no. We were terribly *nice* to each other. We were terribly *reasonable*. We sat down and discussed our problems like two rational human beings.'

'And with Grace?' I say.

'Oh that bitch,' Jake says. 'I'd like to kill *her* twice a week.'

Grace, who is half-listening in the other room, calls, 'You almost *did* once.'

'That's right,' says Jake, 'and I'd do it again too.'

Grace comes in, slim, elegant, and lifts her cheeky face to his. 'Vicky said you'd never apologize. She said you were in the right. She's as bad as you are.'

'I *was* right to slug you,' says Jake, looking pleased with himself.

'It's because Jake *knows*,' I say in my Eeyore voice.

'Knows what?' she says, but she is laughing at him. Their bodies fill up the room. You need a lead shield for the radioactivity.

'What it's all about. *Sex*.'

'What *is* it all about then?'

'Killing,' I say, gloomily.

'That's right, Vicky,' says Jake, 'let me get you another.'

THE NUT LADY SAID TO ME, 'Why someone like that?'

'Well, I can't destroy Mik. He's been destroyed by experts.'

'And he has such a charming record of mayhem.'

'Yes, it's really quite promising,' I said.

'And this man he's supposed to have killed?'

'I expect they were lovers.'

'You seem to have that on the brain.'

'Yes, I seem to pick them, don't I?'

'He doesn't sound homosexual. Mik.'

'Well, he's got quite a thing going with his buddies from Ortona. And he was, too, in the Pen.'

'Is your ex-husband still coming around?'

'Oh yes.' Long-suffering.

'Why?'

'He's doing a head of me. My hair turns into snakes. Medusa.'

'I didn't take an Arts degree. You'll have to explain your references.'

'Medusa's one of the gorgons. One of the three sistie uglers. Her face turns men into stone. She had snakes for hair. And Perseus killed her by looking into a mirror to do it.'

'The three sistie uglers. That's what you call yourselves, isn't it? You and Jocelyn and Francie.'

'Yes,' I say, surprised. I was surprised. She had a damn quick way with her sometimes, my Nut Lady. 'But Ben doesn't know. I mean, it's all very Jungian for Ben.'

'Why do you let him come over?'

'Well, I can't stop him, can I?'

'Why not?'

And, 'How about Paul? Does he still come over too?'

'Yes.'

'You play them all off against one another very cleverly.'

'Do I?'

'Yes, like you play me off against your producer. You manipulate very cunningly. He phoned me about the therapy, you know. Said it was affecting your work.'

'My stories don't have anything to do with me. I make them up. After the last one, when you said that, you know, about the mother, I couldn't write! You made me stop writing!'

'I simply said that the hostility you feel toward your mother ...'

'I am not angry at my mother. That was someone else. In the play.'

The Nut Lady sighed, and looked at her desk clock.

'I'll be going away for a month. In October.'

'Good for you.'

'I thought I'd give you plenty of notice.'

The time was up, so I said, 'How do I manipulate you?'

'You make me laugh.' And she smiled. 'I wonder how you're going to punish me.'

'Punish you?'

'For going away. For rejecting you.'

'You're only going on holiday. You've got to have a holiday from the nuts.'

'From you, you mean. I've got to have a holiday from you. That's what you mean.'

'Me and all the others. I don't mislead myself that I'm that important. You need a rest.'

'But it is a rejection, to go away and leave you. And you will punish me.'

'Of course not. That would be stupid.'

'I'm going away, I'm leaving you, just like your mother.'

'My mother didn't leave me. She just kicked me out.'

'I see. I'm not like your mother.'

'Not in the least.'

'And Mik isn't like your father. Mik isn't queer.'

'My father wasn't queer.'

'Your mother told you he was queer.'

'No. Someone told *her* he was queer, and then she told me what they'd said. She never believed it.'

'That's the facts, eh?'

'Yes.'

'And he killed himself, and Jason too.'

'No! I told you. That was an accident.'

'But your aunt said.'

'She wasn't well. I told you.'

'I see. It was an accident. That's a fact.' She comes to then. Looks again to her watch. Rises. 'You've done it again, haven't you?'

'What?' All innocence.

'Made me run over.'

YOUR FATHER KILLED HIS LOVER and now you want Mik to kill you.'

'It's interesting,' I say, 'how you can make a perfectly feasible pattern out of the details. You can take reality and tell it a hundred ways.'

She smiles. 'Tell me about the abortion.'

'I've told you.'

'You've told me the facts.'

I feel sheer rage. 'You want me to tell you a *story?*'

'I want to know how it felt.'

'All right. I will tell you how it felt.' And I do. And when I am through, her eyes are moist.

She looks at me and says, 'You never cry.'

'No. I've done that.'

'Didn't you feel anything when you told me all that?'

'No. I was making you feel.'

'And, this ability, to make me feel, it is part of your sickness, isn't it?'

'Yes. Don't cure me too much. Don't melt it.'

'Melt it?'

'The jewel. Inside me. What my mother saw from the first. Don't take it all away, just the part that hurts people.'

'I can't melt one without the other. I can't melt it at all. You must do it. You must give it up.'

162

'It's too much. It's all I have.'

'Then you love it too, this power. You want it.'

'I don't want to hurt people.'

'Maybe you do.'

'Maybe I do.'

'Wouldn't it be interesting if it melted and you could still tell stories anyway?'

And, 'I'm always right, aren't I? You always agree with me.'

'I respect you. Sometimes I don't see your point at first.'

'You respect your mother too.'

'Yes.'

'She's the lady, you're the slut. Like I'm the lady, you're the nut.'

I laugh.

'She never had sex.'

'As it happens, she didn't. Except with my father.'

'And all those years since he died, never once.'

'Never once.'

'And she never did anything wrong.'

'I explained about that. I explained why she had to get rid of me.'

'And you were never angry.'

'Yes. I was. But now I understand.'

'Now you understand.'

'Yes. She needed a rest.'

'From you.'

'Yes. I was always so sick, you see. My mother can't bear sick people.'

'So she let your grandfather take you away.'

'The doctor said I had to leave. The house was too damp.'

'I see. The house was too damp.'

'Yes.'

And, 'But you said that was when you were five.'

'It was. I was five.'

'But just now, you said you were nine.'

'Just now?'

'What happened when you were five?'

'I was kicked out.'

'No. That was when you were nine.'

I sit there a long time. 'I've lied. I've lied.'

'What happened when you were five?'

'I was sure it was when I was five, but you're right. You're right. I was nine. I've lied.'

'What happened when you were five?'

'I lied.'

And the hour comes to an end and she half rises.

'All right. Maybe she was jealous of me. Maybe she was trying to hurt me. She said he didn't love me, not like the others. Because of the way I was. When I was born. Maybe it wasn't right to tell me that. About not sucking and so on. I had to suck, I see that. I had to or I'd be dead. I mean, I had to suck on a bottle. I see that. You're right. But you see, she felt rejected. When he died. I mean, it was an accident and everything, but still she felt he'd done it on purpose, so she just struck out, and I was handy, that's all. She went through a bad time. She was only thirty. It was a terrible thing. She was angry at him, even though.'

She is smiling at me.

'I've done it again, haven't I? I'm sorry. I don't know why. I always seem to start to talk at the end. It's strange.'

'Yes,' she says, 'it's quite interesting, isn't it? How you keep me on beyond the time.' And, dryly, 'I wonder why.'

And, 'You're really very good at it,' I say to her. 'When I get out of here I'm wobbly for hours.'

'Why do you want to reassure me?'

'I'm not. I'm just saying you're getting to me. You're good at it.'

'And that's what I'm supposed to do. Get at you.'

'It's your job.'

'I'm being a good therapist, aren't I?'

'Yes.'

'You think I'm in need of your protection?'

'No! Why should I have to protect you?'

'From the nuts maybe?'

'Well, it's good you're going on holiday.'

'Yes, it is, isn't it? I might crack up. You might drive me crazy. I need a rest, don't I?'

'I expect you need a rest.'

'I wonder,' she says, 'how you're going to do it.'

'What?'

'Get back at me. For going away.'

I laugh. 'Well, there's still lots of time for me to think of something.'

'Hmmm.'

'THE NUT LADY SAYS if I can get you to kill me, that means my father really loved me.'

'She's sick.' Mik frowns at me. 'Why do you go anyway?'

'I like to see what she'll say next.'

'There's nothing wrong with you. Nothing wrong a man couldn't cure.'

'She says I've got a nitch for homosexuals.'

'Yeah? Who?'

'Well, when Ben left Crease, the psychiatrist said ...'

Mik guffaws. 'Him? They thought he was a fairy? No way.'

'Well, he said it was latent, but.'

'You bet your sweet ass it was latent. It was so latent it pointed the other way! Listen, that guy wouldn't bend over for a real piece of soap. He's got his cheeks so tight you couldn't give him an enema.' Mik considers me. 'Your ex is no fairy. He's just a ... a nothing. He wouldn't have the guts to do it, one way or the other. How many times did you and him do it anyway?'

'Well, at first it was quite normal.'

'On the average.'

'I don't think it's proper to discuss intimate details ...'

'You don't have to tell me. I knew the moment I laid eyes on the creep. Once a month, if you're lucky, right? And you had to start it. Right?'

My mouth gets tight, like my mother's.

'Don't worry. You didn't marry a fag. You just married a zero. He comes around here and he's just a poor creep, is all. I've seen his kind. They crawl around with their guts in their hands and ask you to be sorry for them. And if you don't watch out, you step on them with your boot. You don't mean to, you just don't see them. You know your problem? Eh?'

'I have a feeling you're going to tell me.'

'You bet your sweet ass. You needed a man, that was your problem. That's sweet fuck all, baby. You just needed a real man. You were just all screwed up and that's all you needed.'

'A real screw up.'

We laugh.

'But, you did say, when you were in the Pen ...'

'You tell her that? Shit. Sweet Jesus. You tell her everything?'

'Not everything.'

''Cause she wouldn't understand. These social worker types, they got filing cabinets for cunts. Look. I wasn't a fag. I was hard up. You get hard up, is all. You close your eyes and you grab some guy, and he's got perfume on, and you say, ah shit. So the Nut Lady's got me pegged for a queer, has she?'

'No. Actually, she said you don't sound like a ...'

'You bet your sweet ass!' He takes me by the arms, hard, and looks me in the eye. 'Listen. Don't make it complicated. You got a thing, you like to make things complicated. You're all woman, you are. If you're hung up, then it's just you don't believe it. You just don't believe your good luck, is all.' He grins dangerously down at me. 'You think I'm gonna do you dirt, so you think, this can't last, how do I screw it before he does. I know all about it, tough guy. I'm three steps ahead of you.' He hesitates, then gives me a love tap with his fist. My teeth jar in their sockets. But I don't pull away. 'Ten steps ahead of you. I'm out-thinking you, tough guy. You got pretty fancy footwork, but I been in the ring longer.'

'Are you saying I try to manipulate you?'

'You try,' he says, grinning. 'You give me a hard time.'

'You don't usually complain of that.'

He looks at me. 'Yah!'

'But I'm honest with you. I've always been honest with you.'

'Go get your sexy swim suit.'

'No. If I'm deceptive or dishonest, I want to know.'

'Dummy up, tough guy.'

'Why won't you be serious?'

'You want to know what I really think? Really?'

'Really.'

He leans toward me and says, very seriously, 'You got a tight twat. Never met such a tight twat.'

I THOUGHT TRUTH was something you could work out, like the

logarithms upon which a slide rule is premised. I thought if you could once discover the base, you could work it out from there. I thought if I could ascertain facts, it would all come clear. Multi-dependent, multi-causal perhaps, but there in some solid and satisfying way.

When Sister Mary Joseph said to me, 'It's you who should have been the nun,' is that another dimension or another template?

Or is it all just a story and would Sister Mary Joseph's be just as real as the Nut Lady's, or Mik's, or Ben's if he could tell it? And is Jeff right when he says I fictionalize everything anyway and no one need fear, for I could not ever tell the truth? 'You insist on living,' he said, 'in a plethora of emotion. The rest of us are satisfied with the solid meat and potatoes of life, but for you the plethora is all that counts. What we turn to for respite, for diversion from the humdrum of our days, you insist must be the All.' And, 'No one could live with you.'

I don't know what happened at five. Perhaps something truly did. It's not fashionable now to write psychological novels. I lied.

They were laying. I was lying. I was hearing. He said I was lying and laying and listening to them laying. To this day I have trouble with the forms of the verb. Lie lies lied, lay lays laid. He pulled my hands from my ears and he said, 'You're laying there listening to us lying.' Lays layed laying. Lain laid laying. 'You're lying there listening to us laying.' It is the transitive which gives me trouble.

When I finally had my baby, I decided to write an anti-Aristotelian novel. I would write each day exactly as it occurred. I would not lie.

The last paragraph goes like this:

It is obvious that this 'journal' will have no literary merit ... simply because I haven't weighed words, balanced truth, selected facts, designed and controlled. I've always found diaries 'written for posterity' rather pompous, but of course ... if they're written to be read at all, they must be written for posterity. Maybe now I can get back to work—without feeling I'm betraying something. I wanted to be honest, but honesty comes out of contrivance ... the truth of the thing is felt because the artist has designed his creation so that the spirit of honesty, if not the data, is there. To be recognized. It's work, it's hard hard work ... and it comes out of the tradition of deliberate, methodical workmanship, threaded through with that sense of something else ... that desire to honestly portray ... which is inspiration or what you will. The beautiful lie.

Sister Mary Joseph said to me: 'You were always seeking God. That was all. You sought him in the flesh of men. That was what went wrong. Why He has denied faith, I do not know. I do not yet understand. But perhaps there is a reason. But it is you who should have been the nun and I the ...'

She didn't finish, and we laughed at that. 'The sinner?'

'We are all sinners. Don't glamourize yourself. It is self-indulgent to consider yourself a greater sinner than me. And it smacks of pride.'

Sister Mary Joseph cannot suffer fools gladly. She is out of the silent order now, but she is still the bride of Christ. Her mother says it is all because 'something' happened to her when she was ten. And I could tell it that way. I could tell what happened to Sister Mary Joseph at ten and it would all be quite clear. Except that, of course, that is not the way it was. God came to her like a killer. There she was, her, high school degree at fifteen, her BSc at seventeen, her MSc at nineteen. Brilliant, irascible, dedicated to reason. And God came and did not ask her name.

People say to me, 'Why is she a nun? Is she afraid of sex?' and I feel such rage for their ignorance. I, who never believed in God, believe in that, what happened to Sister Mary Joseph. I know her name is not Jane anymore.

'You dramatize everything, Vicky,' Momma said.

MIK HAD GONE TO WORK at a logging camp and Mom, on an urgent summons from Jocelyn, had come to see what could be done with the eldest daughter who seemed to have gone mad after the divorce. Who was 'living common-law' with a man who tore telephones out by their roots.

'If I thought that, I couldn't bear to go on,' Momma said.

I had asked her, in a quiet moment, to tell me again how he had died. My father. 'I had this idea,' I said, 'that it was, you know, on purpose. Then, when Jason went in after him, it was Daddy who caught him and held him and brought him down. Under the water. In his arms. Miss Haggerty says I should get it clear. What really happened. Once and for all.'

It was a lie. The Nut Lady had never suggested any such thing.

'It was an accident,' my mother said.

'But do you remember how you said, the night before? He asked you would you make a baby with him? How he was going away for a long time?'

'He had a premonition,' Momma said. 'I'll always believe it was that. He had a feeling something was going to happen. He said, "I have to go away," and I said "Why?" and he said because he had to. I asked him how long he would be and he said it might be a long time. It was a premonition.'

'But you remember,' and this is the hardest part, I can feel the clutch at my throat, and I bring it out past the spasms lurking like inquisitors, 'you said someone told you, Jason and Daddy, someone said they were homosexuals.'

'I *never* said that!'

'Yes, you did, Momma.'

'When?'

'Right after.'

'I never.'

'I have to know, Momma.'

'You always dramatize, Vicky. I remember now. It was Joe Price. He said it wasn't *natural* for Daddy and Jason to be together so much. That's what I told you. Joe Price said their relationship wasn't natural. For men.'

'But ...'

'I *never* said they were homosexuals. How could you think such a thing?' And her lip is quivering. 'And I never paid it a bit of attention. Never. I don't even know why I told you.' And, 'If I believed that, life wouldn't be worth living.' And now her face crumples and tears stand out in her eyes. 'I couldn't go on.' And she cries.

She always cried. After a beating or when she had gone away because she couldn't bear the wheezing. After, she would come and kneel beside my bed and ask me to forgive her. And cry. I would put my hand on her head and say, 'It's all right, Momma, it's all right.'

'She says it was just an accident.'

'Do you believe her?' says the Nut Lady.

'I do and I don't.' I am enormously weary. 'What I feel now is, it doesn't matter, whichever way it was.'

'It doesn't matter.'

'No. It doesn't matter.'

'What does matter?'

I don't answer and then it comes, in a long howl. 'He died.' And now it is I who am crying. 'I loved him and he died.' It is the first time I have cried. In front of anyone.

I cried once before. When I went to feed his chickens. Six months later. Coming over from my grandma's to feed his chickens. Knowing somehow she wasn't doing it. There are three of them in the coop, dead, and the maggots are crawling out of their feathers. Two half-dead birds are huddled well away from the stench. They will die tomorrow.

I buried the dead ones and fed the live ones. And then I cried. But that was the only time. 'You never even cried,' said Momma. 'Not once.'

'I loved him,' I said and I hunched forward and let it all out, all the old years, like rotten yellow crusts.

'You hold it in,' Momma said. 'You even hold your pee in.' I was, inside myself, a mass of dried pee like crusted sulphur, hard and dry and impossible to wash away because I did hold it in, the tears and the ahah. Only a thousand tiny elves working day and night with picks could chip the pee away. Then, with buckets of water, they could wash it down the gulley of my body. But I did not believe in elves anymore. I did not see the inside of my body corrupting and soft with decay, but only as hard and dry and yellow.

Inside my head it was different. If you cut my head in two you would find rows and rows of exactly placed electric light bulbs, like the ones on the marquee of the

Isn't that odd. I've forgotten the name of that movie house. The. The. It will come. I won't think about it. If I don't think about it, it will come.

My mother is still crying. 'Where did I go wrong?'

And, 'You know why I let you go to Grandpop's, don't you? Because you were so sick and the doctor said the cellar was so damp and if you didn't get out of that house you'd die.'

'Why didn't you move to another house?' I want to ask, but don't.

'But when I did come back, that time,' I say, 'you told me to go away.'

'But that was After,' Momma says. 'I wasn't myself then.'

'It was you who rejected me,' Mom says, her voice rising, all the old anger. 'You wouldn't even suck. Right from the first you were different. Not like the others. Right from the first you pushed me away.'

I sucked Mik. His nipples, his penis, his toes. I loved him all over. His great thick body like a whale. In the deep salt sea he rose and spouted and I rode him like a dolphin. Deep under the air there were fairy castles, Gaudi cathedrals, elaborate, ornate, made of shells and limned rock, and one day I would go there, in the dim green light I would breathe. I was out of my element, that was the trouble. They took seventeen days to find him. And nineteen to find Jason. And yet they had gone down together. In each other's arms.

It was called the Plaza.

'What you have are hypnagogic experiences,' said the Nut Lady.

'"Hypnagogic,"' I say, trying the consonants over again as if in their atomic depths I will find the irreducible fact.

AND MIK CAME BACK from the logging camp.

We had written every day for those three weeks. I had sent him a toy boat with a man at the wheel.

'What's the toy in aid of?' he wrote.

'It's the man in the boat,' I wrote back. 'So you'll have it with you.'

He had taught me many expressions. Muff diving and hunting for oysters and the man in the boat. 'I like to see him sit up and take notice,' he would say, tickling it.

Now he was coming back for the weekend. Or was it over, the job? I don't remember. Tonight he was coming back on the ferry. My flesh yearned across the water to his. I dragged a bed down to the cellar, so my mother would not hear us that night. I set it up beside the pile of briquettes. It was cold down there, and smelled of mildew.

He came down the CPR dock and my guts gave a great thud.

There he was, a thick heavy man in an Indian sweater, humped over from the weight of the duffel bag, grinning crookedly at me. He had a buddy with him.

'This is the missis,' he said.

The buddy said, 'Hello, Mrs O'Brien.'

It was only what we had to do. It didn't mean anything. It was what we had to do to stop the furies.

Later, when I was having the baby, I dreamt of them, black hags with long knives rushing at me, slitting open my stomach, dragging out puppies and kittens and monsters of deformity. And I hadn't read Aeschylus yet.

We are in a café, Mik and I, in the back booth, grinning at each other like madmen.

'My mother's here. I've made us a bed in the cellar.'

'That buddy, he's got a cabin, up the coast. He says we can have it if we want.'

My thighs are wet with wanting him. I can feel my nipples straining out to him through my sweater.

'Jesus, I want you.'

He never said he loved me. Except for the first time. And perhaps that's a lie.

A short thick girl with curly hair comes toward us. I recognize her with a kind of terror. Marcie. From the lab.

'How are you, Vicky?'

'All right. You?'

'Okay. I'm in teachers' training now.'

'That's nice.'

'I see Ben sometimes.'

'Oh yes. How is he?'

'Well ...' She darts a look at Mik. 'He's all right.'

For some reason I don't want her to know I see Ben.

'I looked over and I didn't think it was you. You've lost a lot of weight.'

'Yeah. I went on a diet.'

'You're looking well.' She keeps sneaking looks at Mik, her eyes resting briefly and then pulling away as if the sight burnt them.

And I see him through her eyes: a big red-faced thug.

'This is Mik O'Brien. Marcie Davis.'

'Hi.'

'How do you do.'

'I do okay, how do you do?'

'What?' And she laughs nervously. 'Well. It was nice seeing you again. Are you still writing?'

'Trying to.'

'See you sometime. I ...' She hesitates, glances at Mik. 'I'm sorry, for, you know, what happened.'

'Yeah. Okay.'

'I was going through a sort of bad time myself then.'

'Are you all right now?'

'Yes. I'm all right.'

'Who was that?' Mik says.

'A girl I used to work with. She said I filled her with moral horror.'

'Yeah? "Moral horror."' Rolling it over the way he does. And he laughs. 'We sit here much longer I'm gonna melt the Formica.'

And we creep back to the sleeping house, my mother upstairs with Jocelyn, Mom's boyfriend sleeping chastely on the sofa. We come in the cellar door.

Yes. Mom had a boyfriend. He'd driven her out, to see what could be done with me. But they were very proper.

And in the cellar:

'Jesus, I like it when you say "Oh boy!"'

'I don't say "Oh boy!"'

'You do. You say it every time, "Oh boy!" like some kid. You said it the first time. "Oh boy!"'

'I never.'

He turns over and growls into my stomach. 'I could eat you. I want to get inside you and never get out. I want to wrap you around me.'

'Like an overcoat.'

'Like an overcoat.'

'That's what you said, the first time.'

'What?'

'That you'd like to pull me on like an overcoat.'

'Yeah?'

'I don't know why I love you. You're so damn ugly.'

'You're no great shakes yourself. You got calluses on your feet. And a pot belly. And your hips look like moon craters.'

It was he who told me that then. Yes. Now I remember.

'We're gonna go up to that island. I'm gonna get you alone and fuck you to death. And we won't have to be quiet. We can holler our hearts out.'

'Mmm.'

'No Paul and no Ben and no mother and no damn sister.'

'Nobody.'

'Nobody in the whole fucking world.'

'I used to think you were having a heart attack, the way you carried on.'

'I carry on? How about you? "OOoo Eeee." Like a stuck pig.'

'Sh. My mom.'

'You didn't think about her ten minutes ago. "OOoo Eeee!"'

'Shhhh!'

'Up on the island, I'm gonna yell. I'm gonna bring the moon down. "OOooo Eeee!"'

'Shhhh.'

I COME TO THIS NOW, like a lover. Guiltily, as if it were sinful. The book.

Last night I had a dream. Aunt Carrington. She said to me, 'Isn't it strange, how we never call and yet we're not angry with each other.'

'I need your advice,' I said. 'I have all these houses, and I don't know what to do.' It's the house dream again. So many houses and where are we to live, Anna and I. And what am I to do about the others.

'I can't concern myself with your problem,' Aunt Carrington said. 'I'm dying.'

'Oh you mustn't die,' I said. 'I couldn't bear it if you died. I'm selfish, I know, but I couldn't bear it.'

And we hold each other and cry, like children, the spasms wracking our diaphragms, helplessly, like children.

Her sun room is all different. There are pages printed, up on ribbons, rather like a show room. 'Yes, I've taken up the printing press,' Aunt Carrington says. 'It's something to do till I die.'

Then she looks at me. 'One thing I've learned. It's foolish to cry over spilt houses. What house do you want to live in?'

'The one on the hill.'

'Yes, well, live in it then. Forget the others. So you've lost money. Forget it.'

And she looks at Anna and says, 'Yes, me all over.' And, 'So am I in the book or not?'

'No. How could I? It would take another. A whole book. To tell, I mean,' and I try to placate her, as of old, 'you tried so hard, you went all the way, and life did it to you. Over and over. But of course, it's wrong to anthropomorphize, isn't it?'

She is climbing a ladder up to the kitchen sill. 'I never said life did it to me. It was you who said that. It was what happened. I never said It did anything to me.'

'Yes, but you suffered so.'

'Right now, I just don't want to die.' And she goes away, mingling with all the guests, it is a cocktail party of some kind.

And there is a fight, somehow. A pimp. And an Indian girl I've brought home. Yes. And the pimp is a Negro and he has a knife. My kitchen knife. And we fight and I break off his knife and I push him out the door. I say, 'You rotten bigot.'

And I wake up. And I cry for Aunt Carrington, who didn't want to die, and who did anyway, saying, 'I think there's something wrong.'

And Anna wakes up too. She has been counting numbers in her dream. I tell her about Aunt Carrington. 'Do you think there is a heaven?'

'I don't know.'

'Susie says when I die, I'll have to go on the cross.'

'I don't think so. Susie's got it mixed up.'

'No. Susie said when I die, I'll have to go to heaven. And I said,

No way. So she said then I have to go on the cross.'

'I don't believe that.'

'No. I don't either. Do you think there's a God?'

'I don't know.'

'I don't know either. I've never seen a god. Except in the Parthenon. There're an awful lot of gods, aren't there?'

'Yes. People have always thought about gods, and they've taken different forms. I mean, people have seen them differently.'

Anna sighs. 'But it would be nice.'

'Yes. It would be nice.'

BEFORE I LEFT for the first island, Momma said to me, 'It's just sex, you know.'

'Oh Mom, sex is never "just."'

Bert, her boyfriend, said to her, 'Your daughter's not ashamed. If she loves a man, she comes right out with it.' Bert's wife was mental and he couldn't get a divorce.

'Maybe I'm too concerned with social opinion,' Momma said.

And so, after we left, she drove back home with Bert and let him move in. 'I decided,' she told me later, 'what with your divorce and everything, what was the use? I'd been good all those years and what was the use?'

'That's ridiculous,' said the Nut Lady when I told her. 'As if you were supposed to set the example.'

But I was. And I did. My mother entered what she called a life of sin because I led the way. She still says it, and I believe it. 'But I couldn't brazen it out,' she said last summer. 'I was too ashamed.'

My mother. My mother. When I brought the Indian girls home from church camp, she put them up. Saying to me, 'But how am I supposed to afford it?' But doing it anyway. My mother, who stopped the car last summer because she thought she saw a go-pher twitching in the road allowance. Backing up the car, she said grimly, 'It's got to be put out of its misery.' But it was only a piece of tumbleweed. My mother, who took me to see the badgers at sunset, and the Indian rings, 100,000 years old. My mother. Who said, 'All my girls are failures.'

'But Jocelyn isn't.' I know what she means about Francie and me. I don't debate that.

'Well ...'

'But she's married and happy and David's certainly a success in the world's eyes. And Joss isn't doing too bad either.' Joss is the director of a clinic now.

'We were no better than anyone else.'

'And I know Francie's divorced, but, again, in terms of just achievement, it's pretty good, at her age. A church newspaper.' And we laugh a bit about that. Francie putting out a church news-paper. Francie?

'But Joss has a nice home and a good husband.'

'All the university degrees in the world don't make a person happy. All I wanted was for you all just to have good husbands and a good family life.'

'But what would you have liked us to *do?*'

'Wouldn't that be enough? Just to be wives and mothers?'

'I guess not. I guess we had to do something too.'

'It's my father all over again,' Mom says. 'What good was Latin and Greek when he couldn't put a decent meal on the table.'

'But we all make *money,*' I say.

'Oh yes, that's you all over. You never really loved anyone, you just gave them money.'

I say, 'Do you remember the time I poured the whiskey down the sink?'

'I never bought that bottle. Grandpop brought it over.'

'But you must have wanted to kill me. Pouring it down the sink!'

'No. I'm glad you did it. I might have become a solitary drinker.'

'Oh Mom! You? I was a pompous prig.'

'I never bought that bottle. It was Grandpop.'

'I know.'

'Your Aunt Carrington, she took you away from me. I could never get close to you. They all took you away from me. The family.'

And, 'I'm glad to see *your* house gets messy sometimes. I'm glad to see you aren't all that organized either.'

'I know. I was awful.'

'You used to say if I'd only get a system. A system. I used to think, Wait till *you* have kids.'

My mother. Who read me the stories of Theseus and the dragon's teeth when I was three. I never knew what book it came from till last summer, when she found it: Hawthorne's *Tanglewood Tales*. Persephone and Demeter. Only she was called Ceres then, when I was three. Circe's Palace. The Golden Fleece.

My mother. Who made me a red riding hood coat and a sailor's dress and who said I was never never to call Sam-at-the-store a dirty Jew. It didn't matter *what* my father said.

WE CAUGHT THE FERRY to Vancouver Island. And stayed in a Nanaimo hotel. And Mik stole the towels.

But there was something else before the towels. I'm trying to avoid it.

Before we left for the island, Mik bought himself a hat and me a ring.

It was a smart hat, with a small brim. It made him look silly, like a dancing bear.

The ring was gold and set with chip diamonds. It fit my finger perfectly. He'd got it from People's Credit Jewellers, and before two hours were up, one of the chips had fallen out. He went back down town with blood in his eye. He'd never been cheated on anything before: I suppose he'd never paid for anything before. They gave him another but he was annoyed about it all day. 'You pay good money,' he would say, 'and they try to Jew you.'

And, later, still muttering, 'I told him, I said if anything goes wrong with this one I'll shove it up his ass.'

And we went across the strait, the water blue and gold and white, furrowing behind the ferry. And booked into the hotel. And Mik stole the towels.

I must have known with some part of my responsible self that Mik couldn't have a week off from work. I must have known it would cost him his job.

He'd worked three weeks and he had some money and now he was going to spend it on me. I can't remember even asking about the job.

And the next morning, waking up in the hotel room, I saw him packing the towels in the suitcase.

They were fluffy and white and they had the name of the hotel written in red cotton. I won't say the name, for I still have one.

'What are you doing that for?'

'Ah, they expect you to.' Tossing in some wrapped soap as well.

'But we don't need towels.'

'Haven't you ever lifted anything?'

I don't answer.

'I don't believe it. When you were a kid? Penny candy.' He thinks about it. 'Stamps. When you worked in offices. Stamps is the same thing.'

'No.'

'You never did anything buckshee?'

'What?'

'Slugs in phones.'

'No.'

Years later, I do it once, to see. Thirty-two cents of liver from Eaton's meat counter. Walk right out, expecting lightning to strike me dead.

'Did you do that too?' Francie laughs. 'So did I. A lipstick from Hudson's Bay. I had to. We were always so damn superior, you know?'

I refuse to speak to him, and he refuses to put the towels back.

When he pays at the counter, I am sure the clerk knows. I'm sure it's all over my face.

We catch the bus to Campbell River. I don't say anything for miles.

'For christ sake, a couple of measly towels!'

'If I ever decide to sell my soul,' I say loftily, 'it won't be for a pair of towels. It'll be for a million dollars. It's too petty, it's undignified.'

'You lost your soul now, eh?' He snorts. 'Do you good. You're so fucking high and mighty.'

When I was six, the devil came to me and said, 'I can stop all this. In the twinkling of an eye.'

But I knew all about his being able to quote scripture. I was on the floor, rocking back and forth. It had gone on a long time. More than a week.

He was dressed all in black satin, with a great cape, and the cape was lined with red. Just like in the funnies, except for his face. A wise dark face, full of suffering. A small thin man, he smiled at me. Not at all like Epstein's Satan. More like his Michael, spare and muscled with denial, rising sorrowfully above. He seemed so sorry for me. I could see he really did want to stop it, the asthma.

My mother came in to see what I was yelling about. She said, 'You were saying "No" over and over.' I didn't tell her this time it was the devil.

But sometimes, I worry. I've always been so damned lucky. And the wish is equal to the deed.

Before I was kicked out of confirmation class—the second one—I asked about the text that goes 'But I say unto you that whosoever looketh on a woman to lust after her hath committed adultery already in his heart.'

'Does that mean thinking is as bad as doing?'

'Yes.'

And so it seemed to me that, logically, if you thought a thing, you might as well do it: since each was equally as sinful as the other. In fact, not only ought you to acknowledge the thought, but in some way you were compelled to perpetrate the deed. Not to do so made one into a whited sepulchre. It was arguments like these that pissed the Reverend Manfred off. And so he told me to leave. I had too much pride in my intellect, he said. 'I've done everything I can for you. I allowed you to refuse confirmation last year.'

'That was the Trinity issue.'

'Yes. And I put you into an adult class, and you still think you're too clever for God.'

I think, at the end, we agreed that faith was a matter of grace and God in His divine wisdom had not seen fit to grant me grace.

But I've always been lucky.

At Campbell River we caught the sea plane to the island. I don't remember its name but we came down at a cove called Miller's Landing.

The island had one taxi and we took it to the buddy's cabin.

It was on an inlet. The cabin stood on a bluff above the sea.

Below were oyster beds, and out in the ocean, a dry rock with gulls wheeling over it. Behind the cabin was a wooded ravine. I never remember the names of trees. The ones that burst into flower in spring and fall. Little tips of blood rust on their white petals. In memory of the crucifixion. And thin white trees, delicate, their bark chewed off to the waist by something. Deer? We never saw any. And the ones with strips of burnt orange peeling away like origami paper. A stream ran down the bottom of the ravine. Among the lush green grass, tender as snails. And tiny blue flowers were everywhere. It was all green and blue. Deep green, forest green, velvet, lime, grey blue, mauve blue, royal, ink, madonna. And out there, the sea, falling away to the bottom of the sky.

Mik had the key. Inside everything was spare and neat and clean.

There were bunk beds. We had bought groceries when we landed, but we took no liquor. I never thought of it then, but for Mik it must have meant something. I'd never go to a cabin for a week now without at least two bottles of something.

In the mornings, the leaves and the blades of grass had great teardrops of dew on them. You'd soak your jeans to the knees just walking to the stream for water. The gulls swerved and hooted like boisterous kids and the wash of the ocean below made me feel as if we were on a great ship, rocking softly through abandoned seas. The air was so clear and fresh it could have come from an artesian well. You drank it with your mouth.

We picked oysters and made stew. We swam. We made love.

The first night, in the soft light, like clear tea, from the kerosene lamp, Mik held me for a long time. He kissed my nipples and then took them in his mouth. When he came into me, he said, 'No. Lie still. I'll show you something.'

His breath was warm and slightly tobacco-y. We lay together

185

very still, his love swelling in me, his arms around me, his hands cupping my buttocks. Mik never made love like a gentleman, on his elbows. We lay so still the bed went away, and the cabin, and we were in the great deep, suspended. Golden light, dimly green, filtered through the shifting fronds, and all was baroque with time never seen, great arches encrusted with starfish and cornucopias of porcelain. Towers and steeples soared up until you could not see them anymore, lost in undulating mists far above. I was under the sea at last, slippery and silk, silver and single, whole, not moving, as salmon do, resting in their element, gills moving imperceptibly, breathing.

His sweat on my tongue. The Russians say you never know a man until you have eaten so many pounds of his salt. When we came, we came together, still silent, still immobile, the great long crest taking us together in the molten dark.

We did not speak of it. We passed into sleep.

Ben had said, 'There is nothing in the act of love which is degrading. Everything done in love is pure,' reading the chapter on experimental foreplay. Last night, talking to Edna, I remembered suddenly Ben's Great Experiment. He'd shit in me but he wouldn't give me a baby. And then he asked me to douche with Lysol. I'd forgotten that. Dear god, I'd forgotten that. And they say you never forget the first one.

WE MET THE blind girl.

We'd gone out to the rock island in the buddy's boat. In the middle, in a natural cup, was an aquamarine pool of water, and there we made love. The sun was white, the sky noisy with glare, and we made love to each other in the blues and greens of the pool.

When we are leaving, I see the sail boat.

'Oh look. There's somebody there. In that cove.'

We walk over and find them, the large Danish family and the blind girl.

I saw her again, in the doctor's office. We went on the same day, every Saturday morning, at the same time. I would sit, large and pregnant, and not speak to anyone for fear she would recognize my voice. I was so ashamed. Once she sat right beside me on the leatherette bench, and looked into my eyes. I thought, My god! She's got her sight back. As if somehow she had seen me that summer.

They are clambering over the rocks looking for oysters. In the forest above their cove stood a huge timbered house. They are not allowed to live in it, and so they live in the sailboat moored in the water. It is a Welfare regulation. So long as they live in the house, which they own, they are not eligible for assistance. They are required to sell it, and it is up for sale. Impossible on this lonely island. They never go inside, except to get tools or cans of food or books, which they then carry out to the rocks and row across to the sailboat. Ten children. They are brown and strong, with white hair and good teeth, and the eldest girl is a mule deer, leaping from rock to rock, her long hair flying behind her, her voice calling to the others. They see us now and come running toward us, delighted. Now they are standing in a circle, subdued, grinning, nudging one another to shush.

'We're over to Jackson's place,' says Mik.

They smile.

'For a holiday. He gave us the key.'

They smile.

'I'm Mik O'Brien and this is the Missis.'

They shake hands with us, introducing themselves separately, overcome with shyness and joy. When the eldest girl puts out her hand, it is two degrees off. Her blue eyes stare past my head. 'Ingrid's blind,' says one of her brothers.

'Come with us,' she says and we all go out to the sailboat—in bunches of five and four and three—for tea.

It is a large ship. Perhaps they call it a sloop, I don't know. It has a library and an organ, and a round smiling mother baking bread. The father is lean and tall and brown, and he too smiles all the time. They give us a concert on the deck, before tea. The youngest children sing, their clear voices rising into the still air. Ingrid plays the organ and her father the violin. One of the brothers has a recorder. Another brother tells me he would have brought his guitar if he'd known, but it is in the house.

They stay there all winter round, on that boat. The children take lessons by correspondence.

'And you never go into the house, not even in winter?'

'No. It is a foolish regulation, but I have given my word.' The father has been hurt in a logging accident, and cannot work yet.

'The Missis here, she's a teacher,' says Mik. 'Taught at the university.'

'You're a professor?' There is such awe in his voice.

'No, no. A teaching assistant. It's not the same.'

'You taught at the university,' says Mik. 'Same difference.'

'She's a writer too.' Yes, they listened to the radio. Yes. They'd heard it, did I write that?

''Course, Ferris is her maiden name. Now she's O'Brien.'

'You are on your honeymoon,' says the mother, smiling.

Mik goes red and denies it, and they all giggle.

They come over every day after that, bursting into our field with laughter, knocking carefully at the door of the cabin. Bringing us buns and cakes, and once—from Ingrid—a rose done in luminous red satin, the petals perfect, a calyx of green ribbon, one tender leaf. I kept it for years and Anna wore it for dress-up. But one day I threw it out, dead and bedraggled, like a real rose. In one of my passions of clean-out, feeling guilty for having so much.

I turned it over in my hand and wondered at it. It was vulgar, really. The leaf was out of a kit. Like a vase made out of shells.

'Me? I'm an engineer,' says Mik.

I look at him.

'Well, I studied for a boiler makers' certificate,' he says to me later. 'That almost makes me an engineer. Maintenance engineer.'

'I wish we hadn't lied.'

'So, it don't hurt them,' he says, getting mad.

'It makes me feel ashamed.'

'Which lie you talking about?'

'All of them,' I say, lying.

'Yah? Like saying we was married.'

'You don't have to put that on. All that rotten grammar.'

'All right! We're not married. You know what you can do about that.'

'They're so good, it shines out of them.'

'So, are we hurting them?'

'No.'

She sat beside me, a large-boned girl in dun and city dust, her lovely hair caught back somehow into plaits, messily, coarse, little frizzled bits sticking out around her freckled face. Her sweater had balls of wool all over it and her stockings were thick, the kind Grandma wore. She turned her great blue eyes on me and I thought, in panic, My god! She can see.

I REMEMBER SOMETHING ELSE. One morning we went out to pick

oysters in the cove beneath the cabin. The tide was out, and the miraculous orchard of shells lay exposed all along the shore, it seemed a special harvest, meant for us alone. The sky was white, although it would be a royal blue day. And hot. But now it was almost cold, and bloodless. Luminous, like the first morning of the world. A snake moved among the shells and I stooped and picked it up in my fingers. It seemed as if nothing could be alien to me now, I was so fitted into my skin.

But the snake turned and bit me. Its serrated, hard-ridged gums caught my flesh and wouldn't let go. Blood streamed from my hand onto the oyster shells. I tried to shake the snake off, but still it clung. It was terrified of me. Then it dropped back into the strange miniature prehistoric forest. 'But I've never been afraid of snakes,' I say to Mik. It seemed an omen.

One night, Mik said to me, 'I'll teach you how to play poker.'

It was just growing dusk. The sun was making the sea red and oily. I was tired of always being beaten at chess. Mik filled the kerosene lamp and lit it, setting it on the oil cloth. It seemed very easy, poker.

'Yah. It's easy,' Mik said.

When we'd played a few hands, he said, 'Let's make it interesting.'

'Okay.'

'Let's play strip poker,' Mik said.

Twenty minutes later I was sitting there, stark staring naked.

'Here,' I said. 'I've still got the ring. I'll bet the ring, okay?'

'No,' said Mik. 'You leave the ring on. You can bet a curl.'

I was proud of my hair and Mik knew it. But I was furious too, and so I said, 'You're on!' Mik was stone-faced, but I could feel him smirking.

But when I lost again and he came toward me with the scissors he said, 'No. Stand up. On the chair.'

It took me a moment to get it. Then, cold with rage, I stood on the chair.

He snipped the curl away and wrapped it in a piece of toilet paper. He laid it on top of my jeans and T-shirt, my panties, my brassiere, my runners. I picked up the deck. 'My deal.'

'You never give in, do you?' And he called me a name. Not 'tough guy' ... Something like that though. I don't remember. I won't think of it. It will come to me if I don't think of it. Like the others. Like remembering why I could breathe under water and why petals are maroon. I've built myself a trap with this book. I thought it was going to be simple. But the book makes me remember. I'll remember the name Mik called me. And it won't be what I thought. It will be more terrible. It lurks there like Raskolnikov's detective and I come to it, afraid, and wanting to know. The book, I mean. Or do I mean the name.

I wouldn't give in, and the pile of toilet paper envelopes grew. Mik played solemnly, not smiling.

Which of us threw the ring? It seems to have been me. But I don't remember.

It was very cold now, and I was purple with goose bumps. But I played on until, gradually, I won them all back, the little curls in their packages.

Edna says to me, last week, 'I don't see what's so hard. If you want to tell the truth, just tell it.'

'Oh, you think it's easy, getting past all the lies? All the lies you make up to live with yourself? You think that's easy?'

Edna says, 'Well, of course, I'm not a writer. I suppose you have to make it "artistic."' She is in a shitty mood, and I am so furious with her that I decide not to see her again until it is done, the book.

I won them all back. Mik built a fire in the stove and when it was roaring up through the mica windows, I stalked over, opened the door, and threw them in, all the packages.

The toilet paper flares up, easily, as paper does, without any further brilliance. I stand there, staring stupidly down at the open door.

Mik begins to laugh.

'You switched them?'

He throws back his head and roars.

'You switched them! You cheated!'

'I let you win, too,' he says, holding up the other packages, the ones with the curls inside.

'You let me win?'

'You can't beat me,' says Mik. And starts to put the curls away in his wallet.

'You let me win?' It is terrible. It is absolute. I could kill him.

He laughs at me. I know I look a fool, shivering in the dawn, unable to stop my teeth chattering.

'You never give in. I had to let you win.' And, 'I knew you'd play till hell froze over, not to mention your ass.' And he laughs again. Mean laughter. He throws my clothes at me, like a guard at Auschwitz.

I get into them. I am crying with sheer rage. I get into the panties and the brassiere, awkwardly, dressing in front of him defiantly, not turning away. I wish I could strike him dead. The denim is hard and raspy against my legs. Even the runners hurt going on. I open the cabin door and go out and stand beside the ravine. The birds are beginning to chitter. I am so ugly. My breath steams out of me. After a while, he comes out too, and stands a little ways off, watching.

I take off the ring and hold it out to him. He takes it and with a great curving arc of his arm, throws it into the ravine.

I thought it was I who had done it. Thrown the ring away. But it was Mik. I can see his arm now, curving against the pink-ridged clouds, dark, like some primeval weapon, in a long unhesitating sweep. Yes. Mik threw the ring. I had thought it was me. It was me. And we fly back to Campbell River, our week not up. Not saying goodbye to them. Leaving everything neat and clean, the way we found it. But not leaving them even a note.

It is a hot muggy day, the sea as dull and slick as mercury. It curves under the plane in a grey oily meniscus. The sky is hot and leaden from forest fires on Vancouver Island. Campbell River is full of people. The RCMP is conscripting people to cut fire breaks. Mik takes me to a shop and buys me a pair of brief white shorts and a nylon blouse with rickshaws all over it.

'I can't wear these on the street. I look like a chippy.'

'Well?'

We go into a beer parlour and Mik sees someone he knows. A buddy from the camp. We sit with him and drink beer. It is noisy and crowded and everyone seems drunk with beer or fire excitement. A woman comes up to our table and pulls out a chair for herself. Neither man pays any attention to her. She just sits down, uninvited. She is old. Forty, anyway. And thin. Her face is ravaged and made up in a ghastly way. Rouge spots stare out from her cheeks. Her hair has a funny orange look, as if it has been burnt. Her legs and arms are covered with sores. She smokes all the time.

Mik and the buddy go on talking. The woman leans over to me and says, 'He beats me. He beats me up. He only loves me on Welfare day.'

I draw away. I can't help it. Whatever it is on her arms, I don't want to catch it. I look at Mik but he doesn't look at me.

'I do everything he wants and he beats me up,' she says.

She begins to cry, her face crumpling, and black stuff coming down from her eyes. In the corners are thick yellow sleep deposits. Her dress is pink.

'I don't know what to do,' she says, over and over. 'I don't know what to do.'

I look to Mik again, trying to signal, but he won't see me.

Men pass the table and look at my legs in their shorts and grin at me.

Horrible. The pink dress was horrible. Rhinestones. Cute.

She puts her hand on mine and she says, 'Men. They're just animals. That's all they think of.'

I get up and say, 'Excuse me,' and try to find the washroom.

I stay in here a long time, combing my hair and washing my hands over and over, where she has touched me. Washing my arms. I take a paper towel and even wipe my legs. An Indian woman is sitting on the bench in front of the mirror. Fat and ugly with very red lipstick. She is spraying her hair with something in a can. Her hair is back-combed and teased into a monstrous pile on her head. The spray gets into my lungs and I cough. She gives me a cold look, she hates me. She smiles at me, and the red is on her teeth, and her teeth are brown and rotten.

She has pock marks on her face and she is trying to cover them with something hard and pink in a pale blue box.

'You want a hassle?'

'I'm sorry? I beg your pardon?' Perhaps I was staring. I look away from her, to myself in the mirror. My face without makeup. My long brown hair, gold from the sun.

'You want a hassle, I'm the one to give it to you.' Her hands are on her hips, and she is glaring at me.

'No, I'm sorry,' and I go back out to the beer parlour.

A man puts out his hand and strokes my thigh. 'Hey, baby, what's the hurry? Hey, where are you going so fast? Hey, you guys smell hair burning?' They are all laughing at me, and I can't find the table in the smoke. The waiter comes up and says, 'Let's have your ID.'

'I'm with someone.'

'Yeah yeah. Your ID. Your identification,' he explains.

'Just a minute.' And I get out my wallet. But as I hand him my driver's license, I say, 'I'm twenty-seven.'

He reads my driver's license. 'Got anything else?'

I give him my university library card.

'He's right over there,' I say, but Mik isn't looking my way.

The Indian woman pushes past us. 'Thinks her cunt's too good· for some people. Fucking cunt!' she yells back at me.

The waiter says, 'Is this you?'

'What?'

'What's the address?'

'Twenty-nine fifty-two, West Eighth.'

'That's not what it says here.'

'It's written in over the top, see? I used to live there, but I moved.'

'Yeah.' And he hands me back the license and the card.

A man goes by and says, 'Fourteen years.'

'I'll have to ask you to leave,' the waiter says.

'Why?'

'You're not twenty-one.'

I laugh.

He takes my arm and starts to propel me toward the door. 'My friend,' I say, 'he's right over there. Ask him. I'm twenty-seven. Please.' And I pull away and half run back to Mik. The woman in the pink dress has her head on the table. Her eyes are closed and her mouth is drooling.

And we have to leave. Out on the sidewalk, in the bright hot glare,·Mik looks as if he wants to kill me.

'I told him I was twenty-seven.'

'Dummy up,' Mik says and takes me across the road, his hand on my upper arm, the same grip as the waiter's. We register in a hotel and upstairs in the room, Mik says, 'You think you'll never be like that?'

'Like what?'

'Like her.'

'Who?'

'Her. The old bag.'

I think about it. 'No. Never.'

'It could happen to you,' Mik says.

'No. No, it couldn't.'

'It could happen,' Mik says.

I sit there on the edge of the bed, a big double bed with a washable cover. Grey and blue. I shake my head. 'No.'

'Easy,' Mik says, and comes over to me, pushing against my chest, so that I fall flat on my back with my legs still dangling over the edge.

'I want a shower.'

But he is undoing my shorts and pulling them off. And my panties.

He spreads my legs and comes into me, not even taking off my blouse, or his trousers, just unzipping himself. I am dry, and it is rough and mean and I hate him.

And after, I go into the shower and stand there a long time.

When I come out, he has taken off his clothes and is lying on the bed, almost asleep in the smoke-filled room. The late afternoon sun is coming in under the venetian blinds like a threat. He lies there naked, a thick fat oaf. His skin is too pink, and there are blemishes on his back. An old fat man lying on a hotel bed, his mouth open, his sex limp and disgusting. I go up to him and touch his shoulder and he brushes me away. 'Fuck off,' he says.

I draw my tongue down the scar along his spine. Even my tongue is dry. 'I said fuck off.'

I am still wet outside from the shower and I bend and let my hair tickle his face. 'Aw, for christ sake.' I bend and kiss and lick him all over, taking it in my mouth till it rises in spite of himself. He sits up abruptly. 'Shit.' Then he gets up and slams me against the wall, so that my feet are dangling somewhere near the top of the baseboard. 'I could break you in two,' he says, but whether it's a threat or a statement I can't tell.

I put my arms around his neck, now that we are face to face, and kiss him on the mouth.

'Aw, christ,' he says and loves me. It is a kind of victory. Over what I'm not sure.

ONE OTHER THING about that island, the first island. In another version, number four? I wrote: 'I look back and I think, How many times did I do that to him? How many times did I make it impossible for him to stay at a job, to become respectable?' But it was fire season. Mik was laid off because it was fire season. Sister Mary Joseph is right. It's a sin to blame yourself for everything.

AT HOME, JOCELYN and I decide we must sell some of the kittens. She is to keep two of the first batch, Lolita and Humbert, but the rest must go. Especially Pieface, a stray who howled her way into the place and then proceeded to suck on Sally. Now that I've got Sala for Jocelyn, it's just too much. 'Besides, Sala thinks he's a cat too,' says Jocelyn, 'and that's ridiculous in a seventy-five pound German Shepherd!' It is, too; he's always getting caught in the cat hole, or trying to jump on top of the radiator. And Lolly, seductive wench, is constantly getting Sala all excited. 'It'll still be too much for his ego,' says Jocelyn, 'with four cats and just him.' She's right. To this day, he persists in his identity crisis and chases cats madly, not from canine instinct but *amour*.

We put an ad in the paper and the auction commences.

'It's like you're doing interviews for adoption,' Mik says. 'What was wrong with them?' jerking his thumb at a couple going down the sidewalk. Rejects.

'They wanted Siamese for prestige,' I say.

'And yesterday you wouldn't sell because they said they'd spay the female. Already you've got so many rules ... you sell them only by twos.'

'One would get lonely, after this house.'

'But what's so wrong with spaying the female then, if you're going to insist they go as couples?'

'Well. Spaying's as bad as a whatsit. A vasectomy.'

Mik doesn't answer for a while. Then he says, 'My sister's husband's got one.'

'They get neurotic if they're alone. They need company.'

'Not a Siamese. A vasectomy.'

'You're kidding!'

'Twenty minutes. Never felt a thing.'

'Does your sister know?'

'Sure. It was her idea. She gets pregnant every time he hangs his pants on the bedpost.' Mik laughs.

'It was *her* idea?'

'Hell,' says Mik, 'he says it's even better now.'

'You mean she still does it with him?'

'Sure. Why not. It doesn't affect a man's ability.'

'I couldn't.'

'Couldn't what?'

'I couldn't, not with a man who had that.'

'*You're* kidding,' Mik says to me.

'No. It wouldn't feel right. It'd be like, you know, with a eunuch.'

'You've got to be kidding.'

I shake my head. 'No. I could never go to bed with someone like that.'

'But, Jesus, they've got four kids already.'

'But what if she dies? What if they all get burnt up in a fire?'

'Jesus!' Mik says. 'You really mean it.'

'You're damned right, nobody's going to spay my pussy,' and I hug Lolly. But he doesn't laugh. He is looking at me with that funny look. As if he's working something out. As if he's measuring me for the drop.

THE PROFESSOR PHONED to say he was having guests the coming weekend, would I care to come? 'He's John Straussen,' he said. But I didn't recognize the name. 'The CBC big wig?' I still don't twig. 'His wife's Marguerite Prentiss.'

'Oh sure. I've seen her on television.'

'Come on Thursday and then we can have a quiet day before they get here. They'll be coming with Iris.'

Iris was, is, the professor's wife, a woman of formidable wit. Once, at the professor's house, she had introduced Ben, saying, 'And this is Mr Victoria Ferris.' And to a magnificent lady professor whom I adored, 'How wise of you, dear, to give up girdles, they only stop the circulation.'

'Yes, well, can I let you know? I'm sort of working on something.'

It's a lie. I should be working but I'm not. I should be finishing up the one about the man from the sea, and all the complicated chess crud. People had talked so much about the symbols in the other that now I thought I was a symbol writer, and I was putting them in like capers. Anyway, I wasn't working at all. I was screwing around.

And the promise to the Festival man was hanging over my head too.

Jocelyn had announced she would be leaving soon, for the East. David was going to get his PhD and she was going to be with him.

Ben had finished the head. It sat on the coffee table. The best thing he ever did, but rather foreboding. Now he had no more excuses for coming over.

I think I said that. 'Well, I'll be seeing you sometime.'

'Yes. I guess you'd rather I didn't come over.'

'Yes. I guess so.'

'How's the asthma?'

'Nonexistent. I threw the stuff all away. The day of the divorce.'

'I refuse to accept the divorce.'

'Yes, you've told me.'

'People don't stop being married because of a piece of paper.' And,

'How's the Nut Lady?'

'Fine. She says I'm not destructive. She says if I press a button the world will not explode.'

'You never were destructive, I was the destructive one. You're a good person.'

Somehow this sort of talk from Ben makes me feel even more sick.

'Do you realize we never fought?' I said. 'We spent our time telling each other how wonderful we were. We never got cross.'

'Why should we have done?' said Ben. 'We agree on all the basic matters.'

I threw back my head and eyed him archly but that sort of ploy never worked with Ben. 'And what were they, the basic matters?'

'Socialism, for one,' Ben said seriously. 'We're both socialists. And God. We don't believe in God. And the inherent dignity of the individual. The possibility of free will in spite of determinism. That's why I didn't interfere.'

'With what?'

'With what you're doing now. Maybe you need it. Maybe you need a man like that. I mustn't stop you. It would be a breach of your individual liberty. All I can do is stand by.'

'For what? Stand by for what?'

'For whatever happens.'

'What do you think's going to happen?'

'I think he'll hurt you. I think you want him to hurt you.'

'Why should I want that?'

'Because you want to punish yourself. For the abortion. You see it as murder.'

'It was murder.'

'That's a matter of opinion.'

'It's a matter of fact. It was alive.'

'Is life the same when it's uterine, as when it's ...' He pauses.

'Aer-e-o?' I supply. 'Yes, for me.'

Ben sighs. 'I've given it a lot of thought. I was wrong to encourage you. I mean, about the abortion. In many ways, it was my fault.'

I feel a tremor of terror and I hear myself say, 'You couldn't come in me! That time! You couldn't do it in me. You pulled out!'

'I know,' says Ben. 'It haunts me. But you see, I didn't want to hurt you.'

'Hurt me!'

'No, that's true,' he protests. 'I couldn't bear to think of all that suffering. All that blood and pain. It was terrible to think of you like that.'

'You think there wasn't blood? You think there wasn't pain?'

'Not as much as there would have been, at nine months. You were only about two months gone, you know.'

'I was five months gone!'

Ben smiles, his superior smile. 'No. I checked. The foetus was only ...'

'Oh, I see. That's what you were doing. With the scalpel. Checking.'

'Scalpel?' He is genuinely puzzled.

'When you took the scalpel in. To the bedroom. You were checking?'

'I never took a ...'

'Whatever it was. What you use on the silk-screen.'

But he denies it. He denies the whole thing.

'You're very lovely, Vicky,' he says. 'You know I love you, don't you? And you're a good person, basically. Try to remember that. I know you're hurt and bitter. But we all love you, try to remember that.'

'Who. You and who else?'

'All your friends. Ivan and Marie and Paul. Even Marcie. Marcie would like to make it up with you. She's very sorry. I've talked to her about it.'

'Thanks, anyway.'

'It's true. Marie was saying just this morning what a wonderful person you are.'

'*Was* she? Does she sleep with you too, as well as Paul? To comfort you?'

Ben's face gets that hurt look. 'Marie is a very fine person. And Ivan understands about Paul. They don't believe in possession.'

'The more fool Ivan,' I say. 'It's going to happen all over again, you know. It'll be Wilma all over again.'

And at the moment, something goes zonk inside me and I know what the Festival play is about.

'They believe in free love,' Ben is saying, but my mind is going

202

whing whizz zip-azap. 'Marie says you're terribly romantic.'

'Oh yeah? What does Ivan say?'

(I find out years later. After I've written the Ivan-Wilma play. 'What week end?' Ivan says to me in the caf. 'You know. That weekend. When you went on the motorcycle. And you left Wilma alone with Lionel. I always thought it was on purpose. You know. That you sort of wanted it to happen. Because if she did it, she'd *have* to leave you.'

'No. I never expected anything to happen. God, women are romantic,' Ivan said gloomily. 'I don't know what it is you all want.')

'The trouble with us was,' says Ben, ignoring my Ivan-question, 'the trouble with us was I treated you like a child bride, always protecting you from everything. I wouldn't let you grow up. I see it now.'

'I can see you've all gone into this thoroughly,' I say, 'you and Paul and Ivan and Marie. Sitting together over home-made saki discussing poor little Vicky.'

'I've given up liquor,' says Ben, 'and meat.'

'Does it work?'

'What?'

'Oh, you know. Rod. He said it got rid of lustful thoughts, giving up meat.'

'That isn't why,' says Ben. 'I just can't bear to think of the animals. Neither can you, Vicky. You know you can't. You gave it up for eight months; you were stronger than me then.'

I'd read *The Jungle* and driven everyone mad. Grace said of that time, 'That was the real test. If I can stand you as a self-righteous vegetarian, I can stand you as anything.' But that was before I started proselytizing motherhood.

'What's, uh, Mik doing now?'

'Looking for a job.'

'Oh. I thought he had one, in a logging camp.' Ben makes it sound like Siberia.

'That finished.'

'Little Ivan asked me what meat was,' Ben says, 'and when I told him, he threw up. Now he won't touch it.'

'Did he really throw up? Oh Ben.'

'Yes. He cried for the cow.' Ben looks at me severely. 'You can't lie to children.'

'I know you, you made it very real. You didn't just tell the truth. You made it ... you drew a cartoon. Yes, and you gave it a name, that cow. And a baby calf. And you told him each and every grisly detail. Oh Ben.'

'When I'm a teacher, I'll tell the truth to children,' Ben says.

'Oh I bet you will too.' I think about this. 'Did you give the cow a name?'

But he doesn't answer. He sighs.

'How are you doing, for money?'

'I'm getting a government loan.'

'Oh that's good.'

'Well, I'd better be going. I'm glad you like the head.'

'It's the best thing you've ever done. Full of anger.'

'Anger?' He is really puzzled.

'Well, it's Medusa, Ben. Look at it. Look at the eyes. And the way the neck cuts off, and the face sags in ... and the hair, like snakes.'

'That's how you look.'

'I know. That's how I look to you.'

'That head is full of my love for you.'

I laugh. 'I know it's me. But look at it, Ben.'

He says, in a wondering voice, 'It does. It looks like you're dead.'

And, after a while, he says, 'Well, I'd better be going. I don't have any more excuses to come here,' and he smiles, to show he's admitting it.

'Yeah.'

'That's the way you want it, isn't it? Me not to come around.'

'Well, you'll be busy with school and ... Yes. I'd rather you didn't, Ben. I'm sorry.'

'All right. Just remember, I'm always there. Whenever you need me.'

Mik lumbers up the stairs and bursts into the front room.

'I was just going,' says Ben.

'Yah?' And to me: 'Get dressed. We're going to the Old Lady's.'

Ben says, 'How are you getting along, Mik?'

'Okay.' And to me: 'Wear that dress with the spots, like a giraffe.'

'For your mother?'

'Yeah.'

'Any other instructions?'

'Wear your hair up, you know, like you did Tuesday.'

'What's the matter, you're huffing and puffing like a walrus.'

'I humped it across the bridge,' Mik says. 'Come on, for christ sake, she's expecting us for lunch. I phoned her.'

'Lunch! It's eleven-thirty.'

'Yah, so how come you're not dressed yet?'

'God, what a bloody tyrant.'

Ben gives me a pitying look. 'Well, I guess I better go.'

'You're a slob,' Mik says to me. 'Go on, for christ sake.'

So I run upstairs and have a quick bath and all the time I can hear from below, 'Get your butt moving,' and Ben's murmurous voice, polite, interrogative.

I come down and he's still there. Ben. Mik holds the door open but I stand back, waiting. Ben has got to go. Ben moves edgily in front of Mik. 'Can I drop you anywhere?' He has a car somehow, again.

'Nah.' Mik is jiggling the door knob.

'Well, if you need me, Vicky ...' and he goes, smiling at me sadly.

Out on the street, Mik says, 'Here,' and shoves a cellophane box at me. A corsage. He's been holding it behind his back all along. I forget what they are. If I don't think about it ...

'Mik, I can't wear a *corsage*. To go to *lunch*. To your *mother's*.'

'You wear it.'

'On the bus? A corsage on the bus?'

'Here,' and he pins it to my dress.

'No, well, at least, put it on the left side.'

'Yah? It goes on the left side?'

'Of course it goes on the left side.' Now he is taking my hand, walking very fast ahead of me down the street.

On Broadway there is a cab, and Mik opens the back door for me. The whole bit. 'Get in, for christ sake.'

'Oh, we're going in style.'

He gives the driver the address and we light cigarettes. I'm smoking now. I started one day with the Nut Lady. Took in a pack just to keep me company. After the big crying session. Thought if I smoked, maybe. One pack every time I saw her. Now I'm on two packs a day. Not now in the cab. Now. Now, in the cab, I do it because Mik does it. Not inhaling.

It's somewhere near Commercial, his mother's house. A neat white and green bungalow, with careful flower beds and a pocket handkerchief lawn. Inside, the front room is dominated by a massive TV, and the chesterfield is new and extremely red, with silver threads running through the upholstery. There are pillows all over this chesterfield. Elaborately tucked and gored and gusseted.

Mrs O'Brien has Mik's face. It's strange seeing it on a woman, the wide mouth and the long upper lip, with the indentations so marked. Her hair is very blonde and has a patina to it, as if it were ironed this morning. Lots of waves, but puffed up somehow at the same time. Her skin is red and flushed and the pores on her cheeks are huge. She is wearing a flowered crepe of some kind, and a frilly organdy apron that I bet hasn't come out of the bottom drawer since Christmas.

The table is laid in the kitchen. A linen tablecloth and paper napkins in a plastic holder. You take your own as you need it.

I am wet under the arms. I'm smiling so much I think my cheeks are going to cramp. We are all horribly polite. Mik doesn't speak to me the entire time. He refers to me in the third person, as if I were dead. .

'She's got all these cats,' and he laughs.

'I like cats,' she says, 'but they do destroy the furniture.'

'She's a teacher,' Mik says.

. 'Oh? What do you teach?'

'English,' Mik says before I get a chance to deny anything.

'Oh my,' she says, pouring out the tea into very new-looking porcelain cups, all different. 'I'll have to watch my grammar!' And she laughs.

'Or would you rather have a beer? Would she rather have a beer?' to Mik, as she hands me the cup of tea.

'She doesn't drink.'

'Oh my,' she says, 'she doesn't have any vices, hey?' I'm dying for a smoke all of a sudden. The first time I ever felt it, that Jesus-give-me-a-fag feeling. But I know I'd better not.

'Just the major ones,' Mik says and laughs. And his mother laughs and I smile.

'Don't you let him teach you any bad habits,' she says.

'I'll have one,' says Mik, getting up and going to the fridge. There are a lot of beer bottles in there.

She sees me looking and says, 'My husband. He likes one when he gets home from work.' And, as Mik raises the bottle to his lips, 'Oh Mik! We've got lots of glasses!'

'I like it like this. She's not the Queen of England, for christ sake.'

She doesn't seem to be able to sit still. She keeps getting up and going back and forth. 'Do you take cream?' And, 'I'd have put the milk in first but it isn't done in the best circles.' She laughs.

'My grandma always put milk in first.'

'Yes, it's called Mif, isn't it?' And we laugh, common ground at last. 'I guess it happens in the best of regulated families,' she says. And, to Mik, 'Well, stranger! They done a good job on your back, looks like.'

'Yah.'

'It was terrible,' she says, really talking to me now, 'the way they left it all that time. He was all hunched over. It broke my heart.'

'Yah, well, it's okay now,' Mik says.

'It's a wonder what they can do,' she says. And, 'Your father'd like to see you sometime, Mik. You could give him a call.'

'I bet he'd like to see me. So how's Dick.' The last very casual.

'Oh he's fine. He's a first lieutenant now. In the Navy. My other son,' she adds to me. She says it 'loo.'

'Yah?'

'And they've got a new baby. A boy. He's almost a year now, Mik. Can you imagine?'

'So how many does that make it?'

'Three now. Two girls and a boy.'

'My brother the rabbit,' says Mik.

'Oh he's so cute. They brought him over last Sunday and he's just such a little man. They're over to Victoria, they can't get over too often.'

'My brother the first lieutenant,' says Mik. 'Real book man.' And somewhere to my general direction, 'Never saw action.'

'Well, you know Dick was too young to see action.'

'Not too young for Korea.'

'Now, Mik, you know Dick ...'

'I know he got himself a cushy job, sat it out on his butt,' Mik says. 'I seen his type.' And when she doesn't answer, 'So how's the Old Man?'

'He's fine. He has this lumbago, when it gets damp,' she says to me. 'He's at work now.'

'Same place?'

'No. This is a new place, over to Millardville ...'

'Got bounced, eh? Old Man boozes,' to the air.

'Mik!' And after pressing more fruit cake on me she says, brightly, 'Why don't we all go over to see Millie? I told her you were coming and she said, Why not come over and see the house? They got a new house. It's real nice. Brand new.'

So Mik calls a cab and we go over to Millie's. It's one of these development houses, the ground all raw and torn from bulldozers, not a tree left in sight.

'We haven't painted yet,' Millie explains, indicating the white walls. 'You got to wait for the cracks first.'

There are four children of various sexes, and we play on the front room carpet. 'Don't get the lady's dress dirty,' she says to them.

And, 'We got this rec room but it's not finished yet. So how you doing, you big lug?' to Mik.

He laughs and then she laughs and then, abruptly, he picks her up and swings her around.

'Mik! You stop that. You put me down! Oh.' And back on the floor, 'I'm an old married lady now. You bugger. They didn't knock it out of you, hey?'

Her mother gives her a look and she says, 'How about some tea?'

So they all go out to the kitchen and leave us alone in the front room. I can hear them laughing and snorting and beer bottles opening.

The floor is wall-to-wall beige, and there are orange and brown geometric designs on the drapes at the big picture window. The chesterfield is an exact replica of the mother's, only brown with silver threads. But the TV is even bigger, and above it is a painting of a green Chinese girl. Very sexy. I'd never seen one before, although I've seen it many times since. And on the TV proper is a studio photograph of a woman with a big smile, turned slightly sideways. The photograph has been tinted. It has pink cheeks and pink lips and there are highlights of some sort in the hair. After a while, I see that it is Millie.

About five o'clock the husband comes home. He is young and slim and doesn't look as though anything terrible has happened to him. He puts out his hand to me and then says, 'Just a minute,' rubbing it on his trousers. 'Got to wash first.' I am embarrassed to look at him, the Man with the Vasectomy.

'So, you old cock-sucker!' he says to Mik, laughing and clapping him on the back, hitting him in the stomach. 'So, long time no see!' Mik is laughing too, and punching him back. 'So, give the man a beer, Millie. Hey, you kids, leave the lady alone.'

'So, you're doing okay for yourself?' Mik says.

'Hundred-year mortgage. Up to the ass in payments for everything. Your frigging sister, she keeps me hopping all night. And the damn basement's giving already. I phone the contractor? And he says he can't do a fucking thing about it, it's not his fucking business.' He glances at me. 'They give you the run-around, these bastards.'

Then they all go into the kitchen again and I can hear them talking about the basement and how it's been leaking and the fucking shit the husband works for and the cocksucking bastards he works with and the whole frigging mess his life is in, except of course that's not what he's saying at all. 'So what the hell you doing, you cocksucker?'

'Rigging,' Mik says.

'Yah? Rigging, hey? There's good money in rigging. I'd go up north only I couldn't leave babydoll alone for a minute. Can't trust her outa my sight.'

'Oh you!' Millie says. 'You keep a civil tongue or I'll tell a few home truths myself.' And they are all laughing and having a great old time, in there.

The kids and I aren't doing too badly. We've done most of the jigsaws, and now we're on the hockey game. Orchids. That's what they were. In the corsage. 'Is them orchids?' one of the kids asks.

'Yes.'

'They're real pretty.'

I'd give them to her only I don't think Mik would appreciate that.

And then, all of sudden, Mik is standing by the door, giving me a nod. It's time to go. He hasn't said a word about leaving. I say thank you, and they say come again and it's too bad we couldn't stay for supper, and we're off.

About five blocks away, Mik breathes out a great gust of air. 'Hoo,' he says. 'Hoo hah!'

'Were you mad at me?'

'What now?' But I can see he isn't mad.

'You didn't say anything to me. The whole time. You kept saying "she," and then you all went into the kitchen. Did I do something wrong?'

'Ah, sixty-five,' and he gives me a playful punch on the thigh. 'Hey, driver, drop us off across the bridge.'

'Oh Mik,' I say, 'I'm hungry.'

'So I'll get you a sandwich. Hoo!' And he laughs, a great Mik laugh. Throwing back his head and letting it all come out.

'You're in a good mood,' says the driver.

'You bet your ass,' says Mik.

'You just go to a wedding?' says the driver.

'No,' I say quickly.

'I was just noticing, the corsage and everything,' the driver says.

'Buddy,' says Mik. 'You keep driving and don't look in the mirror and see what Santa brings you.' And he kisses me, right in the back seat.

We go to the Castle which, as Mik says, is ritzy enough for anyone. And he gives the driver a bill besides the fare. It looks suspiciously to my eye like a five. But I don't say anything.

'I'm still hungry.'

'Boy? Boy? You got something the little lady can wrap herself around? Something big and juicy and running with gravy, all the trimmings; don't let her fool you, she's got an appetite like a horse.'

'Did it go all right?' I say when the waiter leaves.

'Yah.'

'Was I all right?'

'Ha!'

'No, was I?'

'My dumb broad sister,' he says.

'What? What did she say?'

'Never you mind.'

'What'd your mother say?'

'You passed short arm inspection,' Mik says.

'Short what?'

'Short arm. It's an army term.'

'Did you tell them I'm divorced?'

'Nah.' The waiter brings Mik's whiskey and my sandwich and

Mik takes a long drink and says, 'Nah, you done all right.' And to the waiter, 'A pink lady for the boozer here.'

'Oh Mik. No! Not with a sandwich. A ... a gin and tonic, please.'

'You watch her, she's a real lush,' says Mik. 'Fell in love with her 'cause I thought she was Oriental, but it turns out it was yellow jaundice all along. Don't trust women, buddy.' The waiter laughs.

'Did ya see his eyes bug out?'

'Well, if you will talk to waiters ...'

'Not him. The prick my sister married. Hundred-year mortgage. Hoo!'

'I take it I performed creditably,' I say. 'I take it they consider me a fine upstanding citizen who will encourage you to tread the straight and narrow.'

Mik has finished his drink and holds up his finger for another.

'I take it I am seen as "A Good Influence."'

'The prick was dying to know if I'm putting it to you.'

'Did he ask?'

'Nah. He was just dying to know.'

'You didn't say ...'

'Come on.' The waiter brings my gin and tonic and Mik's new whiskey.

'What did your mother say?'

He shakes his head.

'No. Mik. Tell me.'

'Ah, she wouldn't believe it if I drove up in a Cadillac.' He drains the glass and stares at it. 'I caught her once. With this guy.'

'Oh Mik.'

'I come home from school and there they are, humping it in the front room. On the sofa.'

'Oh Mik, you shouldn't tell me.'

'Rotten bitch.'

'Aw Mik, come on, you don't know what ...'

'I hate her guts,' he says and holds up his finger again.

'Don't get drunk.'

'What's it to you?'

'Well, for one thing,' archly, 'it impairs your faculties.'

'"Impairs my faculties,"' he says, and then hoots. 'Okay,' and he calls me the name I can't remember. 'One for the road.'

After a while, he says, 'I got married once.'

'You never told me.'

'I don't tell you everything. It was when I got back from overseas. She lived down the street. Her mother and my mother, they were big buddies. Her mother used to have me over, feed me up. 'Course I looked all right then. I wasn't so bald. I had this big patch on the top of my head but I looked okay. From the silver plate. Girls used to go for the uniform. I wore it even after.' He grins. 'Big hero. I had all this salad up here,' and he touches his breast. 'You know, good conduct medals. But I looked okay. Anyway. I knew her six weeks ... like I knew her before, but this time, it was six weeks, and we got married. Big wedding. The whole schmozz. White dress. Navy blue suit. Rice.' He swirled his glass.

'What did she look like?'

'Blonde. She was blonde.' He drinks. 'A real bitch.'

'How old was she?'

'Eighteen. I took her to this hotel,' and he names it but now I don't remember. 'In Winnipeg? I didn't touch her, see? The whole six weeks. Like she's glass. Like she'll break if I lay a finger on her. And she says, when we get into bed, she says ...'

'What?'

'She's up the stump. Some other fucker.'

'Oh Mik.'

He laughs. 'Yah. I'm waiting there, the big punk, the sucker, and she gets in beside me in this nightie, all white and frilly, and she says, "Mik? I got something I better tell you."' He laughs again but it comes out like a grunt.

'She didn't have to tell you,' I say finally. 'She could have let you think ...'

'She took me. What a punk.'

'You need never have known.'

He gives me one of his looks, long and considering.

'Oh yes. I know. We're all alike. I know what you're thinking. All I'm saying is, she didn't have to be honest.'

'I just got up and humped it out of there, left her right where she was. Crying her guts out.'

'Sometimes I think it's all a story. Everything you tell me. The whole thing.'

'She got a divorce. I got the papers. Out here. Maybe she annulled it. I don't know. I tore them up, when they come. I never read them. Anyway, we're divorced, don't you worry.'

'I wasn't.'

'Yah, well, don't.'

We walk home through the late August night. The air is soft and warm, below the bridge the tugs are moving out to sea, lonely, their riding lights red. Down the shaded streets, the air so thick with blossom that it's like moving through water. I take off my shoes and run ahead of him, down the cool sidewalk. He is laughing. I am laughing. People look at us and smile.

And in bed, he says, 'Don't you worry. I'm divorced. It's all legal.'

'I wasn't worrying. I'm not trying to trap you.'

'Yah. That's right. Keep it up, tough guy,' or something like that.

I would wear the diaphragm all the time. I'd take it out and wash it and wave it in the air to dry and then I'd squeeze out more goo and pop the whole business back in. Mik would make jokes about me going all mildew but I couldn't depend upon him not to arrive home in the middle of the day. And we made love every night.

But one afternoon, I took it out and left it to dry on the window ledge in the bathroom. I was vacuuming our bedroom and so I didn't hear him come upstairs. I heard the bedroom door bang against the wall though and I looked up and there he was, and he said, 'I'm gonna give you a baby.'

'like hell,' i said, but he threw me on the bed and started to pull down my jeans.

I was furious. I hit him in the face and he whammed me back.

'Hey, that hurt!' I said. I was surprised more than anything.

He looked so strange, not like Mik at all. 'You look like Ghenghis Khan,' I said, still half-amused. 'Hey Mik. Don't be crazy.'

He had me half sitting up in the bed, my T-shirt around my head.

'Hey Mik! Hey.'

And I felt my brassiere rip away. This convinced me more than any wham could have done. Tear my clothes? Hey.

'Oh no you don't.' And I rolled over toward the edge of the bed, but he caught me and hauled me back again. I was all dangling straps and jeans down around my ankles, and very aware of how silly I looked.

'You leave me alone or I'll scream.'

And his hand came up and covered my mouth and nose and eyes. I could feel his other hand getting all the bits and pieces off me and then trying to spread my legs. I clamped them together, and his hand went away. I'd always read that no one could be raped if she didn't really want to be. And I kept my legs firmly together, grimly trying to breathe under that hand. I decided he must be drunk. I heard his zipper go down and could feel him wrestling with his own clothes. It was getting hot and dark under his hand and I started to feel sick. 'Mik?' But it came out all muffled. It was a bit like going under ether, the darkness going round and round and trying not to fall into it.

And all the time, the vacuum was roaring away like a siren. I tried to get my teeth into his palm, but couldn't manage it. I don't think I was taking it very seriously even then.

And then the cats thumped onto the bed, had to see what was going on.

Mik took his hand away from my face. He was naked now. And reached down to pull out the vacuum cord. This struck me as hilarious. All the serious business of rape being interrupted by vacuums and Siamese cats.

Mik gathered them up in a bundle and threw them out the door, slamming it behind them. All through the next part, they were whining and snuffling and scratching away.

I said, 'How dare you!' about the cats. I know this because he teased me about it later, "How dare you!"' laughing at me. But I was really indignant about the cats, throwing them out like that, so rough.

I said something like 'Don't look like that, Mik. You're scaring me.'

And then I was almost afraid of him. My body seemed to draw itself in, all the soft edges going somewhere deep inside, to some hidden core. I scrabbled up to the top of the bed and grabbed a pillow to put in front of me.

He was standing there, swaying, his penis thick, engorged,

purple. I sort of laughed. 'Now Mik ...'

And he jumped at me.

I didn't waste my time yelling. There was no one to hear. I raked his face with my fingernails and felt the skin gathering under them. I put my thumb in his eye. I kneed him once and he gave a grunt. The struggle went on in a grim silent way. Both of us breathing like gladiators. I kept clamping my legs together and he kept pulling them apart. I kept writhing to one side just as he was about to make it. I think I laughed at one point, it was so difficult for him, it was just like the books said. So he fell on me full length and put one hand to my throat and squeezed. That was different. Things got very black and very sick. And my legs were apart and it was smashing against me, still not getting in, but smashing against the inside of my thighs, my pelvic bone. I pressed my hips down into the bed but it just kept on smashing and missing. He took away his hand, and I could breathe but I wasn't fast enough. He lifted my bum with one hand and tried to guide it in but I was too dry and the fight had made him limp. He swore. I think I was crying. It was awful, little whimpering sounds like a coward. He ran his hand up and down his penis until it was hard again, and then, gripping me like death, pushed it in. I stopped making noises. I just went rigid and held my face in.

It went on and on, like a bad movie. And when he came in me, he came silently, not like Mik at all. Pulling my thighs back and forth to his movements, and just coming. It felt so hot, and molten, like sulphuric acid. And he pulled out and just went to the bathroom.

I was more astonished than anything else. Astonished and indignant. And mad. And I hurt, and this made me even madder. And I whimpered. And this I could never forgive him. I hated myself.

When he came back, his bare feet thudding against the floor, I

218

said, 'You *raped* me.' He was picking up his clothes, putting them on. He didn't say anything. He just got dressed.

'You left your shit in me,' I said.

This made him stop for a moment, but then he went right on, getting dressed.

And then, he just went down the stairs and out of the house. Not even slamming the front door.

The cats came roaring in and jumped up on the bed, sniffing. What's going on?

I went to the bathroom and ran a hot tub.

Somewhere in the other bedroom, Jocelyn's, was my douche kit. I found it finally, down at the bottom of the drawer. I always hated douching, even before I read it wasn't good for you.

I had to kneel at first, inching down into the water, it was so scalding. Letting the water rise gradually. Down there it hurt like billy-oh. I took the nail brush and scrubbed all my thighs, even there. I could have torn the flesh off the bones.

I got out at one point and went down to the kitchen to mix up something good and strong for the douche, but all I could find was Javex and I wasn't having that. I didn't hate myself that much. I finally mixed up some salt and soda, thinking it was better than nothing. I couldn't think what women were supposed to use anyway. Lysol? I kept on douching until my muscles wouldn't let the syringe go in anymore. Then I took all the bedding and my ripped-up clothes and shoved them down the laundry chute. 'Oh no you don't,' I said because Sally had leapt up and was teetering on the ledge, ready for her free fall all over again.

Then I got dressed in something and phoned Paul.

'Have you still got your rifle?'

'Yes?'

'Bring it over,' I said and hung up.

219

He was over in minutes. 'What happened?'

'Nothing yet. I'm just going to kill the son of a bitch.'

'I knew this would happen. Did he hit you?'

'Just give me the rifle and get the hell out.'

But Paul said No, he was staying. If there was any trouble, he would kill Mik.

Jocelyn came home and said, 'Oh god,' looking at Paul sitting there on the chesterfield with the rifle across his lap. 'You're all mad,' she said and went over to David's for the night.

We waited a long time, Paul and me. Then we watched television. Then I went to bed and left Paul there, on the chesterfield, with the rifle on his lap. He stayed like that all night. Watching the front door.

In the morning I was stiff and sore and I ached in every bone.

'Oh go home, Paul,' I said when I got downstairs. 'It's all right.'

'But what if he comes back?'

I made us some coffee. I said, 'Paul? Look. You don't understand. If he doesn't come back, I'll go looking for him. Take the stupid gun and go home. Work it out with Marie.'

'You're trying to destroy yourself,' said Paul.

'Look. I'm sorry I dragged you in. Okay?'

'Look, Vicky,' said Paul. 'I know all about it. I know this sort of man. And I know about you, too.'

'What do you know?'

'How you feel about contraceptives. For an atheist, you're a bit RC, aren't you?'

I sighed. 'Did Ben say that?'

'I know you don't use anything. And, Vicky, Mik's going to get you pregnant, don't you realize that? And then he'll just walk out. And then what?' He was drinking his coffee, his face full of concern for me. 'That's all he wants, you know. And if you get knocked up, he won't waste a minute on you.' He shook his head. 'Up to now, you've been lucky. That's all.'

'Paul?' I said. 'You're a prick.'

And that was the end of Paul—for that year.

I cleaned the house from top to bottom. The cord to the vacuum was ripped but I fixed it with mending tape. That mending tape's still on, now that I think of it. I vacuumed and I scrubbed and I polished. Attacking the corners like enemies. I always do that when I'm mad or if the story isn't working. I used a whole box of Spic· 'n Span and two cans of Dutch Cleanser. And all the Javex. I did the windows with Windex and oiled the mahogany panels in the dining room. I did a wash and hung it flapping out in the wind. A good brisk day for drying.

My fingers got that cracked puckered look. And my knees were all red. When there wasn't anything else to scour, I had another bath and got dressed and went down to the Safeway's. Bought enough food for an army. Ten pounds of potatoes. Trundling it home in a cart I snitched from the lot.

No one came. I made a Busy-Day Cake, a recipe of my mother-in-law's. I peeled a great cauldron of potatoes. I garlicked the steaks. I went out into the garden and picked every rose in sight, great cabbage roses, pink and white and red. Putting them in vases and bowls and even milk bottles. I even laid a fire in the fireplace, though it looked like a warm night coming up. I took in all the wash. It smelled so clean and good. I made up the bed.

Everything smelled of lemon oil and roses and Javex. And I waited.

Jocelyn didn't come home. And along about nine o'clock, bang crash thump, here he comes, the Thing from Outer Space.

He stands there beside the dining room panel doors, looking at me, stone-faced. I stand there, just out of the kitchen door, looking at him. Our lips quirk at about the same time. Mik guffaws. '"How dare you!"' he says.

'You bastard!' And we stand there, five feet apart, snorting and roaring like two fools.

'"How dare you!"' and he slaps his thigh.

'That was because of the cats!' And this sends us off again.

'All we needed was that great hound,' he says, meaning Sala, who was at the vet's or something, or maybe with Joss.

'Paul sat up all night with a gun!' I say.

'A gun!'

'You know, a rifle. Waiting to kill you when you came in the door.'

'Lucky I didn't come home. I'd've rammed it so far up, he'd be spitting bullets.'

And we laugh and hold our stomachs and hold onto each other to keep from falling down. And then we have dinner and make up the fire anyway.

Somewhere around midnight he pokes the fire and says, 'So you'll have to marry me now.'

'Who says?'

'I says. I humped you good. I humped you real good.'

'Ah, you did before and I never got caught.'

'Yah, but I put my mind to it that time.'

'Your mind, was that what it was!'

'I made a good job of it.'

'Nevertheless ...'

'"Nevertheless,"' and he tickles me.

'Nevertheless, I have no honourable intentions about you, buster.'

'We'll see. I never met a woman yet didn't hit the panic button, she missed the curse.'

'Don't worry. I wouldn't marry you if you were the last man on earth.'

'Yah yah. Keep it up.'

'I am not kidding, Mik.'

'We'll see when the time comes.'

'What an influence *you'd* be on a child.'

He doesn't pay this any mind, but I go cold for a moment. I stare into the fire and I go fish cold. It's true. He'd make a terrible father.

And the next day I catch the bus to Horseshoe Bay. The ferry is pulling out when I get there and I phone the professor. 'I'm sorry,' I say, 'but I've just missed the boat.'

'But there isn't another tonight,' he says. 'Look, get a water taxi.'

So I do. We go zipping over the water, me standing all the way, feeling like a figurehead, the spray drenching my hair. He's waiting for us at the dock, and insists on paying. Twelve dollars. I feel guilty about it, but oddly pleased too.

The sea is that painful blue, that terrible heart-aching blue, and the sun glitters our eyes. At the cabin, everything glows. The mugs on their hooks, the thick rugs, the piano. It is a perfect, still blissful day and I say, 'God, what a place. I'd give my soul for a place like this.'

We swam and he read me something he was writing, a complicated exegesis of Hume. But when I said, 'Aren't you still falling into Kant's trap?' he got all upset, and explained the same thing over to me again. He was reading Malcolm Lowry and he said, 'Let us go through the forest to the stream.'

We took machetes and hacked our way up, clearing the foliage that had grown around the thick black hose that ran down the hill to the cabin. Once, he stopped and said, 'This is known as Conception Rock,' and I looked and saw a moss-covered piece of granite.

'Why?' and knew what he would say.

'Because lovers come here.'

Then we went back to hacking the undergrowth with the machetes and once I struck the thick black hose and laughed hysterically. 'I've cut it right through, I think,' I said, giggling. I thought, Oh god, it's all going to be Symbolic.

We found the source of the stream and he stood there in a terribly portentous way. I think I kept giggling. I was horribly embarrassed. He looked so old and white, his scalp showing pink through his hair. I thought Ah, don't. Don't. For I did truly like him. In a way I almost loved him.

And that night, watching the sea, he said, 'Would you consider marrying me?'

'I don't know,' I said, hugging my arms between my knees.

'I know how much you want children,' he said in an even, reasonable voice. 'I can give you three. We can manage three, and when I'm dead, you'll still be a young woman.' It was terrible, terrible. I think I knew as soon as he paid for the water taxi.

'What about Iris?' I said.

'We haven't lived together as man and wife for years. I have a mistress.'

'Oh.'

'Of course I'll provide for Iris. I'd have to give her a decent living allowance. And if you want, I'll give up my mistress.'

I think I laughed.

'Is it because I'm too old?' he said.

'No, no,' and then, ashamed, because he honoured the Real, 'yes, in a way. I never thought of you like that. I mean, I'm sorry, I just never ...'

'I waited until your divorce,' he said.

This I felt was a lie. I just did not believe he had harboured a

224

silent passion for me all those years at university. No.

And the telephone rang.

'It's for you,' the professor said, holding the receiver out to me. Walking to the French doors and looking out at the sea again.

'Hello?'

'Hi,' and he said the name I can't

'Oh hello,' I said in what I hoped sounded a surprised tone.

'Is *he* listening?' said Mik.

'Yes, all right,' I said.

'Hey, tough guy, I'm horny for you.'

'Oh yes?'

After a pause, Mik said, 'Say something.'

'All right, I'll see to it when I get back.'

'You bitch, do you love me?'

'Oh yes?'

And he hung up.

And to the professor's back I said, apologetically, 'That was the boarder.'

'He's in love with you,' he said.

'Oh no.'

'Yes.'

'Has he got you in bed yet?'

'No, my goodness. No.'

'You'd better watch out then.' He sounded so angry.

'I'm sorry,' I said. 'I really am. I do love you, in a way, you know.'

He gave a short laugh and said if we were going to get any work done tomorrow, we'd better go to bed.

I slept like a baby, in the guest house.

The next day the CBC big wig and his wife came with Iris.

We'd put in a good morning. I was finishing the play about the man from the sea. A bad play. There were so many symbols in it, one man (an English teacher) phoned and said he'd worked everything out but the bishop, in the chess game. What did the bishop represent? I mean, it was that bad. People played games with it. But I wanted to get it done. This other one, about Wilma and Ivan, was knocking at the door. Lines were already in my head.

Along about four in the afternoon, they came down the path.

'Vicky!' Iris cried. She always seemed terribly pleased to see me. 'Did you come up yesterday?'

'Yes.'

'Get lots of work done?'

'Not bad.' I was awkward with her. I thought she could see right through me.

'This is the delightful child my husband's taken up with,' she said to the couple. 'She's awfully brainy. You know. She's the one who does those plays on radio. *The Carson Family* out of Ibsen?'

The man shook my hand and smiled. Said I looked younger than he'd expected. The woman smiled. I liked them right off, they were so lovely together, so well-mannered and yet easy at the same time. You could see they'd make terrific parents.

'I liked the last one, dear,' Iris was saying, 'but of course it's not *great*. It was a good story, though. I like a good story, I can't bear all these clever little things they do now. It's nice to find someone who isn't ashamed of simply *entertaining* people.'

'It was a damn fine play,' said the professor.

'Yes, well, it didn't break any new ground,' said Iris, 'but we all know how you feel about Vicky. Don't breathe a word of criticism, sweetie,' to the wife, 'he won't have it.' And, 'Isn't it a shame nobody listens to radio anymore? I love it myself. I listen to everything, even the crap.'

A lot of things happened that weekend. It doesn't matter really, or maybe it does. I'm finding it hard to sort the non-causal from the causal; in a way, everything's causal.

When Iris got up Sunday morning, she came into the kitchen where I was washing up the dishes from last night and she put her hands on my bum and said, 'It's only youth, you know.'

I was wearing the old bathing suit, size twenty. It was that or the leopard skin, and I was embarrassed about the leopard skin.

That afternoon, everything broke into pieces. Marguerite fell down a cliff, and her husband was horribly frightened for her. The professor drove madly down the gravel roads to arrange for a water taxi to take her into the hospital. He kept saying, 'Iris will be so upset!' But, oddly, when the water taxi had taken Marguerite and her husband away, Iris was not at all upset.

When she drove me down to catch the ferry at five o'clock, she said, 'He asks everyone, you know.'

'What?'

'To go to bed with him. He asks everyone. He's asked all my friends, you know. First he offers to marry them, and then he suggests a trial run, to make sure everything will work out.' She glanced at me. 'You haven't done anything foolish, I hope, Vicky.'

I wasn't going to tell her one way or the other. But I said, 'I have a lover actually.'

'Does he know?' she said with a jerk of her head back along the road.

'No. But I'll tell him.'

'Yes dear, you do that.'

We drove for a while in silence and then I said, 'Iris, do you say things like that on purpose?'

'What dear?'

'You know. The sarcastic things you say.'

'I? Sarcastic? Vicky, I tell the truth and the world calls me a bitch for my trouble.' She pulled the car into the long line waiting at the dock. 'Marion said that to me too. She says I say awful things to people.'

'Yes, you do,' I said. 'And I can never make out whether you mean them or not.'

'Like what?' said Iris. 'Give me an instance.'

'Like, "This is Mr Victoria Ferris,"' I said. 'That time you introduced Ben.'

'But he *was*, darling!' she said. 'That's all Ben ever was, your husband. Like I'm *his* wife. Wasn't that the whole trouble with you and Ben?'

But I wasn't getting caught like that. 'And when you said to Marguerite, that she fell down the cliff to get her husband's attention.'

Iris smiled. 'Well?' she said. 'She is getting on, you know. And you're young and fresh and almost beautiful because of it. Oh, your face is too broad for real beauty. Later on, it'll get a real Irish jut. But now, since you've lost all that weight, and you're young, you see. You'll get old, we all get old, but we can't help hating your guts right now.' And she jerked the emergency brake.

'Am I? Almost beautiful?' I would have believed anything she said at that moment.

'Almost. Like your stories. Not great, but very good.'

I laughed. 'I like you very much, Iris.'

'Yes, I grow on one, like artichokes.'

We were inching slowly ahead now, car by car, but at the barrier, the guard stopped us. 'No more cars,' he said.

'Oh shit,' she said.

They hoisted up the ramp. I half-opened the car door and called, 'Can I come on anyway?'

The guard grinned at me. I could see now he was really a sailor. 'If you can shimmy up a ladder!'

'Iris? Thanks.' I got out and slammed the door. 'Listen, do you mind?'

'No. I think I'll go back to the cabin for the night.'

'Don't tell him. Let me.'

'I'd like to tell him,' she said.

'I know. But, don't, eh? I will.'

'Okay.' And I ran. The sailor waved to the captain up in his little house at the top of the ferry, and everyone waited until I clambered up the ladder and over the rail and jumped down to the deck. Then a cheer went up, and the captain blew the great horn, and everyone laughed and waved. It was like walking onto a great empty patch of floorboards and finding you're standing on the stage of the Old Vic with a full audience out front. But I laughed and waved back.

I'm probably a fool, but I believe she never told the professor. Not that night.

I was very happy. I went up to the café and had a mug of coffee and looked at people. And they spoke to me. They said, 'Hey, that was something!' And, 'You're quite a girl.' Men. Yes, it was men who said this. I was bubbling inside. I couldn't remember anything like this ever happening before. No. It had never happened before. I'd grown up ugly and I'd married ugly and I'd spent a lot of years being too disgusting to touch. And now men were looking at me with grins and a kind of love, because I was almost beautiful.

I know this sounds all out of kilter. I know I bought the suit and the dress that day with Edna. I know how I've described it ... looking at the girl in the mirror.

But I had never felt beautiful, or almost beautiful. Not in my whole life. Till that evening, sailing back across the strait, with the gulls circling and weaving overhead and people, men, grinning at me and laughing. Iris was right. It was only youth and I knew it, but youth is never 'only.' It was nothing I could take credit for, nothing I had accomplished or won. But I loved Iris for telling me before I was too old. How awful if now, for instance, she were to say, 'That summer you were twenty-seven, you were almost beautiful.' And I sat there with my coffee, thinking. But I must have been at least pretty then, when I was eighteen. I must have been, and all the years since, even when I was fat, if I'm almost beautiful now.

And then I thought, Oh to hell with it. I've found out before it's too late. I can be almost-beautiful for three more years, and then, when I'm old, at least I'll have known what it was like. For at thirty, of course, one's womb fell out, dropped with a great clank, like a rusty old carburetor, and everything was over. No one could possibly look at a woman of thirty.

I sat there and I thought, I'll love Iris till the day I die, and I might make it yet.

WHEN I GOT HOME (a lot of people offered me rides, but I took one with a nice married couple), Mik wouldn't speak to me. 'What have I done?' I kept saying, though I knew very well. And in bed, he punished me.

He sent me to Coventry. He turned his back to me and it was worse than anything.

'What is it? What's the matter?'

'You know damned well.'

I did. I knew. I had denied him.

'But you don't understand.'

'I understand.'

It occurs to me now that Mik might have been hurt about the phone call to the island. It stops me. Even writing the line stops me. I stare at it a few seconds. Well, what had I thought until now? I had thought it was a matter of principle—I had denied him, which is not done amongst friends or lovers. Mik was disgusted with me. Properly so. But hurt? Yes, he was angry, because I was such a chicken-shit, but hurt? Mik?

'You see, it was, well, it was a peculiar situation, just when you phoned. He had ... well, he'd just that minute asked me to marry him and I ...'

'You accept?'

'What?'

'You accept his proposal?'

'Oh for god's sake, Mik!'

'Yeah, well, tell me about it in the morning.'

'No. I want to have this out.'

'Look. I got to get my rest. I got to hustle a job tomorrow.'

'No, you're refusing to discuss this logically ...'

'I'm tired.'

'I'm going to tell him.'

But Mik was breathing heavily, rhythmically.

Jocelyn was getting ready to go, all her stuff piled into boxes for the Salvation Army. The grey blouse she'd worn for four years, a hand-me-down when it started; the black skirt I'd given her at Christmas. That was a pang. I stood there, pawing through the things and, in the end, salvaged the skirt.

Sala was being crated down at the freight office, and of the two kittens I'd given Jocelyn, only Lolly remained. Humbert had gone one night, telling me goodbye from the garden. 'What's the matter, you idiot?' I yelled out Mik's window. Humbert was standing right below the cat door; he could get in if he wanted. But he stood down there, yowling up at me in the moonlight. I knew it wasn't an ordinary cry. There are all kinds of cries, and this was different. But I just said, 'Oh, come on in,' and went back to bed.

And he went away. That day, in the afternoon, Jocelyn had picked Humbert up by the tail and swung him around, for the hell of it. Jocelyn never does things like that. It was so terrible, I hate to write it even now. And Humbert flicked his back paws fastidiously and went off to lick himself under the radiator. Thinking it over. We advertised in the papers, and offered rewards, but we never got him back. So now there was only Lolly. When she left, Sally and Peter would be alone.

The professor took me to lunch in the faculty club. I dressed carefully, trying to look sedate and mature with my hair done up. He came to the house and I introduced him to Mik. I told him just before we started lunch, after the martinis. I thought, Oh god! I would have to spoil his appetite, too! What a thing, just before he eats! But I wanted it over and done with.

At first, he was good about it. But then he said, 'I know these types. Basically, they despise women. Their true loyalties are always given to men friends. I saw this sort in the war. It's a form of homosexuality. And if they don't outgrow it then, in the war, it just carries on. I would bet you Mik has tremendous ties with old friends ... isn't it true?'

'Yes. From Ortona. They hang around beer parlours and remember the good old days.'

'You see? I could tell, the moment I saw him. He's what they call "A man's man," which means he can never really relate to a woman. You're a symbol to him, something to show his friends. And, basically, now that you've slept with him, he'll come to despise you for it. That sort of man is terribly romantic. There are two sorts of women for him: the kind who do and the kind who don't. And now that you have, he'll despise you, Vicky. He will. He'll knock you up and he'll probably beat you and then he'll walk out, because you're a slut anyway.'

'I sort of have trouble in that area myself.'

'What?'

'Oh, the slut-lady distinction.' I laughed. 'We're a lot alike, Mik and me.'

He drove me home, being terribly calm and wise. But at five o'clock he phoned from the island: 'You used me. You used me, you got me to introduce you to important people. You just used me. You used me all through university, to get the scholarship too. I got you that scholarship and I got you the teaching assistantship, and all along you've just been using me.'

It was terrible, to hear him humiliate himself like that. I kept saying I was sorry, over and over.

Jocelyn called a taxi and we stood together like strangers in the dining room. Everything looked dusty. 'I've done all I can,' she said, almost crying, 'but I've decided. I'm through with you, Vicky. I really am. You deserve everything you get!'

And she went out to the kitchen and emptied the tin bread box and started punching holes in it with a chisel and hammer.

'What's that for?'

'Lolly,' she said.

I let her do it too. I even helped. Punching holes.

And we put Lolly in, and shut the lid. I even let them get out to the taxi. I even let Jocelyn put the bread tin on the back seat. And then I couldn't help it, I rushed down the walk and grabbed the bread tin and opened it.

Lolly was already hot and dry and half asleep with terror.

'I'll send her,' I said. 'I promise. I'll send her. You can't, Joss. Look at her. She'd be dead before you got to Mission.'

And she could see it was true, and I could see she would never forgive me, and that was how she left, all the violence still between us.

THERE IS SOMETHING I've got to put in. I can't place it. It was when my mother was there. The three of us, Jocelyn, my mother and I, are in the dining room. There is music playing. A record on the hi fi. It is about seven o'clock at night, and suddenly my mother starts to dance. And Jocelyn is dancing too. And I am dancing. The three of us, like fools, dancing in a circle in the dining room, laughing, a little embarrassed, but dancing, going around and around, dancing, not alone but together, the four of us, Jocelyn, my mother, Francie, and me. It must have been after one of those awful strained truth sessions. I saw it happen in Greece once. A girl, Georgia, jumped up and began to dance and I jumped up too, not able to stop. In a tavern. And after, Maria, Georgia's friend, said, 'You see. Her brother. He was burnt to death by fire. Last week.'

And that was how we danced, Jocelyn, Francie, my mother, and me.

Francie? But Francie wasn't there that summer. Francie was somewhere else. Where was she then? That summer? If Mom was at my place, where was Francie?

It used to happen often, in the days after my father died. My mother would suddenly leap up, music on the radio, and begin to dance, and we children would dance too, all four of us, and would laugh at ourselves because of course it wasn't done, women dancing together.

And when it was over, Francie said, 'You're still the best, Mom,' and Mom laughed and said, 'At least I gave you all straight legs.' She is still the best, our mother. She outdances all of us. And she married a man whose religion forbids dancing.

Why did I have to put that in?

AFTER JOCELYN LEFT in the taxi, I took Lolly back into the house. It was so empty. The windows were filthy. The garden drooped. Dishes in the sink. Salvation Army boxes everywhere. Scum and crud and confusion. The end of the summer.

I don't remember. What happened then?

The buddies came over. Yes. And got drunk in the front room. I am upstairs marking papers. Yes. And Mik comes upstairs and says to come down. And I do, and one of the buddies, a fisherman who'd made it across the bridge, took hold of me and pulled me down beside him. 'Have a drink,' he says.

'Don't touch me!' I say, and pull away.

The buddy is surprised. He says, 'I wasn't going to hurt you.'

No one says anything about it. I have a beer and listen to them talk about the war. Mik is shooting me flashes of lightning. But I don't care. I'm tired. I am tired of the noise and the mess, the fake Sarukhan rugs are littered with beer bottle caps and ashes. Someone has spilled an ashtray.

'Well, I've got work to do,' I say and go back upstairs. The professor for whom I was marking had said, 'Just form not content,' as if you could mark one without the other. 'Fallacy of the Undistributed Middle,' I print in large red letters. 'Circular Argument.' 'Non Seq.'

Someone comes up and goes to the bathroom. I am just so immensely weary. It comes over me now, as I try to write it. That heavy, bored, moving-through-molasses feeling.

And I think, My god, I'm pregnant!

My god. When was my period? My god. I've missed it already. Dear God, I'm pregnant. Oh god, please God, if you let me off this time, I'll be good.

Caught. Up the stump. A bun in the oven. In the Family Way. Expecting. Knocked up. Stagnant.

Oh my god, I'll die. I'll kill myself. It's not true. It's just late. Is that a spot? I won't think about it. It'll come if I don't think about it. I've been upset, that's all. God, look? I know I don't believe in you, but if you just ...

My breasts ache. They are sore to touch, heavy and swollen. And I am so tired. Do I feel sick to my stomach? Oh god, yes I do. I'm caught. Oh the bastard. My life is ruined.

So much for my intensely maternal drive.

Mik calls up the stairs. It's the telephone. The professor's voice, thin and embarrassed, comes distantly over the wires: 'Vicky? I was upset. I know that's not true. What I said. I don't know what came over. Yes, I do know. I was furious. You and that ... thug. I still think you're wrong. I still think you're heading right for disaster, but I'm sorry for what I said.'

And I want to cry out, sitting there, with the buddies only feet away, 'You were right. I am pregnant! It's horrible. Help me.'

But I say, 'It's all right. It's all right.'

SIX MONTHS LATER, picking up some papers, I stop at his office and he says, 'Oh yes, it's Mrs uh ... it's Mrs Ferris, isn't it?' And is polite and distant. He forgot my name. In six months. I didn't understand it then, I don't understand it now. It happened.

WHEN THE BUDDIES LEAVE, I come down and start—my lips compressed like my mother's—to pick up the debris.

Mik says, 'You bitch.'

'They broke one of my glasses!' I say, discovering the shards.

'I'll break your fucking glasses!' Mik says and hurls another across the room where it shatters against the wall.

'So what am I supposed to have done now?'

'"Don't touch me!"'

'Well?'

'Don't you ever talk to a buddy of mine like that again. Never.'
He thrusts his fist under my chin.

'Look. I don't like being grabbed by strange men.'

'"Strange men."' He is really very angry. '"Strange men!"' And,
'That's my buddy!'

'Oh you and your buddies. What do you want me to do, lie
down for a gang bang? That's what you do, isn't it? Share and share
alike? God, any decent man would've told him to get his hands
off me.'

And Mik takes me by the hair and swings me around the room.
My feet ricochet against the mantel, knocking off a vase and
the candles.

He just grabbed my hair below the nape and swung. Zoom!
Centripetal force, baby.

It hurt like hell. But I have to laugh now, thinking of it. Zoom.
Ah Mik, you were lovely, yes you were. Are you dead?

And whee, he lets me fly. Thud.

Well, there goes the bath water, I say to myself.

But it isn't over yet. He grabs my hair again and drags me like
a sack across the floor and thumpety-thumpety-thump up we go.
Ho hum. Up the stairs. And screws me.

So what was new. God, I was tired.

What am I trying to prove anyway. Ah how I have suffered.
Nice little Anglican girl. What a terrible thing! Imagine.

But I get him. Boy do I get him.

I am sitting up in the middle of the bed, smoking furiously. I
say, 'Incidentally, it appears I am pregnant.'

That stops Mik cold. Ho ho. Thought I was dumb, thought I

couldn't take care of myself, hey? Frigging clot.

And, of course, love blooms eternal in the wasteland of the brutish heart. He stops punching me out and kiss, kiss.

'Ah,' he says and ... why can't I remember the name!

'It'll be a boy,' he says, going all mystical with the thrill of it. A man at last. Proof positive. God, I hate men.

He has him all dressed in a football uniform and taking little girls into the bushes. He has him swiping penny candy at the corner store. He has a real boy there, a real boy. 'Don't you give him poetry,' he says. 'Don't you turn him into a namby-pamby.'

'I don't actually see how it concerns you,' says I, puffing away madly.

'Har har de har har,' Mik says.

'No. I'm being perfectly serious,' and I am, sitting up stark starers, smoking like billy-oh.

'Put that out,' Mik says. All concern for the kid.

'Because, if you're interested, I have no intention of marrying you. Fart face,' I add.

That came out of the blue. Fart face. Yes, by god, I said it, like a jewel. I remembered that one. The perfect moment. Fart face. Oh you good little book, you bugger, you're going to do me in, aren't you?

'You'll marry me,' Mik says, smiling in a superior way.

'I'd like to see you make me,' says I.

'I'll drag you to the marriage bureau, if I have to,' he says.

'"Do you take this man to be your lawful wedded husband?" And I scream "No!" And then you hit me. I don't see the ceremony coming off somehow.'

He considers this. It hasn't really occurred to him before that he cannot make me marry him. Now it occurs. I can see the light bulb going on inside his head. Eureka.

'And if I'm unconscious or dead, they'll never sign the register,' I say.

After a while he says, 'I'll sue you.'

I double up and almost roll off the bed, I'm laughing so hard. I've never heard anything so funny, so beautiful, so fantastic.

'For what?' I shriek, when I get my breath. 'Maternity? You'll go down in history. The first man ever to bring a maternity charge!' It's hilarious. Oh lord, it's gorgeous. Ah sisters, we never thought of that one, did we? All the time we had it right in our crotch, the real solution. Back to Mycenae. Oh Zeus, watch out. Sisters, let us re-inaugurate the holy spring festival. Ride them in the ditches. Ah Pentheus, you bad boy, we told you not to peek. Rip snort chew him up. Here comes Mama with his prick in her mouth.

'That is beautiful,' I am saying. 'Oh lovely. Oh Mik! Good luck, you big stupid lug. Take me to court,' and I'm off again into peals of laughter. It's heaven. I've never enjoyed myself so much. I almost forgive it, this parasite, this worm, this leech, this real boy, sucking my innards.

'You can't get away with this!' says Mik, clenching his fists.

'Oh that's weak. Oh you can do better than that, a big strong male like you. You can surely do better than that, can't you? "You can't get away with this." Oh paltry!'

He says, 'I'll take you to court and prove you're an unfit mother.'

'So? So they take the kid away. They won't give him to you anyway.'

'There's blood tests,' Mik says. 'I can prove I'm the father.'

I'm becoming hysterical. 'Oh god, Mik, you're so funny!'

And, 'Unh uh uh.' Because he is making punch-out motions. 'Don't hurt the baby.'

I don't remember what happens next. I suppose we calm down.

Then there's the party for the actress. In West Van. An engagement party, and we're invited. Sherry and a swim before supper.

I go like Lady Godiva, daring anyone to make the slightest comment.

Mik behaves himself.

The blue blazer boys glance uneasily at him.

Splash, off the private dock.

The actress says, 'Vicky. You look smashing.' In my vulgar suit.

Mik's tattoos loud and clear in the evening air. He jumps in and stays up to his chin.

I go far out and wish I could drown, but I swim too well.

I say to him later, 'But I don't belong either. The welfare brat. I don't belong to the upper crust.'

But he doesn't believe me.

He stuck out like the proverbial. And everyone was terribly polite to him.

What a treatise on the Canadian social scene one could do, with paradigms of frigid courtesy. 'How interesting!' And, 'Logging must be fascinating work.' And, 'The outdoor life is so healthy, isn't it?'

I've heard it applied in various forms, this Canadian courtesy: 'Really? A PhD from where? Kalamazoo? Where is that exactly? Oh, a southern state? How interesting.'

Back in her bedroom, the actress says to me, 'It's folly, Vicky. Sheer folly.' We are getting dressed. 'But you'll probably get away with it. You can be put down as eccentric. Still, it can't go on too long, you know. Right now, it's a bit like parading a tame ape through Buckingham Palace. It's all right for you. You're Victoria Ferris, but isn't it rather hard on the chimp?'

And, 'Of course, he's really terribly attractive, in a way. I can see the appeal.'

And Mik goes on a bash. This time I do not look for him. I am fed up. I am tired. I haven't really written for weeks, months. I can't remember. I mark papers and I sleep. It is doom. I've had it. I'm caught. I wake up in the mornings and I think, 'I'm wet!' but it is only optimism.

I trot to the bathroom, casually, pretending not to care. Then I drop to the floor, sliding off the toilet seat, my pajama pants around my ankles, saying, 'God! God?'

We have had interminable talks, of course. Without laughter. I have said, 'Of course, you'll be fine biologically.' Pretending this really concerns me. 'But what sort of father will you make? How would he feel, seeing you swing me around the chandelier by my hair? Such gay moments can be terribly traumatic.'

Mik has been grinding his teeth a lot.

While Mik is out on the bash, I clean the house. It's a solitary four days. I wouldn't even mind seeing Paul. Or even Ben. But they are banished.

Edna comes over. With news of her own.

'My god,' Edna says. 'A medical student!' She has crabs. She has had to ask the druggist for blue gentian. 'He gave me such a look!'

Later she is to find out the medical student has given her more than crabs.

I don't tell her my glad news. It isn't true anyway. Was that a cramp? Hmm. Yes. Ignore it. I won't go and look. Let it be a surprise.

I tell Edna to iron her sheets. 'I heard it on CBC Matinee.'

'They said iron the sheets for crabs?' Edna says.

'No. For infections of any kind.'

'It's not an infection, Vicky. It's animals. Like creepy crawlies. It's horrible. I'll never live it down. Crabs!'

'You mean they look like real crabs?'

'Yes! Horrible. Ugh.'

And we giggle and shudder, two nicely brought-up girls, and all the time I'm thinking: It's not possible! He'll give it a switchblade before it's even latched onto the nipple. He'll throw it up and down to teach it to be tough. And all the wrong locutions. *Irregardless.* Yes, he says *irregardless!* It'll say, *I feel badly.* Tea with Grandma on Sunday afternoons, sitting on the red chesterfield with the silver threads. And Mik coming home drunk and me in a housedress with rips under the arms. Mik saying, 'You trapped me.'

It won't happen. I won't let it happen. I'll go to Timbuctoo. Or Toronto. But I'm so tired. God, Edna, go home, I'm so tired and in a minute I'll tell you. Edna go home.

And she does, saying, 'For god's sake, never tell anyone.' And, 'Do you think I should burn the mattress?' And 'Damn Sam anyway. I'll never forgive him.'

And one night the telephone rings and it's the hospital. The nurse says coolly, 'Mr O'Brien asked us to call you.'

'But what is it?'

She won't say. Her voice drips disapproval.

I walk down from the house. I'm furious. It's just like men, cowardly and weak. Go on a drunk and get yourself so sick you have to go into hospital. And then have the nurse phone. Oh yes, you're not too sick to make a dying request. And now I'm supposed to feel all guilty, eh? Oh you great weak cowardly clot. And your sister has a green Chinese girl on her wall too. I mean, that's in poor taste, Mik, that really is.

'You're the fiancée?' the nurse says. And I have to say it. Oh the bastard, he makes me say it or I can't get in to see him.

She takes me to a cubicle in the emergency ward. Curtains around the bed. People puking left and right. Calling 'Jesus.' Drunks and dope addicts.

He lies there, looking really vile. I have to admit it, he looks ghastly. But am I sympathetic?

'What idiocy have you committed now?'

He pretends to be unconscious, too far gone, his last gasp rattling in his poor throat.

'Don't pull that crud on me.'

He moans, fighting his way up through the blackness. I know it's a lie. He had to give the nurse my name and phone number, didn't he?

'So? What have you done now?' Just like Mom.

'Took some pills,' he says.

'Oh god! You tried to kill yourself? Oh god.' I am so disgusted you could scrape me off the floor. 'Congratulations. You have now been fully initiated into the Loyal Order of Victorian Victims. You and Ben should enjoy group therapy together. Well well. You do look charming. I just can't understand why you boys can't do a proper job of these things. Inefficient, I call it.'

'Threw up,' he says. 'Ulcer.'

It's true, he has a bleeding ulcer. There's a kidney pan on the bed table, looking rather messy.

'And you'd been destroyed by experts. Hunh!'

He starts to get mad. I can feel it stirring in him, his muscles bunching beneath the white coverlet.

'Get to hell out,' he manages.

'And you told the nurse I was your fiancée,' I say. 'You felt well enough to tell her to call me. You great phony. What a big phony. Oh no, you don't want me to feel sorry for you. Oh no. That's the last thing you wanted, wasn't it, me trotting down here all sorry for you. Oh no. Oh you great disgusting phony. "Don't worry about me. I've been destroyed by experts." Oh brother. You're just like Ben.'

'Go to hell,' he says, a little more firmly.

'You get up out of that bed, you clot, and come home.'

'Never want to see you,' he says, a fine thin shine of steel in his voice. That's my Mik.

'You rotten creep, what a bandstand play. You and Ben can do the libretto, with Paul on the piccolo. "How We Died for Queen and Country."' This catches my fancy and I elaborate, singing to the tune of 'America the Beautiful':

> Our little band of red coats
> So loyal and so true,
> We lived and died
> Without our pride
> And she can screw you too!
> Victoria! Victoria!
> She rules our native land,
> A sceptre in her navel
> And our balls in either hand.

He grunts. He is trying not to laugh. It's marvellous, I just keep making it up out of the blue.

> The thin red line of valor,
> We march on, side by side,
> And drop and fall,
> In honour all, The Noble Suicide.

The lyrics are getting weak, so I do the chorus again.

> Victoria! Victoria!
> Our belle dame sans merci.

It's hard to crawl without your ball,
But wait until you pee!

Mik guffaws. I am inspired. Doing it right off the top. I would
like to go back and rewrite the second stanza.

Oh trample us to ashes,
Oh trample us to dust,
We'd live for just a peek at
Her splendid royal bust.
Victoria! Victoria!
Eunuchs rise and stand!
A sceptre in her navel,
And our balls in either hand!

I've lost it, but it doesn't matter. He lies there, his eyes closed,
chuckling.

He says the name I can't remember. Then he snorts. Then he
says, 'Fuck off. I'm getting dressed.'

We walk home. I have refused to get him a taxi. Suffer, you bastard. You lousy crud. He can hardly stand upright, let alone shuffle.

Back at the house I get him into bed and make masses of black
coffee. He tells me the rest of the story.

'So Taffy and me, we got this gun, and I take a turn and he takes
a turn.'

'So what happened?'

'I don't know. It never went off.'

'You probably forgot to put a bullet in.'

'I put one in. Maybe Taffy took it out. We're in back of the
Helen's, and he's helping me. That Taffy.'

'What a buddy,' I say. 'What a friend, helping you commit

suicide. What's he want to die for?'

'Keep me company.' Mik's still not speaking very clearly. His eyelids are so puffed together he doesn't seem able to see. But he must be seeing because he says, 'Jeez, shut that light off.' And, in the dark, holding the coffee mug with both hands, 'So I took some Bennies and a twenty-six, and then I start to puke blood so they called the ambulance.'

'That's twenty-five dollars right there!'

'You got under my skin.'

'I thought you could take it.'

'I'd punch you out,' he says, 'but it'd hurt too much. Me.' And he laughs. I laugh too. It is all right.

He can't stay awake anymore. He lies there, a great baby, his mouth open, snoring gently. 'Oh I love you, you rotten crud,' I say, and I cry now, great crocodile tears, smiling and hugging myself. I sit and smoke, and watch him.

He wakes just once and says, 'You had to say. When you came in. You had to.'

'What?' but he's off again. I know anyway. I had to say I was his fiancée.

And I say to myself, Well? That's what you wanted, wasn't it? You imagined it just that way. 'I'm gonna give you a baby.' Wham bango, the whole bit. So what's all this tum terror in aid of? You got what you wanted, Vicky.

In three days he has a job and is off up North. Very businesslike with his duffel bag and his boots. It feels like he has won after all ...

Someone honks for him outside and he gives me a uxorious peck on the cheek and says, 'I'll call you.' And he's gone, away away into the world of men.

'WELL, YOU DIDN'T HAVE to go to the hospital,' the Nut Lady says. 'You didn't have to bring him home, even if you did go.'

'You don't understand,' I say.

'You'd better have a urine test,' she says.

'All right.'

'You remember? I'm going in a week.'

'That's all right. I'll be okay. I've got an idea for something.'

This is true. The Ivan-Wilma play is cluttering up my head. Odd bits and pieces of dialogue dropping like pennies. I'm getting that depressed feeling, I'm sitting around watching TV all day. It's a sure sign. I see the opening shot clear and bright: test-tubes in a refluxer going burble burble.

'I think maybe it's going to be funny,' I say. I feel shy.

'That'll be a change,' says the Nut Lady.

ONE MORNING I WAKE up and there's blood everywhere. Blood. Oh blood! Oh blood blood glorious blood. If I'd known you were coming, I'd have given up mud.

I am bleeding. I am not preggers, caught, up the stump, expecting. I am not.

Free.

In the meantime, like the Bobbsey Twins, Edna has discovered that the medical student gave her more than crabs. She phones and says, 'It's for tomorrow. Look. Can you come and stay overnight?'

So I go and we drink vodka and orange juice and mutter darkly about men. I tell her about Mik's suicide, and my close call with destiny.

'God. How bloody ironic,' Edna says.

'That's the operative word.'

'How did you feel?'

'I was scared to death.'

'Yes.' She is sitting there, looking terribly wan, her hair limp. 'Yes.'

'So much for my protestations of motherhood.'

'You wanted the other one,' Edna says.

'Yeah. Okay. Yes I did.'

'I don't want *his*,' Edna says, her eyes filling. 'He's just so damn *dumb*.'

I feel a bit scared when she says this. It's true. I didn't want Mik's. But not because he's *dumb*. Because ... oh god, I don't know. But I didn't want his.

Edna tells me she's had a brief affair with Paul. And that Ben chased her around the apartment.

'You're kidding! Ben?'

'I couldn't,' says Edna. 'It'd be like incest.'

Ben? Chasing a woman! For sex!

'He must have changed,' I say.

'He was all leery,' Edna says, half grinning, but eyeing me all the same. 'Does it bother you?'

'No. Sure. Nah. Yes. I don't know. Sure it does.'

'He's gotten all aggressive,' Edna says.

'He must have. So, how's Paul in the sack?'

'Surprising.'

'Yeah?'

'Really.'

'No kidding. Paul?'

'It's marvellous, until after. When he opens his mouth.'

'Don't tell me. He picks up your dangling modifiers!'

Edna giggles.

After a while, she starts to cry a bit, thinking of the baby so soft and safe, feeling comfy in there. Never dreaming what Mummy's up to.

'I know you don't approve,' she says.

'I know it's not the same. I mean, this time I really didn't ...'

'But you'd have gone through with it,' Edna says. 'Wouldn't you? I feel such a coward.'

I don't know what to say.

'I know. You think it's murder.'

I don't answer, and so she says, 'But for me it isn't, you know. It's not really alive yet. I mean, for me, it isn't,' but she is crying.

And then she wipes her nose and says, 'What really gets me is, he borrowed ninety bucks from me. I'll never see that again. And now $250 for this. He should pay half.'

'Damn right.'

'He won't though.'

'How did it happen, Edna, for god's sake.'

'He said he wouldn't come in me but he did anyway.'

'It isn't Paul's?' And she gives me a horrified look. 'Sorry,' I say.

'No, it's the med student's. I know. God, Vicky, what do you think of me?'

'Sorry. It's just you said ...'

'That was before.'

And she talks about her psychiatrist, who's arranged all this—good doctor, real operating room, nurse in attendance—and says, 'I'm sort of in love with him. I know it's only transference, but all the same ...'

'You know,' I say, 'what you said, about him coming in you, how it happened. I don't think anyone's ever told me before. I mean, ever said anything about what really happens. I mean, we never really say, do we? Oh we talk about good or bad or indifferent, or about orgasms, that stuff, but we never really say anything *real*. Like. In books. I mean, if you believed the books, it's all fire-crackers. Up like a rocket. Zoom.'

'That's because men write them.'

'Yeah. Well. No. I mean Henry James has one line, about white lightning, in *The Portrait*, but that's as close as I've ever come to reading about it, the way it is for us.'

Edna is embarrassed. 'Well, it's private, I guess.'

'Yeah, but listen, Edna, if you think about it ... I mean, we're really ignorant. Women don't *talk* to each other. I mean did your mother ever really tell you about birth control?'

'God no!'

'You see? Or about having more than one. Orgasms. You know?'

'Do you?'

'Now I do. Don't you?'

'Sometimes. I thought I was over-sexed. Sam says I am.'

'Maybe he's just saying that. Maybe there's a big conspiracy. Tell us we're abnormal if we do, then we'll be guilty. I mean, I've heard women talk about *not* having them. Like Wilma used to say it didn't matter if you loved a man enough, but what about the rest of us? Maybe it's not that we're the different ones, maybe we're in the majority. Only we're too scared to compare notes. Like, did you really know anything about your clitoris?'

Edna laughs.

'Well, I didn't. Don't. I mean, if you asked me to draw a diagram, I couldn't even now. Where and what happens, and all that. I mean, it's all a big mystery.'

So Edna draws a diagram and I put it in my purse to check it with myself, when I get back home and can use a mirror. 'I think that's right,' she says.

'All these years, you and Grace and me, and we've never really *said* anything. We don't know anything really. Like, I could never imagine what you meant when you said I should have trapped Ben. I mean, how could I? But then, I never thought that maybe every man didn't act like Ben. Like, Ben was normal for me, see? I thought that was *everybody*.'

'It makes me nervous, talking like this,' says Edna.

So we go to bed.

In the middle of the night, she shakes me awake. 'Vicky!'

'Hunh?'

'Hey Vicky.' All embarrassed. And I realize.

'Oh god,' I say. 'Oh lord. Edna!'

I've been making love to her leg! Arrrgh.

'I thought you were Mik,' I say. I've been dreaming of him.

'Yeah. Well,' she says, and laughs nervously. 'Too much sex talk, I guess.'

'I'm sorry.' And we each hang on our respective edges for the rest of the night, terrified we're lesbians.

In the morning, she is white with fear. One of those damn clichés you resent so much when they happen. The original lurid, ghastly pale, gleaming like the outside of my grandma's plum duff when she took it out of the boiling cloth. We walk up to Dean's and order pancakes. But Edna can't eat. She sits there, staring at the blueberries and the whipped butter. I don't know what we were thinking of, trying to eat at all. But that's what we do, order a full course of blueberry pancakes. She gets up suddenly and says she'll go on ahead.

'No, I'll walk you, for god's sake.'

'No, you're not finished.'

'I'll tell them to keep it for me.'

So we pay the bill and walk through the September morning light, up to the exclusive university homes area. Manicured lawns. Manicured lives.

'Is that his house?' We can't believe it. A big rich house. An expensive house.

'It must be. It's the address.'

And we stand there staring at it.

'You go back to the apartment. Here. Here's the key.'

I take it. 'Hey,' I say.

'Yeah.' She tries to grin. 'Hey.'

'Hey.'

'Hey. Hey, it'll be okay.'

'Sure. Hey.'

'Anyway, I'm zonked to the gills,' she says.

'How many'd you take?'

'About five.' She giggles. 'Won't feel a thing.'

And off she goes, up the curving walk past the neat flower beds to the grand front door. I know they're going to kill her.

They haven't kept the pancakes for me so I wander down to a shop and buy the brown pleated skirt and the forest green sweater. It's a beautiful golden day. The sky is blue and the trees have turned. The same sort of day when my father died. As if there were no harmony in the universe at all. Everything bright and fresh and impervious. I'm young and alive and not pregnant. Edna's dying on some illegal table, bleeding to death in a $100,000 house.

I go back to Edna's place and try to wait. Then I start washing dishes. Then I get out the vacuum. Then I clean the stove. I think about Mik and my nipples start up like traitors. Everything's in a conspiracy of life. She's never coming. They've killed her.

God, I say, I'll give Mik up, only let Edna live. Oh please, God, I know I don't believe in you, but just this once.

It's only eleven-thirty when she comes. The doctor has driven her home. She looks wonderful. Because she's breathing. I make her a cup of tea and she gets into bed.

'You've cleaned up,' she says reproachfully.

'Had to do something,' I say. I know it drives her mad. I show her the skirt and the sweater. She's shivering. She takes some more pills.

'It sounded so awful,' she says.

'Look. Vicky. Understand this. Look. I can only say it to you. Because you'll know. Will you leave me alone?'

'Sure.'

'He was nice,' she says, as if this is a surprise. 'Not what I expected. A nice man. I'm not rejecting you.'

'I know, for god's sake.'

I don't cry until I'm on the bus. Either.

And on the telephone to the island: 'It was all sound and fury, signifying nothing.' But he doesn't get it so I say, 'I'm not pregnant,' and everyone in the cookhouse hears. A radio phone. I've humiliated him.

Mik says, 'There's a house up here. You come up next Thursday.'

I say, 'Yes.'

I know. The Nut Lady's going. Maybe I'm doing it on purpose, to punish her. It sounds too easy to be true. It doesn't grab me. I don't feel sick when I say it.

I want him. I want Mik. And I say, 'Yes.'

I pack up my bags like a lady, nerves shrieking so high that only the mad dogs of the universe can hear. I've said that all before. I am calm. I am going to put myself into his hands. It is irrevocable. It is final. I am committing myself. A woman at last.

MAYBE IT'S ONE HUGE orgasm, this book. Maybe I just want to remember it once more before I go menopausal. Maybe I just want to feel young again and real and alive. The Victorian era. Repressed lust. But to the girdle do the gods inherit. Down from the waist they are centaurs. The fitchew nor the soiled horse goes to it with a more riotous appetite. The wren goes to it. Let copulation thrive.

Perhaps I shall go mad and run naked down the streets at night, waving my bum behind me like a flag. Perhaps I shall leap on beautiful young men, a moustache on my lip. Oh god, it's not fair to grow old. It's not fair. I hate it. I really do.

THAT DAMN PLAY. That damn clever play. I sat there like a zombie, clackety-clacking in the misty mornings in the shadows beside the lagoon. The fire going out. The cats went berserk in the forest. And I wrote a clever little story about civilized people doing uncivilized things to one another. And Mik would come home, and there wouldn't be any supper.

'I was working, I didn't notice the time.'

We've never talked about the writing. He's never seen me at it. He's never seen me in it. Perhaps he thought it was something cute and feminine I did, like crocheting doilies.

'For christ sake!' And he bangs around, opening cans of beans.

CLACKETY-CLACK. Anna says, 'Here, I've written a story.'

'Once upon a time there was a little girl and nobuddy liked her not even at school, the raisin was she alwass said jest a minit.'

'Who says, "Just a minute"?' But she won't tell me.

'Sometimes I think that'll happen to me,' she says. 'I'll be writing my stories and I'll say "Just a minute."'

'Oh lord, is that me? Do I say "Just a minute"?'

IN MY DREAM last night: Jocelyn comes in shorts and a very brief top. A red-headed baby on her back in a carrier. She says, 'The Jaks came over.' I take the baby and hold it against me. It is very hard and solid and it laughs at me. 'You don't know anything!' Jocelyn says. She is very brown and her hair is caught up in the back with a rubber band. She looks Amazonian. 'You sound like Francie,' I say, but hate like fire is coming from her mouth.

'All right, what are the Jaks?'

'You don't know anything,' Jocelyn says. 'You live here and you never go out and you think you know everything.'

'Well, tell me then. What are Jaks?'

'I see,' she sneers. 'From your great height, you will condescend to ask what are Jaks. I see. They sound the Alert and the Jaks come over and you say, "What are Jaks?"'

'Is it some American plane?' I say. 'Have they attacked?'

She sneers and starts to get ready to go.

I think, Oh, she mustn't leave him. The red-headed baby. But I want to keep him. Oh Jocelyn, I say, but not aloud, you're his mother. I hope she leaves him anyway.

But no, she hoists him into the carrier and she is gone with one last look of disgust in my direction, a long-legged brown girl with a baby on her back.

And Francie comes and she too has a baby.

'But didn't you have the abortion?' I say.

'Yes. I never knew about this,' she says.

'But weren't you worried?'

'Why should I worry?'

She too is impatient. I hold the baby. It too has red hair. But of course that can't be. Jocelyn took the other one. This one is hard and solid and he laughs at me.

Francie slams about. We are in some sort of farmhouse kitchen.

255

Crowded with broken furniture. She too is disgusted with me. I hope she will leave her baby, but I doubt it.

She looks so thin and tired, Francie. I want to feed her and make her have a nap before she leaves, but I know I mustn't say anything.

I hold the baby against me and she comes for it. She too has a carrier on her back but before she can leave I am in some large stone place. Arches. And two men are saying hello. And then I have to be introduced. There are suddenly many people. Men and women and children. Children in Orlon fur coats. I try to remember all the names but I can't.

'Yes!' cries one of the men and he is holding the book.

'But what place is this?' I say.

And it is quiet and only one man remains. The other has taken the book.

'But you contacted us,' the man is saying.

'Yes, I did,' admitting it. 'But what is this place?'

And then I know. It is a monastery. For men. And women. And children.

And I cry, 'Give it back. They won't understand. They'll burn it. They'll take out the God.'

But he smiles and says, 'It is a very religious book.'

And the children rush by in their Orlon fur coats, and now they have leather webbing across their chests. They carry rifles. They run by and I think, Yes, it would be practical, Orlon. They smile at me and call out. It is war then, the Americans have attacked and we are all guerrillas.

I sleep with the children, so many children. They are very gay and they tell me where the bathroom is. But I cannot sleep. I keep going out to the large flagstone hall and I wake all the children up. I don't mean to. But they are all up now and it's all my fault.

AT CHRISTMAS, Francie says, 'You have a very selective memory, Vicky.' I take things out of context, she says. I twist them to fit my meaning.

And Jocelyn says, 'You can't even stand it about Daddy.'

'What do you know about Daddy? You were six.'

'He was weak.'

'He was not weak.'

'See?'

I AM TEN AND Jane Broughton says to me, 'They caught Errol Flynn doing it.' We are standing in front of Miss Darling's. Looking in the window at the home-made teapot covers crocheted in bright wool. The baby sets. Doilies. Useless pot holders, not for heat, for decoration.

'Caught him doing what?'

'Making a baby.'

'What was he doing?'

'He was sitting on this lady's stomach. That's how they make babies. They're going to put him in jail.'

I walk over to Mom's. Where was I living then?

'Is this true?' I say, stern as Jehovah.

She gets all scared in the face. 'But I've only done it twice, for you and Joss.'

I am very disgusted with both of them. Her and Daddy. I think of my father sleeping in his long soiled underwear.

'You can forgive a person for making a mistake. It was only twice. It's all right if you do it for a baby anyway.'

He has come in but we haven't heard him. In his shiny leather jacket and his cap. When I leave to go back to wherever I'm staying, he catches me up on the sidewalk and walks me home.

'About what you were sayink,' he says. He stumbles over the theta too, so that he says, 'It's nuffink.'

'About your mother and me,' he says. 'We've done it lots of times.'

I am too disgusted to speak, and burning with shame for both of them.

'It's actually pretty wonderful,' he is saying. We are passing St. Jerome's and he says, 'It's like, when you're in church, see? And the choir's singink and you look up and the light's comink through the stained glass window. You know that feelink?'

'Um.'

'Well, it's a bit like that. Only physical. It's the closest we get with our bodies. It's really beautiful.' He stops, ready to turn back, not wanting to see my grandfather. 'You'll understand when you're older. It's not dirty, you know. Don't you ever think it's dirty. Okay?'

'Okay.'

As he turns away, I say, 'When can I come home?'

'It's your mother,' he says. 'I want you home.'

But Momma says it's him.

I SAY TO Jocelyn, 'You didn't really know him.'

BUT THERE'S ANOTHER STORY. Yes. One day I go up on the hill and a man comes to the horse. Yes. I am standing there because of a horse. And the man asks me if I know a Mrs Hoar. I do, she's one of the teachers at school. But I don't have her. The man says the Mrs Hoar he's thinking of has a lot of girls living with her.

He shows me what looks like a milk bottle cap. He asks me if I know what it is. I say, Is it a milk bottle cap?

The dog is with me and when the man reaches, the dog growls and I say, very politely, I must go now. And run like hell, not knowing why.

And I tell Grandma and she tells Aunt Carrington and they laugh a lot in a funny way and say I'll have to tell Daddy. So I go over and tell Daddy, feeling rather important about it now.

My father becomes furious. I've never seen him so mad. He will do this and that, he will kill the man if he ever gets his hands on him.

I come out on the porch to go home and there the man is. Walking by the house. He sees me and I see him. I go back inside and say, He's out there. Going down the street.

My father rushes out. But when he comes back he says, Are you sure?

The man he's seen is Mr Chesterman. Mr Chesterman owns a big electrical firm. He got a VC in a war. He's in the PTA.

And my father doesn't do anything.

Years later, I see the man again, walking with Mom on Sunnyside. 'There's Mr Chesterman,' I say.

'Where?' Mom says. 'Where?'

'Right there,' I whisper. I am cold all over.

And when he has passed us, Mom says, 'But that isn't Mr Chesterman.'

'But that's the man,' I say.

'Oh Vicky,' Mom says. 'Daddy must have seen Mr Chesterman. That day. Oh, and all these years every time I've seen Mr Chesterman I've thought such things about him.' She thinks about it. 'What if we'd brought a charge!'

'But I could have said it wasn't Mr Chesterman.'

JOCELYN SAYS, 'He was weak, Vicky. Why won't you admit it?'

I FINISH THE STORY about Wilma and Ivan. It's late October. I say, 'Want to read it?'

He whips through it very fast.

'Yah,' he says, putting it down. 'I like more blood and thunder myself.'

'More blood and thunder? But there's a lot of violence there.'

'Yah. But I like, you know, I like it more *real*.'

'Real?'

'You know. They all just sit around and talk. Why doesn't he punch her out?'

'What he does is worse.'

'It's all words,' Mik says scathingly.

My lovely funny vicious play.

'Like, I like it when it's real, you know. I mean, I guess you got to do it this way for the CBC. I can see it's right for them if you want to sell it.'

YEARS LATER, WHEN it's finally done, a critic says, 'Nobody talks that way.'

'BUT DON'T YOU SEE, Mik? He does it all without ever losing his temper or being rude or anything. He does it without even knowing he's doing it. It's terribly violent, underneath.'

THE CRITIC SAYS, 'How can you have any sympathy for such disgusting people?'

'YAH,' MIK SAYS. 'I guess it's high brow all right. I guess that's what they want. I mean, if you want to sell it.'

'It'll never work,' I say. 'You and me.' And as I say it, I feel it. The cold enters my marrow. It's true and I have said it. It's out there like a dead baby.

And Mik goes away next day to the place where they get supplies. In a motor boat. With a buddy. They are gone a very long time. I hear the boat coming back about six-thirty at night. When he comes in, his face is hard and shiny. He is dripping wet.

'What happened to you?'

'Fell off the dock.' He is swaying slightly.

'Oh you're drunk.'

'That's right. Bitch.' And he beats me up.

I believe it this time. I believe him when he says he'll kill me. I think, I'll pretend I'm mad. The Arabs don't kill idiots or lunatics.

And I pretend I'm mad, like Ophelia.

'Is he dead?' I hear myself say. 'He's not dead. They'll find him. I won't believe it. Is he dead? Don't bring him in the house.'

And, 'He said he'd take me too. He said. He promised.' It comes out like a wail.

Mik stands there, soaking wet, and his hand stops coming at me. But it is too late. I am really back there now.

I am in the hallway. Grandma's hallway. The floor is polished.

I am saying, 'Both of them? Not both of them. Don't bring him in the house.'

I am in the back porch. Mrs MacDonald is coming down the stairs. She is saying, 'Poor child.'

'Are they coming? Will they bring them in here? All wet?'

Aunt Carrington is out in the back lane. 'Don't touch me,' she says. 'I can hear it coming. Here they are.' She stands there for a long time. Nobody can get her in. She keeps hearing the bug coming. The bug. A cut-down Model-T, painted white. A black eagle on the door.

'Where are they?' This to Aunt Foster. I am in Aunt Carrington's patio. And Aunt Foster says, 'Don't. Someone's got to stay sane. Someone's got to hold on.'

'But where are they?'

'Heaven,' she shrieks as if she wants to kill me.

'No, I mean, where. In the water? Are they still in the water?'

But she doesn't answer. The sky is blue. The clouds are high and fluffy. A perfect day. For sailing.

Grandpop is getting out the brandy. He doesn't cry. Not now and not for a long time. One day I hear something. I can't find it. I look everywhere. But Grandma is sleeping and Aunt Carrington is unconscious from the dope. I find it at last. Grandpop. In the shop. Grunting with it. 'Go away.'

'I have to be the strong one,' says Aunt Foster, her eyes mad.

My mother is at the doorway to my room. She cannot speak. She looks at me from the doorway and then goes away.

'Don't touch me,' says Aunt Carrington, very reasonable. 'I can hear them coming now.' No one can get her in from the back lane. She pushes them away and stands there, waiting.

I am burying the dead chickens. The maggots are crawling everywhere.

'Both of them?'

Someone is saying, 'Lie down.'

'No. Both of them? Don't bring him in here.'

I see the clothes lying on the floor. Wet clothes. I hear a scream.

It is myself screaming. Someone says, 'I hit you too hard. Lie down.'
It is Mik. It is Mik. He is alive.

'Where ...'

'Lie down. I hit you too hard.' He holds me in his arms, but I know they are coming. He lights a cigarette for me.

'What?'

And a long time later, I say, 'Nineteen days, for Jason. Seventeen for Daddy.'

'I missed the dock,' Mik is saying. 'I fell in. That's all.'

'I made it up, you know. To stop you. I only made it up.' But I am the girl who cried wolf. My made-up wolf came and ate me.

'Yah. I forget you're such a little guy. I hit you too hard.'

I trace the letters. CREAM COFFEE. 'What does it mean?'

'Go to sleep.'

'What does it mean? I don't understand.'

'Go to sleep.'

I SAY I MUST GO BACK and pay the rent, the bills. I have an appointment with the Nut Lady. I leave the cats as hostages. Mik knows I wouldn't leave them if I weren't coming back to the island. He knows I know he'll kill them. I do it on purpose. I leave them there and I know I'm never coming back.

A boat takes us to Powell River. We stay overnight. The hotel.

'Come on down,' Mik says. I can hear them below. The men. In the beer parlor.

I am lying in bed in my underwear. I have a headache.

Mik stomps out. A few minutes later he comes back with a buddy.

The door opens and Mik comes in. The buddy comes in after him. Grinning. Mik grabs the top of the chenille bedspread. Beige.

Pulls it down. I lie there in my underwear. The buddy turns to leave but Mik grabs him.

'Look at her!' he says.

'Ah Mik, she doesn't want to.' Doesn't want to what? What is happening? I do have a headache.

'What's happening?'

The buddy goes away and I get up and get dressed. I think he's mad because I won't go to the beer parlor. So I get dressed and say, 'All right. I'll come.'

But when we get downstairs, it's closing time.

'Why did you get me up if you knew it was closing time? I don't understand.'

I DON'T EITHER. It doesn't occur to me what might have been happening until just this moment. But surely not. But what did the buddy mean?

WE GO BACK upstairs to bed. Mik is very quiet.

'I'm sorry. I really do have a headache.'

'Yah.' He is smoking in bed, staring up at the ceiling.

'Mik?'

'Go to sleep.'

Mik is coming back to town with me. On Monday he goes back, I'm to come up by plane on Thursday. I say so. I promise. I lie.

THE NUT LADY SAYS, 'Well? Are you satisfied?'

'What?'

'Have you been punished enough?'

'What?' I don't seem to be able to understand anything anyone says.

'I said you'd do something. To punish me. Yourself.'

'What?'

I phone him on the radio telephone. 'I have to stay in, for tests. At the clinic. They say I've got to stay in for tests.' All code of course. I don't want them to know Mik has a mad wife. In the cookhouse.

'Yah. Okay then.' He sounds uninterested. Because of the cookhouse.

He says goodbye and I say goodbye and we hang up. I wonder if he'll kill them now. Peter. Sally. Lolly.

The house smells of decay.

I look for an apartment. Edna comes with me.

Three rooms, with an entrance onto the garbage cans. I share the bathroom with an old lady, Mrs Leigh. She locks the door on my side when she goes to the toilet; I lock it on hers, when I go.

But I am to forget. I often lock her out and drive her mad. The bedroom window is painted over. One house away are the railway tracks. The front room window stares out at a window across the way. But at least it's on the first floor. The stairs so rickety that one day they swing away from beneath my feet. Fifty dollars a month. I can move in on the twenty-first. The twenty-first of December. What has happened to November? I don't remember.

Ben comes over. I ask him to help me move on the twenty-first.

Mik phones. He's coming down. I don't ask him. I know they're dead.

He'll be here at five. I have nothing in. I go out and get two TV dinners. The house is filthy. Cold. Mildewed. I haven't bought any briquettes. I use an electric heater in one room. In the front room. In the kitchen. In Jocelyn's bedroom. Moving it from place to place. At a quarter to five, I can't stand it. I leave the house and walk around the block. Coming up the back stairs. Into the empty house. He isn't here yet.

I stand in the kitchen and I wait.

I hear him coming up the front porch steps. Not loudly. Not Mik. The door opens. Closes. I hear him put his stuff down.

He comes into the kitchen.

Then I hear them.

'Oh Mik. You brought the cats.'

'Sure.'

I let them out of the Mexican basket and they run around, sniffing, recognizing everything. I had not even put out their dishes. I was so sure.

'What did you think I was going to do with them?' But he knows. And I know. We move painfully through the dusk. 'Jesus,' he says when I take out the TV dinners.

We are like two ambulance cases, tender with each other. Death is a ghetto too, and we are buddies here.

He doesn't go back up north. He goes on a bash.

Ben helps me move. I think Ben always did the moving. I always got sick. Yes. And this time I go in hospital the same morning, to get out of moving. Oxygen tent, cortisone intravenously. Ben stands there beyond the frosted plastic and says, 'I'm staying in your new place. To take care of the cats.' He is there. In my new place. I haven't even slept there myself yet.

Christmas Eve. Beside me, a woman is dying. There are twenty-eight beds on the ward. She cries, 'Jesus, Jesus,' and everyone yells, 'Oh shut up.'

Down at the other end, a woman thinks she is having a baby. 'It's coming! I can feel the head. OOOh. That's the head.' She is ninety.

I lie there and it is warm and wet now in the tent. It is cold only at first. I breathe through water. Up above the bottle drips. They haven't been able to find any more veins, so it is in my finger now.

The woman beside me will not die gently. She is not glad to go. They give me a pill so I won't hear.

But I stay awake with her. It takes her until three o'clock Christmas morning. It is very noisy, her death. She rattles and fights all the way. 'Oh Jesus,' she cries and people mutter, 'Oh for christ sake, shut up.' She says, 'Help me.'

I feel embarrassed for her.

Down the ward: 'It's coming, Nurse. Nurse! The head's coming.'

The woman beside me dies at last. Something spills. I hear it splash. She dies saying, 'No.'

After a while the flashlight comes. The nurse looks. Then the men come and take the woman away. And two more nurses come and clean up the bed. And the floor. Moving quietly on the morn of our saviour's birth.

When they have gone, I unzip the tent, and pull out the needle.

The nurse finds me in the bathroom, smoking.

'What in hell do you think you're doing?'

And I am hustled back, threatened with a restrainer, plugged in, zipped up.

Christmas Day. Mik comes. His face is all scratched. He stands there, looking embarrassed for me. He puts a present down on the bed. The bag says London Drugs. He takes it out and shows me, through the plastic. A salt and pepper set in phony plastic wood. I don't speak and he says, 'Well, I better go.'

I could have spoken. The asthma isn't that bad. But I am so tired. It is too late. There is nothing to say.

I take a taxi to the new place on January 4. Ben is firmly ensconced. He has arranged everything artistically. He is cooking something macrobiotic in the kitchen. The cats look healthy.

'The landlady over at the old place? She came when I was moving you. She said you have to pay damages. She said everything was in perfect condition when you moved in.'

We laugh.

I thank him for the cats. He goes, suffering for me.

'Anytime you need me,' he says. He has taken a place near me. A studio. He can get over in minutes if I need him.

The hi fi is rigged up and there is food, even meat, in the fridge.

In the letters: 'I have just read your masterpiece in the barber's chair. I laughed so hard I nearly got my throat cut.' They pay me for the play. But they never do it.

Mik comes over and we make love but it is different. 'Shh,' I say. He's across the bridge. The other way. Back at the hotels.

He comes over too often. I say, 'Look, this isn't a coffee house.' And, 'Look. I'm working.'

I pack up Lolly and send her to Jocelyn. But she sets up such a fuss, crying all the time, that Jocelyn sends her back again. Always was a bitcher, that cat.

I got the washer fixed yesterday and she tells the man such a story.

'What are they doing to you?' the man says, bending to stroke her. 'Don't they feed you then? Aw.'

I FIND OUT WHY I had to put that in, about Momma dancing.

We go to Francie's. We phone Mom. The four of us on the line: Anna, me, Francie, Mom. Mom says, 'We're going to a shindig tonight.'

'You're going dancing?' I say.

'Yes,' and she laughs.

'Fred's going dancing?' I hear Francie say on the extension.

'Sure,' Mom says. 'He likes it.'

And later, up at the cabin, Francie says, 'But I was there, that summer.'

'You weren't there,' I say.

'Yes, I was. I was with you for months. Don't you remember? I was going to live with you.'

'You were there that summer? You saw Mik?'

'Sure. I was there the whole time. Don't you remember?'

No. I don't. She wasn't there that summer.

'Don't you remember, I climbed out the bathroom window and you said I was "putting it on,"' Francie says.

'I what?' but it starts to come back. No.

'When I climbed out the bathroom window,' Francie says. 'You said I was "putting it on."'

'You saw Mik?' It's not possible. 'You were there?'

'Of course I saw Mik. I was there that summer. Don't you re-member? All those weirdo friends of his? Getting drunk. That one, the abortionist, telling us he'd protect us from Mik? Mik was dan-gerous? My god. And Mik ripping out the telephone? And Joss calling the police?'

'I don't remember,' I say.

But this morning, at six, I get up, stagger around looking for cigarettes. All right. All right, godammit, I'll remember.

Francie lumbers out fifteen minutes later. 'What's wrong?'

'I always get up at this time. Tell me about the bathroom window.'

So we sit in front of the phony fireplace, drinking coffee, suck-ing on air to make fun of our nicotine hang-up, and Francie tells me about the bathroom window.

'I think I had flu or something. I was in Joss's room, and Mom

269

was in Mik's bedroom with Bert.'

'Not with Bert! They didn't sleep together.'

'Oh well, maybe. But they had been, you know.'

'No. She didn't until after she saw me with Mik.'

'That's a lie,' Francie says. 'She slept with him, she didn't live with him, but she slept with him. Anyway, I woke up and the bed cover was *huge*. Like, magnified a thousand times. I could feel all the fibres, under my fingers. And the bones in my hand, beneath the skin. When I went to the bathroom, I could feel the wood beneath my feet. So coarse. All the texture had changed. I was in the bathroom and I didn't think, I'm going to kill myself, I just thought if I could get out into the air ... You and Mik were sleeping in the basement.'

'Oh yes.'

'And so I did, and Mom came to the door and said to let her in, but I said no, I said, "Go away." I knew I was hurting her but I couldn't help it. Everything was so coarse.'

'Do you hear what you're saying? Coarse? I mean, not just in terms of texture.'

'Oh yes,' Francie says. 'Yes. It was Joss who got me to open the door, with her librarian's voice. "Now, Francie, it's going to be all right. Open the door now, Francie." I wouldn't have for you or Mom. Not for either one of you.'

'Yes. Now I remember. I know why I forgot too. I hadn't taken care of you.'

'Have you put in the gun?' she says.

'No. It was duplicated. I mean, I show my attitude toward stolen goods in another part.'

'But you've got to put in the gun.' She turns to her friend, a quiet Japanese-American. 'There was this gun. A real high-powered gun, with all sorts of complicated dooeys on the top. I found it.

Vicky sent me upstairs to Mik's room, and I found it in the dresser.'

'You found it?' I say, still not believing she was there.

'Sure. And Vicky, she wrapped it up in a tablecloth.'

'My god!' I cry, 'a plastic tablecloth, all done in lace!'

'And she put it across the handlebars of her bicycle and rode down to city hall, and took it right in the door and past the commissionaire and ...'

'Not in the door,' I say, 'up to the door.'

'But why?' he says.

'It was hot,' Francie says.

'I didn't want him to get in trouble. He'd stolen it. Or one of his buddies. But you know what I remember? I remember how you all, you and Mom and Joss, how you all sort of sneered when I came back, feeling pleased with myself.'

'Oh you have to put the gun in,' says Francie, 'it's important.'

And she goes on to say that she and Joss had it all figured out. A man had been killed. It was in the newspapers, he had had a collection of rifles. And they were missing.

'I don't remember that. What I remember is ... people honking at me on the way to City Hall. And I thought they were honking because the wind was blowing the tablecloth away, and they could see the gun. But after, when I was riding back, people were still honking, and I realized I was wearing that brown and white dress with the polka dots? And I had no slip on underneath!'

'*What* did you do with the gun?' he says.

'I put it beside the door of City Hall.'

Francie says, 'You know. That summer. Not because you were my ideal or anything, but because it was true, you were really attractive.'

And she climbed on the bathroom windowsill and wouldn't answer the door because the world was coarse. I was coarse. My mother was coarse. Only the air would be finely textured again.

'I didn't take care of you. That's why I couldn't remember. I couldn't remember your being there. I was sure you weren't there. And then, in the book? I put in this part? Where we were dancing? All four of us. You and me and Joss and Mom. All of us dancing, and I couldn't figure it out, how were you there?'

'I remember that,' Francie says.

'You remember the dancing?'

'Oh yes!'

I am quiet for a while, staring into the gas flame that never eats the pretend logs. I think, but how did Mik and I? All that *sex*. With Francie in the house. But I don't ask her.

Instead, I say, 'So, how is it in bed?' Not her and the Japanese-American, but her and the new one. John.

She giggles. 'Good. Fantastic!'

'I never asked you before you got married. I never asked you the important questions.'

'Only, when I first saw it, his dong, I said, "No way!"'

'But was it okay?'

'Yes. Fantastic.'

'Well, you know,' I say, 'it stretches.' And I draw a diagram on the rug. 'Three-quarters more, if you reach a state of excitation.'

'What? The clitoris?'

'The clitoris!' I look at her, my swinger sister who tried to hide last night when she was smoking a toke. From me! 'The clitoris? The vagina!'

'Does it?'

Is it possible? Is she as dumb as I was? 'Yes, of course, if you're relaxed. If you're "flexible."'

'Maybe that's it,' Francie says. 'If I relax, if I'm flexible, it will be okay. I won't push the Reject button.'

'Yeah.'

'*How* much does it stretch?'

'Seventy-five per cent. And the front clamps down. Like this.' I squeeze the diagram and the rug strands lean together.

'No kidding. So that's why it didn't hurt. You know, after the divorce, the doctor said I was almost *intact*. I was so *small*. But with John, it didn't hurt. Not at all. And then, he wasn't like most men, he didn't need it to hurt.'

'He sounds all right.' And then I say, 'Look, do you need any money?'

I SAY TO MIK, that spring in the apartment, 'Look. I've got to get this done. Let's hold down the coffee shop visits for a few days. I'll call you.'

I've forgotten what this is. Whatever it is, it has me in its clutch. Aunt and Uncle Forbes are here, and I go with them to Stanley Park once, but I begrudge the time, the loss of intensity. I move about the cages like a zombie, my head full of words. They are staying somewhere. I forget. A hotel.

I work. I don't call Mik. I fall into bed exhausted. I get up. I work.

The telephone rings. I stagger out to the desk. In a pair of old flannelette pajamas. I see the clock.

'It's two o'clock in the morning!'

'You said you'd call.'

'Mik, it's two o'clock. I was *asleep*.'

'I been waiting.'

'Mik, I was *asleep*. It's two *o'clock*.' It's all I can think of. Indignation rises in me like a pure column of flame. 'It's two o'clock in the *morning!*'

273

'You said you'd call. I been waiting.'

And then I say it the second time. 'Go fuck yourself.' I mean it precisely. 'Go fuck your *self*.' I know what the words mean now.

And I hang up and go back to bed. Falling asleep instantly. Innocent as angels.

Mik comes right through the door. He just comes through it. When I see it later, it is knocked clear off its hinges, and there is a great clean gash of wood where the lock used to be. Someone has leaned it up against the wall by the time I see it.

Mik tells me much later that he threw the knife away as he came down the road.

The man who lives upstairs comes down and stands on the back porch and listens. He is afraid to do anything. He doesn't want to get involved. 'I thought maybe it was a lovers' quarrel,' he says later. 'The language was terrible.'

I don't remember the language. I remember Mik saying, over and over, 'You're just like my mother.'

It is hard to remember pain. When you're in it you don't want it. There is something terribly degrading about pain. It makes you into something sub-human, something just wanting to be let go. A shriek of Let Me Go. You'd press all the buttons in the world, and a hundred million Chinamen would die and you wouldn't give a damn, if only It will stop. Sartre says you never know whether you're a coward or not until you face torture. Well, I'm a coward. I'd have named names, sacrificed the whole world, even my family. Other than that—knowing that—I don't remember. I remember thinking, with a sort of surprise, that I hadn't lost consciousness. I thought you did, if it got too bad.

I remember not wanting to die. That is very clear. I do not want to die.

And then it is over. Mik is gone. I am up. I am wearing a blue blouse. God knows how I did that. Or why. The landlord is standing in the kitchen. He is saying, 'This sort of thing can't go on.'

I laugh.

The police come.

I phone Edna and then a cab. I go to her place. It is dawn now. The birds are chittering as I walk around to the back where her door is.

'Your face!' she says when she opens the door.

I have been beaten up. It happens to women. I've read about it. I thought it had happened before. But it hadn't. Not a real beating up.

I am afraid of Mik. I've never been afraid of anyone in my life. Not that way. Not in my bones.

I go back in the morning. The door is still up against the wall. The telephone is ringing. It rings and rings and rings. It doesn't stop.

The mirror is broken. In the eight dollar vanity. Yes. He brought back the bull and threw it against the mirror. The ear is gone.

Walking down Robson Street. Mik sees it in a window. A carved wooden bull. Red wood. A beautiful thing. So expensive. And I go back, the next week, and buy it for him. Now he has thrown it in the mirror.

I pick up the ear.

The telephone rings and rings. It doesn't stop.

I go down to the corner and phone Uncle Forbes' hotel.

They come.

Uncle Forbes says, 'A man doesn't do that unless he has a reason.'

Aunt Forbes says, 'Well, Vicky said he's got a silver plate in his head. From the war.'

Uncle Forbes says, 'You must have encouraged him.'

Aunt Forbes says, 'Vicky was just trying to be kind. He just got the wrong impression.'

275

She says I must go home to my mother.

I telephone the Nut Lady to say I am leaving.

'I think you'd better come out and see me,' she says. She sounds cross.

I sit there in her office and she is very far away, and very tall. Elegant and tall and her mouth purses like my mother's. 'You'll have to charge him,' she says.

I shake my head. 'Go home,' I say.

'No,' she says. And for an instant, she looks almost frightened. But then she is herself again. 'I'm going to lay it on the line, Vicky. Either you charge him or you're out on your ear. I'll have nothing more to do with you.'

I go away. The landlord is fixing the door. Aunt Forbes says she will call the head of the clinic. A friend of hers. She will protest such nonsense. 'The man is dangerous.' She prescribes poultices.

Her friend tells her he never interferes in his therapists' cases.

I go over to Edna's and sit around.

Finally I go down to the police station.

'Were you living common law?' says the man at the desk.

'Not now,' I say. It hurts to speak. Everything hurts. 'Before.'

He shrugs. 'Look, lady. I've seen this sort of thing before. You'll charge him and then you'll change your mind.'

I think maybe he is right. I go away without signing the form.

The door is fixed. The lady across the way calls to me: 'Your phone has been ringing and ringing.'

I feed the cats.

Aunt Forbes phones the Nut Lady. 'She can't just stay here in this apartment, all alone.' She won't believe it's my fault.

'He's a criminal. He should be put away,' she argues.

'I've been in the Army myself,' Uncle Forbes says, eyeing me speculatively.

'Don't be silly,' Aunt Forbes says. 'You know what Vicky is. Always taking in stray cats. And then, she's a divorcée. He just got the wrong idea. Men do, they get funny ideas about women who are divorced. It's a shame you had to take men boarders, couldn't you have got a woman?'

'He answered the ad,' I say.

'Well, you keep those poultices on,' she says. 'It's really just bruises. Your teeth will probably firm themselves.'

'She was lucky,' Uncle Forbes says gloomily.

He's right. I am. I always have been.

I let three days go by. I can't sleep. I tremble when the phone rings and rings and rings. I start at the slightest sound. I am waiting for something.

The landlord says, 'You had better charge him. I can't have this sort of thing going on.'

Aunt Forbes and Uncle Forbes have to leave. Aunt Forbes goes inveighing against the incomprehensible arbitrariness of the Nut Lady. Uncle Forbes says, 'She must have led him on. I've been in the Army.'

I know she means it, the Nut Lady. If I don't, I can't go back. She'll kick me out. She means it.

I go down to the police station. I speak to the public prosecutor. I sign the form.

I go back to the apartment and I sleep.

I go to see the Nut Lady.

'You can move,' she says grimly. 'But I wasn't having you run home, like a baby.'

'It was wrong of you. To force me to that. It was wrong. It was a bad move.'

'Perhaps,' she says. 'I make mistakes sometimes.'

'I just want to say that this time you've been wrong.'

'All right.'

And the days go by. The phone has stopped ringing, but I get an unlisted number anyway.

I go back to work. The face fades. I can't remember how I looked then.

Ben comes over and takes the Medusa head outside into the area where the garbage cans are kept. He puts the head into a garbage can and, with a hammer, smashes it to pieces. 'I realize now,' he says, 'I was possessed of the devil when I did that. It was evil.' He is destroying everything he has made in the past two years. He invites me to come to see his studio ... to see the portrait of the mad woman before he cuts it. 'It glows in the dark. You can see the devil,' he says. But I don't go.

Paul comes over and brings the chess champion from the university. We draw.

A serious Chinese boy, a political science candidate. Very fond of puns. 'The pigeons are very active in your alley,' the Chinese boy says. 'Foul of them.' Then he chuckles, enormously pleased with himself.

After we draw, he says to me, 'Next Sunday?' And we agree to play next Sunday.

I work hard and on Sunday I play a game of chess. Sometimes Paul is there too. He plays one of us first and then the other takes him on, but it is between me and the Chinese boy. He says to me, 'You are very imaginative.'

'And you care for nothing,' I say. 'You hold no brief for your Queen or your knights.'

'My nights have no queen,' he says and chuckles. Then he considers. 'No.' He watches the board. 'I will tell you. My weakness. I am a Marxist. I care for the pawns. If you are to beat me, you will have to do it with the end game. I care for the pawns.'

It is true. He cares for his pawns. I work on the end game but I never beat him. He sacrifices his pawns. He knows his weakness. Life goes on. Everything passes.

One day I am walking down Broadway and I see a brown khaki shapeless man rolling toward me. I stop dead in my tracks. He stops in his.

We look at each other, from half a block away. I hear him laugh. And I laugh too. We stand there, not able to see each other's faces, but laughing. Like lunatics. Then I turn and go on back to the apartment.

The telephone rings. How is that possible? I have changed the number.

It must have been later then. That I changed the number. Because the telephone rings and I answer it.

''S me,' he says.

I say he can't come to the apartment. The landlord will phone the police. I say I will meet him at a coffee shop.

'I'm back across the bridge,' he says. 'Taking a course. You know. Maintenance engineer.'

'What happened?'

'You dumb broad. Nothing. They put me away for a night, and in the morning my mother put up the peace bond. I could have come back anytime. You think that stopped me?'

'I thought they'd locked you up and thrown away the key.'

'"Disturbing the Peace,"' he says with a sneer.

So that's what I must have signed. Yes. I did.

'I threw away the knife when I was humping it down the road. I threw it away. That was nothing. You think that was something?'

Yes, I had thought it was something. 'I thought you were serious.'

'Nah. All they did, they phoned me up and said they had a bench warrant out for me and to wait, they were coming to pick me up.'

'They phoned you? The police?'

'Sure.'

'How did they know where to find you?'

I forget what he answers.

'I felt such a Judas,' I say.

'Naw. You were just mad.'

'No. I was scared.'

'You? Scared of me?' He doesn't believe it. 'I wouldn't hurt you.'

I was scared. But I don't tell him. I thank him for the coffee and I go back to the apartment.

A week later he phones and asks me for coffee again. I go. This time, there is a bubbling inside me. He says, 'Come to my place,' and I go.

A little bed sitting room, only blocks away from my place.

Cretonne on the easy chair. Bright sunlight through the window. A canary in a cage. And, from the library, a book: How to Write for TV and Radio.

Oh Mik.

We make love. He uses a safe. We are quiet because of the landlady.

'I been seeing this woman.'

'Why are you talking like that?'

'Like what?'

'"Been seeing?"'

'She's all right. Thirty-five. Had a tough time. I fixed her kitchen cupboards for her.'

'Just don't talk like that to me.'

'We get along. It's not the same, but she's had a tough time.'

A week later, he phones and says, 'I'm getting married. Tomorrow.'

'To that woman you told me about?'

'Yah.'

'I hope you'll be very happy.' And 'Congratulations.'

'Look. Let's see each other before, eh? Look. You don't have to worry. It'll be neutral territory. Bring Edna. I'll bring George. See me before. At noon. The Aristocrat.'

Edna and I walk down to the Aristocrat at noon the next day. Mik is already there with George. My stomach won't have anything to do with the food. I have to excuse myself and go to the washroom.

Edna says to Mik, 'Look. It's hard enough on her. Leave her alone, why can't you? Can't you see she's upset as it is?'

'What's she upset about?' Mik says.

'Men!' Edna says.

Walking back to my place, Edna says, 'Do you believe him? About getting married?'

'Why would he lie about that?'

Like Jocelyn about clerkship, I can't imagine why anyone would lie about the state of marriage. One might admit it, but lie!

AND IT IS OVER. Only of course it isn't.

One day, two years later, coming back from the clinic, I stop at an East Hastings café and here's Mik.

'You've put on weight.'

'Yes. How are you?'

'Okay.'

'How's married life?'

'Great.'

'It seems to agree with you.'

'So. How are you, Vicky?'

'I'm all right. I don't remember you ever saying my name before.'

'We're older.'

'Yes. I'm thirty.'

'Yah. We're older.'

He is working at a warehouse on Delta Island. He'd like to show it to me. I say all right and we go, driving in an old clunker. He's a watchman. He shows me the warehouse, and then we drive back. It's night time now. He drives me to the top of Burnaby Mountain and shows me the lights of the city. He kisses me. But I say I want to go home.

That's all. Except I give him my telephone number.

And I go to Berkeley.

While Edna is working and Sam is seeing his analyst, I wash and scrub and scour their basement suite. I cook immense meals, and buy place mats for the table.

Edna says, 'I can't stand it, Vicky. You're just like my mother.'

So I take the bus to Sausalito. I buy a book and a pair of black pants, with those awful elastic things for under the feet. And an orange sweater. I eat lunch at a swanky restaurant. I buy a peace button. I get on the bus to go back to Berkeley.

The book is *Big Sur* by Kerouac.

I'm sitting there, in the back seat of the bus, the paper bag with the slacks and sweater on the seat beside me. The bus has stopped and I look up and see him. Standing at the front of the bus. Looking down toward the end. I shift my paper bag to my lap.

I recognize him instantly. My Mexican doctor.

He sits beside me. He looks at the book. He says, 'Not so good as his first.'

He asks me if I'd like to have a beer when we get to Berkeley. I say, All right.

He looks at me as if I'm lying.

We sit under a trellis of vine leaves. They are real. We have beers poured from a large pitcher. He asks would I like to see Haight-Ashbury tomorrow.

I say, All right.

Of course he isn't my Mexican doctor.

The next day, at three o'clock in the afternoon, I get pregnant. On Russian Hill. He takes me to the Berkeley bus. He buys me a ticket. He kisses me goodbye. I·never see him again. We write letters. I will write and tell him all about the friendly advice I am getting. Iris and the knitting needles.

I will take a break from all this. I will tell the story about Iris and the knitting needles. I will sell my soul for a good joke.

I have gone to an intellectual gathering in the professor's West End apartment. The day Jack Kennedy died. We all sit around in various stages of shock. I say something about a conspiracy, and the professor gets furious. It wasn't a conspiracy, it was one lunatic, alone. People see conspiracies under beds. It's an American disease to see conspiracy. I am wearing the green velvet dress with the cape. A lovely deep emerald green, and the cape is lined with gold.

We talk about it. How the children have been given a day off from school and how they are pleased with this, a holiday. We talk of someone who said, 'Who will be our president now? The man with the barbecue handshake?' It is a good image, someone says. The barbecue handshake.

I'd been lying in bed when the news came through. Then the soap opera came on again. The programming went on as usual, an American channel. Until after one o'clock in the afternoon. Brief news flashes through the inane bright chatter of a woman's show. She was reeling it off, some nonsense about a flower show, as if it had been pre-recorded in her head; but her eyes were mad.

It seemed too much to bear, that terror and my own as well. For I was afraid.

I had been lying in bed because I didn't want to get up. I didn't want to know all over again what I already knew. There would be no blood. I was really pregnant.

The professor asked me to stay behind, after the others left. He made me a drink. He said how was I. I said, pregnant.

'You. Every time I see you, you're into something.'

A couple of days later, he phoned. Iris could help me.

I don't know what I expected. Advice on motherhood perhaps? I go there one bright morning, the air crisp and cool and smoky. And Iris delivers her lecture on Planned Parenthood and the Knitting Needle.

'You take a catheter tube. You can get them in Woodward's. And you put the knitting needle inside. This protects the uterus from the actual tip, you see. You don't actually touch the uterus with the knitting needle. Just a plastic knitting needle, thirty-nine cents a pair. It stiffens the catheter tube. The prairie farm wives showed me. They've used this method for years. You just introduce air, you see.'

'Isn't there a danger of haemorrhage?'

'You have to take that risk if you really want to get rid of it. Look, I've done it thousands of times. Well, hundreds. It's worth the risk, isn't it? Are you surprised? Did you think I was faithful to him?'

One of the apocryphal stories about Iris is that she has said, 'I've always enjoyed sex with my husband. Every one of the sixty seconds.'

'But Iris, you see, I did it accidentally on purpose.' This is the first time I am to say it. It is my story and I will stick to it.

'You mean, you're going to keep it?'

'Yes.'

She says then that she thinks it's wonderful, all power to me.

But last New Year's, across an academic party, she calls, in her high carrying voice, 'Aren't you glad you kept it after all?'

The Nut Lady said, 'How are you going to foul things up?'

I am surprised. 'You don't think I'm mad?'

'No. You've done it half-way. Really, it's a victory. You're almost ready to leave.'

'I'm cured?'

'You want a certificate?' She looks tired.

'You think I'm going to foul it up?'

'Oh yes.'

'Yes,' I say. 'I guess I already have. I write clever letters.'

'I bet you do.'

'Maybe I don't want to get married.'

She laughs.

'I write and say, It's fine, I can Handle It Myself.'

'I bet you do.'

'It's like, you see, there was this woman, she slept with Zeus. I can't remember her name. But he comes to her as a man. And she isn't satisfied. She asks him to come to her in the full glory of his godhood. And when he does, she's fried to a crisp. Only with me, it's just the opposite. I'm afraid ... I don't want to know anything about him. I want him to stay right where he is. I don't want him to tell me his troubles, or his failures, or his ... I don't want to know. I want to be able, always, to say, It was a miracle. Do you see?'

She sighs. 'Yes.'

'A mysterious stranger, a god burnt black from the sun. Not Icarus.'

She says something.

'What?'

'I said, Icarus?'

285

'Flew too close to the sun. He was human.' I am still hearing myself. What I've said. 'His wings melted and he fell.'

'But you already know,' she says. 'You already know a lot about him.'

'Yes.' But I am to deny it. I am to deny it for years. Even to myself. Most of all.

One night Mik phones me and I say blithely, 'Guess what? I'm preggers.'

This has become my story. I am gay, blithe, unconcerned. It is all wonderful, wonderful, I couldn't be happier. In the mornings I brush my teeth and say Courage with a French accent. I am both terrified and yet, oddly, superbly unconcerned. I know if I just hang in there, it's going to be all right. I say that to myself: It's going to be all right, kid.

Mik says, 'Who's the father?'

'I met him in San Francisco. On a bus.'

'What's he like?'

'Tall and dark, and very nice. He doesn't know.' A lie.

Except by this time I believe it.

We chat for a few minutes and I ask him how his wife is, and then we say goodbye amicably.

A knock comes at the door. It is Mik.

We play chess. I beat him.

'You're not concentrating,' I say.

'Out of practice,' he says.

'Doesn't your wife play chess?'

He looks at me. 'I never got married.'

I knew of course.

Then, 'What do you mean, "dark?"' he says.

I tell him.

He says, 'And you said I left my shit in you.' He gets up and begins to walk around the room, swinging his arms.

'Oh Mik, don't be obstreperous.'

'"Obstreperous!"'

'No, really, I must be very calm and very quiet. People mustn't make a fuss around me. I have to take care of myself.'

He goes out into the kitchen and after a moment, he leaves. The door slams.

He passes by under my window, in the alley that runs between the two old tenement houses. And he shouts up at me: 'Nigger lover.'

In a way it is a gift.

After the baby comes, I am swamped with bills. It's strange how much everything seems to cost, even if you are only breast-feeding.

I decide to write everyone who owes me money. I will say, 'Even if you can't pay it all back, half will do.'

I go down the list, and then I think of Mik. Should I? Why not.

I write him in care of his mother. I ask him if he could pay back what I spent on the clothes that time. I mail all the letters off, and I get a rather good return. Almost everyone pays me.

I can't remember what I spent on Mik's clothes. I say approximately ninety, but if he remembers otherwise, that's okay.

LAST WEEKEND, Francie says, 'Over 200.'

'Really?'

AUNT CARRINGTON AND Aunt Foster phone. They hear the baby cry. They're on the extension phones. Aunt Carrington says, 'I'm coming out.' Later, she tells me, 'I went right over to your mother's. I said, "You get on the phone, Ellen, and you forgive her. You do it now."'

I say, 'Was that when she called and forgave me?'

'Yes. I stood over her,' Aunt Carrington says.

'I wish you hadn't told me. I thought she meant it.'

But before Aunt Carrington arrives, driving in her great blue car through the mountains, Mik comes bashing at the door. Thump smash crash. Boom bang.

I pick up the baby and go into the bathroom. Lock the connecting door. Pound on Mrs Leigh's door. She's listening to the eleven o'clock news. 'What is it?' she says but I give her the baby and push her inside her room. Lock her door behind me. And out her door and up the stairs to the neighbour who didn't want to get involved. Call the police. Back down and into Mrs Leigh's room. It sounds like Armageddon through the bathroom. Bish bang crash thud.

The police come but Mik gets away down the alley.

They don't seem to take it seriously at all.

I phone the babysitter. Her boyfriend has a rifle. He brings it over and shows me how. I lean it against the kitchen door, which is not broken down. Mik must have just been kicking it.

I write a letter to the city prosecutor. I explain, logically, why—in view of the lack of concern shown by the constabulary—I shall have to kill Mik O'Brien the next time he comes through the door. Yours truly, V.E. Ferris.

Aunt Carrington arrives.

Two detectives come and sit in the front room and speak politely to us.

'He has a silver plate in his head,' Aunt Carrington says. 'The war did dreadful things to men.'

The detectives say please get rid of the rifle. Accidents happen that way.

Aunt Carrington says, 'There must be something else you can do. I myself don't like guns, but you can see my niece's difficulty.

If you can just do something for the time being, we'll be out of here soon.' She gestures to the high-ceilinged rooms, the Salvation Army furniture, the pile of diapers on the desk. 'I'm taking my niece to Europe,' says Aunt Carrington, 'and when we get back, we're going to buy a house in a better section of the city. But in the meantime, I don't believe my niece can give up the rifle unless she is sure that Mr O'Brien is quite safe.' Aunt Carrington smiles at the detectives disingenuously.

Perhaps they think my aunt is mad. Perhaps they think I am mad. But what they say is, they think O'Brien is mad. O'Brien is well known to them. Has been in trouble before. They explain to us that with someone like O'Brien, you could possibly get in one shot, but that might not kill him, you see. And before you knew it, he could grab the rifle from you, and game over.

'I've seen that happen,' says one detective.

The other detective nods, to confirm. And even goes to the kitchen, to pace out the requisite steps from the door to the place where I would be standing, firing the rifle. He looks at the mended hinges. 'What happened here?'

'That's where he broke down the door,' I say. 'The first time.'

'Someone like Mik O'Brien, you need an elephant gun,' says the first detective. Mik would have liked that.

And they say, for the meantime, until we leave the area, they can arrange to have Mik committed to Essondale.

I return the rifle to my babysitter's boyfriend. He is relieved that the detectives did not confiscate it. We go to Europe, and when we get back, I buy a house. Aunt Carrington wants to buy it with me, but I can't.

Paul offers to marry me, for the baby's sake. I give it a thought. For the baby's sake, I would do almost anything. Uncle Forbes says, 'Oh Vicky, not another one.'

It seems incredible, but I actually do. I wonder if I should marry Paul, to make things respectable. But I don't want my daughter
to have a coward for a mother. I tell him No, and Paul cries. Sits in
my front room and cries. For hours.

Mik never did that.

IN MY DREAM LAST night. I am flying up north. There are two stops.
I am going to see my grandfather. This will be the second visit. My
grandmother has died and this time is for the funeral. He has said
to me, last weekend: 'It's a waste. I can do the embalming myself.'
And I come now, knowing my grandmother to be dead. It is an
empty bare little house, all on one floor, and the linoleum has
maroon fleshy petals. The spare bedroom, where I expect her to be
laid out, is bare. There is still a patch of wet on the linoleum though,
beside her bed. Perhaps he has washed the floor, or perhaps that
is wax. But it looks too wet for wax. Yes, it must have just been
washed. He wouldn't use liquid wax that doesn't need buffing. But
then I think, Maybe it is the fluid from her body. Has he done the
embalming here? I imagine how terrible it must have been, taking
out my grandmother's stomach. I sniff, expecting rotten meat, but
no. There is only the stale mustard smell of old people. I go along
to their bedroom and I see, on a cot beside the big bed, my grandmother's feet. They are twitching convulsively. I look up to her face.
Her mouth is drawn wide in a soundless howl. She is alive then, in
spite of the removal of her stomach. Her wrists are in restrainers.
She jerks and twists and screams in silence.

He says, behind me, 'Now she doesn't make any noise anyway.'
He seems sad. 'I had to cut the vocal cords.'

I wake up.

I come upstairs and plug in last night's coffee. Put on the kettle

290

for instant porridge. Light a cigarette. Go stand at the front window. It is foggy. The rain beats maniacally against the pane. I go to the back window. The sun is coming up, red, behind the mountain. Up it comes, out of the fog and the rain. Now it is casting a strange clear light, like the amber of tea, over the city. The city is lit up, as if the light is coming through stained glass.

I get the heated-up coffee. The radio clock switches on.

I know it's today I finish. My lover, my enemy, my killer.

Anna comes upstairs. I stare out the window. I am crying.

The light is shining through water now. And suddenly, like a message, a rainbow. A rainbow in the clear holy light, and the rain falling through gold like a blessing. It arches through the sky, from mountain to sea. Perfect. A perfect terrible rainbow, like a promise.

What does it matter, says Jeff, if it's a lie? So long as it's a good, a beautiful lie? Oh yes, I remember that first one, after the flood, and everyone dead or drowned, and you said, It's all right, it's all right, it's all all right. Old arch-deceiver, with your rainbow full of promises, and everyone dead and drowned. For our sins.

There is a silly song on the radio. From four or five years ago. From a movie.

And I am dancing. An old fat fool. Dancing. Anna comes out, sleepy still, watching me, starting to move herself, but one eye on the radio clock.

'It's seven forty-four.'

I have taught her that way, thinking 'quarter to's' and 'five past's' not logical.

Lolly yowls.

The water for the instant porridge is steaming up the windows.

And I dance.

'Mom? It's seven forty-nine!'

'Just a minute, for god's sake.'

For years I was guilty about Ben. About Paul. About my mother and my sisters. I shall probably come to feel guilty about Anna. But I never feel guilty about Mik. I think now, My god, they probably put him away for life. If there's anyone you really did destroy, it was Mik.

But I know that's not true. If I think of Mik, right now, lumbering down Broadway in crumpled khaki, I want to laugh.

I know I could say: Look, Vicky, you set this poor bastard up. You made him part of your own personal destruction epic. You provoked him into trying to kill you, then you got him sent to the madhouse for doing it.

Well, that's probably the truth. Only I don't feel guilty for it.

I can *see* Mik, cream and coffee over his tits, his head thrown back, hollering to the moon and bringing down the sun. And I know they never destroyed him. Not Mik. And I know I didn't destroy him. Not Mik. Because Mik had been destroyed by experts.

And now Anna is dancing too. Unable to help herself. And we dance, mother and daughter, in the underwater light.

We dance, and we say, Just a minute for god's sake. Just a minute. Just a minute. Just a brief and dancing minute for the sake of the dark and laughing god.

BETTY LAMBERT (1933–83) was a playwright and novelist; born in Calgary to a working-class family, she graduated from the University of British Columbia in 1957, and joined the English faculty at Simon Fraser University in 1965, where she eventually became professor. She was best known for her prodigious output of plays for stage, radio, and television. *Crossings* was her only novel.